A SHARED HISTORY

ABIGAIL SHEFFIELD

Quills & Quartos
PUBLISHING

Copyright © 2024 by Abigail Sheffield

All rights reserved.

This is a work of fiction. Names, characters, businesses, places, events, locales, and incidents are either the products of the author's imagination or used in a fictitious manner. Any resemblance to actual persons, living or dead, or actual events is purely coincidental.

No part of this book may be reproduced in any form or by any electronic or mechanical means, including information storage and retrieval systems, without written permission from the author, except for the use of brief quotations in a book review.

No AI training. Without in any way limiting the author's [and publisher's] exclusive rights under copyright, any use of this publication to "train" generative artificial intelligence (AI) technologies to generate text is expressly prohibited. The author reserves all rights to license uses of this work for generative AI training and development of machine learning language models.

Ebooks are for the personal use of the purchaser. You may not share or distribute this ebook in any way, to any other person. To do so is infringing on the copyright of the author, which is against the law.

Edited by Jan Ashton and Katie Jackson

Cover Design by Pemberley Darcy

ISBN 978-1-963213-62-1 (ebook) and 978-1-963213-63-8 (Paperback)

For my husband, my children, and my family. You inspire me more than you could possibly know.

CHAPTER ONE

December 1813, Hertfordshire

Elizabeth Bennet sat on the worn sofa in Longbourn's parlour, a novel held tightly in her hands, her fingers beginning to turn white as her grip intensified. She read the page she had been stuck on for what felt like the fifth time, still not completely grasping its meaning. The noise from within her busy house, and her own anguished thoughts, kept her too distracted to progress very far in the story. If it had been a different season, she surely would have been able to retreat out of doors to sit against her favourite tree and better concentrate on the words. Unfortunately, the cold air on this first day of December prevented her from such an escape.

A small thump echoed from somewhere in the house. An inconsequential noise that should have elicited no more than a slight glance instead made her all but leap from the sofa.

She bowed her head, closed her eyes, and took a deep breath to collect herself.

It is only a few weeks. You can do this.

Elizabeth looked up and straightened her back to steel herself. Longbourn's tumult was greater than usual, as the household was busy preparing for a gathering to celebrate the impending marriage of her elder sister, Jane, to Mr Charles Bingley. The gentleman had entered their lives no more than two months earlier when he leased the nearby estate of Netherfield Park. Mr Bingley was young, handsome, friendly, and rich, a fact that Mrs Bennet liked to remind them of any time his name was mentioned. He and Jane had met at an assembly in Meryton, spent most of the evening together in either dancing or conversation, and fallen quickly and deeply in love. It was not long before he proposed, and they set a date for their wedding, now less than three weeks away.

Such a straightforward path to matrimony, Elizabeth mused, a small twinge of jealousy intruding on her thoughts. *If only all love stories could be so simple…*

No, she reminded herself firmly. *Jane deserves nothing less than to have a love match that also answers all of my mother's and society's expectations of a good marriage.*

Soon after the Bennets met Mr Bingley, they learnt he shared a mutual acquaintance with them. Most of her family would consider the gentleman merely a nodding acquaintance, but Elizabeth felt far differently, for he was none other than Mr Darcy. And it was Mr Darcy whom Mr Bingley had chosen to stand up with him at the wedding. The gentleman was said to have arrived at Netherfield the previous evening and was to visit Longbourn with Mr Bingley this very day. Elizabeth knew not if she could bear it.

A SHARED HISTORY

No one, not even Jane, knew how much his presence pained Elizabeth. She had never told anyone of what occurred in Kent more than three years prior between herself and Mr Darcy. They knew only that Mr Darcy had been in Kent at the same time as Elizabeth and that they had been sat at the same dining table on a few occasions. A slight connexion.

Unfortunately for her, it had been so much more than that. He had become her biggest adversary.

It would be a difficult few weeks in his presence, but Elizabeth was determined to remain strong and enjoy her sister's wedding. She was resolved to be unaffected by Mr Darcy and to part from him after the wedding breakfast, after which they likely would never meet again for the rest of their lives.

Elizabeth sighed as she looked out the window closest to her. Her eyes took in all the beauty of the early winter countryside. Though she typically preferred spring's colours and liveliness, today was different. There was a unique loveliness to behold in the faded grey landscape, particularly as viewed from the window-seat in the parlour with a fire crackling merrily nearby. As she wore a mask of composure amidst the cheerful scene around her, she was oddly comforted in having her own sombreness mirrored in nature.

Her thoughts were interrupted by her mother's voice from another room. "Lizzy! A strapping young man is here to see you!"

Her stomach tightened with a jolt. She had been so deep in thought, she had not heard anyone enter the house. Was Mr Darcy here, already? Had he come to call on her? That would be bold indeed.

Her hands shook a little as she shut her book and quickly put it aside. Elizabeth stood, smoothing her gown and wishing she had time to change into another, more flattering one. Before she knew what she was doing, she had turned her back to the parlour door and was again staring out the window. She heard her mother's footsteps coming down the corridor accompanied by a heavier footfall that she feared belonged to Mr Darcy. As the sound grew closer, she crossed her arms and hugged herself tightly to prepare for the moment she had dreaded for so long.

"Here she is, sir," she heard her mother's voice say as she entered the room.

For a moment, Elizabeth thought she might swoon. Was this to be the day that all her imaginings, her greatest fears and hopes, came to life?

Bracing herself, she turned around, only to be met by a different man entirely. In place of the dark, sombre figure she had anticipated, a fair-haired, blue-eyed, robust young man stood before her.

It was Mr Henry Royce, followed by his uncle Sir William Lucas.

"Miss Elizabeth!" He smiled at her with genuine warmth, his countenance open and amiable.

Elizabeth felt all her trepidation melt away as she walked briskly towards her childhood friend. She held out her hand towards him, and his sturdy, firm hand soon enveloped hers.

"Royce!"

Noticing her mother looking a little too excited at the pair joining hands, Elizabeth quickly drew hers away.

"If you will excuse me, gentlemen. There are some matters I must attend to before the gathering begins. I look forward to speaking with you both soon," Mrs Bennet said as she began to walk out of the room. Before she exited, she gave Royce one more long, assessing glance that could only make her daughter blush. Elizabeth could hardly blame her. Her old friend had grown only more deeply handsome since the last time he had come to stay at Lucas Lodge. It took much self-control to refrain from openly staring at him as other women in the neighbourhood, her own sisters, and even some of the household servants always had. If her mother's reports were to be believed, his fine countenance could only be enhanced by the fact that he had also become wealthy in recent years through an inheritance from a distant aunt.

After her mother left, Elizabeth drew her attention back to Royce and Sir William. "To what do we owe the pleasure of your presence? The party does not start for another hour. I did not expect to see guests until then."

"We came to call on your father, but it appears he is out with a tenant," Sir William explained.

"We thought since we were already here," Royce said with an attractive smirk and a glint in his eye, "we simply must keep you and your sisters company until the party begins. That is, unless it is an inconvenience?"

Elizabeth tried to shake off the suspicion that he had somehow orchestrated his visit to spend more time with her alone. "It would be delightful to have your company, sirs," she responded, feeling suddenly shy.

With some silly excuse that could only increase her consternation, Sir William moved to the side of the room and took up the very book that had failed to capture Elizabeth's attention only moments prior. He hummed a little tune beneath his breath as if to announce to her that he was not paying attention to the two younger people.

Royce angled his body such that Sir William was behind him. "I have very much looked forward to seeing more of you since I have arrived at Lucas Lodge. We saw each other but a moment when you came to call on Maria."

"Like passing ships."

"You must inform me at once of all the latest happenings at Longbourn." Lowering his voice, he added, "And all the latest gossip of Meryton." He raised his eyebrows, and she laughed.

He bid her to sit down on the sofa next to him, and they spoke at great length, catching up as old friends do.

CHAPTER TWO

A few hours later, Elizabeth stood next to Royce in the middle of the drawing room. Longbourn was at its most lively with nearly everyone they had invited standing elbow to elbow, almost shouting over the sounds of laughter, the Gardiner children scampering about, and her sister Mary playing a reel at the pianoforte. Although she had been carefully vigilant to the announcement of one particular guest, still she somehow missed Mrs Hill bringing him into the room. It was a jolt to her system to hear her mother crying out,

"Mr Bennet! Jane! Mr Bingley has finally arrived, come welcome him in. He has brought his friend too—Mr Dardee."

"Mr Darcy, madam," he said, his voice still encompassing that haughty sedateness she remembered.

Elizabeth's stomach dropped and she inhaled sharply, then hoped Royce had not noticed. She still could not see Mr Darcy without it being obvious that she was looking for him, but nevertheless she flushed at the sound of his voice.

Quickly she recalled the various greetings she had practised, imagining this, their first meeting in years.

Out of the corner of her eye she saw her father nod at her mother's summons and leave the spot where he had been firmly planted for some time enjoying refreshments. He proceeded leisurely towards their distinguished guests.

Her mother continued speaking to Mr Darcy as she waited for Mr Bennet to arrive, "Oh! Yes, indeed, Mr Darcy! Mr Bingley reminded me that we have met once before. In your aunt's home, in Kent. Do you remember? It was one dinner together some three or four years ago. Such a beautiful house that was—I do not believe I have since been in such a grand house, although Jane and Mr Bingley will be settled in a house that does compare to it. You know, I always knew she would be sure to marry a man of significance. And you also have met my Lizzy and Lydia as well, so you must come in and greet them. They are as beautiful as ever."

Though Elizabeth still did not look over, she could hear her father's voice as he joined their group.

"Mr Bingley, welcome."

"Thank you, sir. Your hospitality in hosting tonight is greatly appreciated."

After a slight pause, Elizabeth heard Mrs Bennet chime in to introduce Mr Darcy and Mr Bennet.

"Welcome to Longbourn, Mr Darcy," her father stated cordially. "I trust you will enjoy our gathering tonight."

Finally daring to peek in their direction, Elizabeth was just in time to hear her mother exclaim, shrilly, "Pray forgive me!"

To Elizabeth's horror, she saw splotches of her mother's

wine punch liberally dotting Mr Darcy's snow-white cravat. Mrs Bennet must have stumbled after she performed the introductions. She had removed her handkerchief from her sleeve and was dabbing ineffectively at Mr Darcy's chest as Mr Bennet called for a footman. Elizabeth's cheeks burnt hot, and she closed her eyes a moment against the scene. Why could her mother not behave respectably just this one time? It was likely she already had drunk too much punch, rendering her unequal to the task of performing introductions without splashing her drink on a distinguished guest. After he spent the next weeks in close company with the Bennet family, Elizabeth was certain Mr Darcy would feel justified in the callousness he had shown towards her three years ago.

However, he surprised her, showing her mother far more courtesy than she expected. "It is no trouble, madam. Please do not distress yourself over it."

Giggling, Mrs Bennet backed away from Mr Darcy. "Ah sir, you are as obliging as you are handsome."

And it was at this most inauspicious of moments that he raised his eyes to meet her gaze. He looked as handsome as ever; age had added more depth to his countenance. What used to look boyish was now angular. Where he had been thin, he was now broad. And had he always been so tall? He loomed over everyone else in the room. At this first sight of him, Elizabeth's humiliation at her mother's clumsiness gave way to jitters, and she scolded herself for feeling anything at all for such a horrible man.

Though there was much commotion between them, it felt for a moment as though they were the only ones in the room. He stared at her with an intensity she had not felt since last they met. She returned his gaze as she shuffled through many emotions: anger, sadness, disappointment, bitterness, and even to her horror, a twinge of excitement.

Elizabeth looked away hastily, trying to find anything to focus on but Mr Darcy. It was uncomfortable to be in the same room as him, and to appear to others—and to each other—as hardly more than strangers, when so much had happened between them. She thought back to the last time she felt his impenetrable gaze and, reflecting on their final conversation, tears began to sting her eyes.

No, no Lizzy, not now. You cannot be distressed by him, not when he is standing right there to witness the effect he still has on you.

Recalling how infamously he had treated her, she felt anger surge within her; it was a comfort, certainly better than feeling sorrow over him. Her courage began to rise. She would not let him win. She was in *her* home, preparing for *her* sister's wedding. He was a visitor of little significance to her and her family. She would not let him come into her house and make her feel uncomfortable.

Elizabeth returned her attention to Royce, leaning towards him and listening with feigned eagerness to what he was saying. Determined not to appear as though she had been anticipating Mr Darcy's arrival, she laughed too readily over a shared joke, which seemed to encourage Royce to position himself a little closer to her than propriety would recommend.

Out of the corner of her eye she saw that Mr Darcy had joined Jane and Mr Bingley and that they were making their way towards her. Elizabeth forced herself to turn away from Royce once the trio was too near to ignore anymore.

She curtseyed to both men, careful to keep her eyes on her soon-to-be brother. "Mr Bingley! How good it is to see you. I do not think you would be surprised to know that your absence was keenly felt."

"Felt by myself as well!" He smiled happily. "The day is finally almost here—I can hardly wait for it. I believe you have already met my good friend, Mr Darcy?"

She met his gaze politely. "Mr Darcy, how good it is to see you again."

He gave a slight bow. When he was upright again, his eyes moved from her to Royce in a curious manner. "The pleasure is all mine," he replied stoically.

Jane introduced Royce to Mr Darcy and Mr Bingley. Everyone was silent for a moment, and Elizabeth felt all the awkwardness of the scene. Royce came to the rescue by introducing a conversational topic.

"Miss Elizabeth and I were just speaking of novels. As with most topics, I am afraid she had much more to contribute to the conversation. I must confess I have not ventured often into that medium. Are either of you devotees of the written word?"

Mr Bingley shook his head. "I am afraid I spend more time out of doors, and am not a good contributor to this conversation either. What think you, Darcy?"

He looked away in his usual aloof manner. "No, I cannot say that I admire the medium. I am afraid I see novels as a shallow indulgence rather than as something intellectually stimulating."

"How could you argue such a thing?" cried Elizabeth, with more emotion than she had intended. She was prickling to quarrel with him and set him down, but it did not mean she wished the entire room to know it. All the heads in their small group turned towards her, so she modified her tone for her next utterance. "I must say that is a rather old-fashioned way of looking at the subject at hand. Of course—"

She faltered, looking at Jane's shocked expression. *This is Jane's night,* she told herself. *Do not ruin it by offending her guests.*

"Of course, everyone is entitled to their own opinions," she said, offering a small, conciliatory smile to Jane before lowering her eyes.

Royce, evidently meaning to play the gallant, said, "Although I have not read many novels, I was vastly entertained by those that I have read."

"Is entertainment sufficient purpose for a written work?" Mr Darcy enquired and with that, all of Elizabeth's resolve to end the subject vanished.

"A well-written novel has the remarkable ability to captivate minds and inspire change in a way that strictly educational text could never do," she retorted.

Mr Darcy looked at her intently. At his silence, she continued passionately, "Consider this—a novel can resonate with and fascinate even the simplest mind, and by including edifying and philosophical material within its story, it can educate its readers. Rather than intimidate its readers as educational texts might, a book that is entertaining can stimulate intellectual growth."

Everyone other than Mr Darcy looked surprised by her lengthy speech. He appeared calm but continued watching her intently. Jane and Mr Bingley exchanged a glance before she pulled her betrothed away to more peaceful circles. Royce remained, smiling gamely at the exchange.

"I suppose I can see your points in this matter, Miss Elizabeth," said her opponent. "However, I wonder whether a novel could truly change the simpleton, who may be drawn only to the sensational theatrics within the pages, into an intellect? Or are those who are learning from the discretely placed intellectual messages within the narrative already inclined to pursue greater degrees of understanding and betterment?"

Elizabeth was quick to reply. "Learning can come only through exposure. A novel can be the gateway that presents the shallowest of readers with ideas that would not be introduced to them if they live amongst an unvarying society."

She looked to Royce to find agreement, but was frustrated to find only a confused stare.

"Consider this book I am reading," she remarked as she picked up *Charlotte Temple*, the novel she had struggled to read earlier. "At first glance, it appears to be a simple romance. But it serves as a vessel for the author to shed light on various social issues. In doing so, it offers readers a different perspective of the world, encouraging introspection and growth."

"I do not believe you actually answered my question," Mr Darcy said, his lips curled slightly in apparent amusement. No doubt he enjoyed knowing he still had the capacity to arouse her indignation.

"Yes. I did. You are just choosing not to—" She stopped herself, urging herself to regain politeness. She was still a proper lady after all, even if she despised the man in front of her. She inhaled deeply and began again. "My answer to your question in plain terms is this: I cannot *know* with certainty whether a simpleton learns from the information presented through a narrative, but what more can we ask than to expose people to ideas to give them the chance to better their minds."

The sides of Mr Darcy's mouth again quirked upwards. Clearly he was enjoying sparring with her again. "I think it is a good argument. I am not completely convinced on all your points, but perhaps I need some time to dwell upon them. I am not a creature who changes his mind easily."

"You are ever the interesting creature indeed, Mr Darcy," Elizabeth responded as she placed the novel on the table again. "Walking into an unfamiliar house and challenging its inhabitants on views they hold closely to themselves."

His smile turned into a frown. "On the contrary—I had no idea which stance you took, Miss Elizabeth, as I joined the conversation late. If you do not remember clearly, I was asked a question, and had no preconceived notions of which consideration my hostess sided."

She noticed Mr Darcy quickly draw one hand to his side and begin rubbing his fingers together, perhaps in agitation. Realising she had become overly agitated on an unworthy topic, Elizabeth took a deep breath.

"Very well," was all she said to him before turning towards Royce, to whom she spoke in a much calmer voice. "Did you not just say before this that you wished to take a turn about the garden?"

"Um, did I?"

"When we were with Mary?" she prompted him. "She told us about the different plants planned for the spring."

"Of course, yes, we had discussed that earlier." His eyes shifted between her and Mr Darcy, looking slightly confused. Likely he also was puzzled by the notion of viewing a winter garden, and at night, but Royce never disappointed her. He offered his arm to her, and they began to leave the room. Once at the door, she risked one last glance in Mr Darcy's direction. He was still standing in the same spot, but was holding her novel in his hands, curiously perusing it as he looked through the pages. Restraining a smirk, she turned and walked out.

It took several minutes to retrieve their wraps, but at length they gained the outside, the cool air a welcome relief to her face. Mary was conscripted to join them and as the three of them walked, Elizabeth was glad her sister was there, for she carried the conversation and prohibited Royce from asking about the odd exchange. All Elizabeth could think about was what had just transpired. She was stunned she had behaved in such a manner. She had not seen Mr Darcy in three years and in their first conversation, she had verbally attacked his opinions on novels. It was not the reunion she had had in mind. She had hoped to meet him as a respectable but indifferent acquaintance, to surprise him with her poise and maturity. Instead, she had behaved exactly like one of the melodramatic characters in the very novels they were discussing. *Foolish girl!*

When the trio returned to the house, they found that Mr Darcy had gone, and Elizabeth was thankful for it. She was not ready to meet him again and would need time to regulate herself. She knew she would need to be more diligent in practising restraint the next time they met. This would not be an easy reunion.

CHAPTER THREE

April 1810, Kent

"Continue straight, Cousin Elizabeth! After you ascend the hill, you will see it," Mr Collins called out between gasps from somewhere behind her.

Elizabeth continued walking energetically up the grassy incline, anticipating the great stone building she had heard so much about. She paused for a moment, welcoming a gentle breeze as it wafted through her hair, carrying with it the scent of freshly bloomed flowers. She pulled out her handkerchief and dabbed her face. The spring air was crisp, but the mild sun, combined with the exertion of the climb, was warm enough to draw beads of sweat on her forehead. However, her curiosity—building since they set out for their destination and growing deeper as they drew closer to the grand Rosings Park manor house—remained undiminished.

She glanced behind her and saw Mr Collins drenched in sweat, trudging up the hill. Charlotte stood only a short distance in front of him. While she fared better than her husband with the physical effort, she appeared wary at the prospect of the rest of the climb.

Elizabeth placed the handkerchief back in her sleeve and proceeded forwards. She had been in Kent for five days visiting the former Miss Charlotte Lucas and her new husband, Mr Collins, before they had received an invitation to dine at Rosings. Her hosts were unreservedly excited and considered it an honour, while Elizabeth began to wonder whether it would be an ordeal. Since arriving at the parsonage, she had heard nothing but of how much the Collinses esteemed—an esteem which bordered on reverence—Lady Catherine de Bourgh. Mr Collins had described in great detail how wealthy she was, and his effusive commendation of even the most mundane things had begun to grate on Elizabeth. In every way that he described her, his patroness sounded to be overbearing, elitist, and arrogant. The overly manicured and manipulated gardens that they trudged past as they finally neared the great home only added to this impression.

Elizabeth paused at the top of the hill and looked down at the gargantuan Jacobean-style manor house that had finally come fully into view. She resisted every urge to let out an audible gasp at the sight. *It resembles more of a castle than a home,* she thought. *In all of my eighteen years I have never seen a house so impressive.*

She continued to gaze at the house until Charlotte and Mr Collins arrived at the peak a few minutes later. After taking a few steadying breaths, her cousin said, "I can see in your silence that you are nervous at such an opulent house, dear cousin. But do not concern yourself. Lady Catherine is all that is graceful and kind. She will not look down on you, no matter the differences in your rank."

Elizabeth resisted the urge to roll her eyes at him but could not refrain from sending Charlotte a look.

He continued, "It is a grand house, is it not? I am certain you could not add up all the windows without losing count. I would tell you how much the glazing costs, but I worry it would only further intimidate you. I would not want you to be so nervous that you would not be able to enjoy our dinner."

Elizabeth looked to the side and held back a smile. *If Lady Catherine is anywhere near as grandiose as her home, I doubt I could take any pleasure during a dinner in her company.*

When they at last arrived at the magnificent front doors, the butler stated that Lady Catherine awaited them. Though he was a servant himself, he gave their small party a sidelong, disapproving look as he said in a drawn-out manner, "This way, please."

He led them through the entry hall into a long corridor. Elizabeth's heels clicked against the marble floor, save for the areas protected by plush rugs, as she followed Mr Collins and Charlotte. Ornate tapestries hung near portraits of men and women who she imagined were de Bourgh ancestors. She schooled her expression so that she would not appear as amazed as she felt by the display of wealth and lineage. The butler stopped at a door and a footman appeared from nowhere and opened it; the butler stepped through and announced, "Mr and Mrs Collins and Miss Elizabeth Bennet."

Elizabeth followed behind the others, surprised to find they had been led directly to the dining room as opposed to the drawing room. Not only that, but five people—two men and three women—were already in their chairs prepared to eat.

Still standing at the front of the room, she quietly surveyed the company with great interest. At the end of the table sat a middle-aged woman whose opulence in dress—a gold silk gown—was outshone only by the elaborate arrangement of her hair. Though no introduction had yet been made, it was clear from her position at the table as well as her superiority of manner that she was Lady Catherine de Bourgh.

Elizabeth glanced at the other two women. *That must be her daughter, Miss Anne de Bourgh,* she deduced as she looked upon the young, but frail woman wearing a lavender gown sitting directly next to Lady Catherine. She sat, her eyes down, without any acknowledgement that they had entered the room. *And that must be the companion whom Charlotte mentioned, Mrs Jenkinson,* Elizabeth surmised, noting the older but much healthier-looking woman wearing a small smile and a blue silk gown sitting beside Miss de Bourgh.

Elizabeth quickly cast her eyes to the other side of the table where the men stood, having risen from their seats upon their entrance. Her eyes were drawn first to the young man farthest away from Lady Catherine; he wore the uniform of an army officer. Though he was not handsome, he carried himself with an easy manner and looked in their direction genially as they walked in.

While the first man's military uniform initially caught her eye, it was the second man who held her gaze. He appeared to be only a few years older than herself and wore a dark jacket and waistcoat and an intricately tied cravat. He was deeply handsome, almost in a classical manner, with dark hair and eyes.

However, his reception of their party quickly undermined any admiration she felt towards him. He glanced at them with a blank and disinterested gaze before quickly darting his eyes away. *I wonder whether he can be as haughty as he appears.* Elizabeth barely concealed a laugh at his expense. He must have noticed as he snapped his head back towards her and gave her an unreadable expression.

After they had fully entered the dining room, Lady Catherine surveyed them for a moment and then, without performing any introductions, said, "Now it appears that we may finally eat. Mr Collins, has punctuality become obsolete in the parson's world?"

Mr Collins immediately began to bow and scrape, stuttering, "M-m-my dear Lady Catherine, we must b-b-beg your forgiveness for our unpardonable tardiness. I-I can assure you, that if you allow us to make amends, it shall never happen again."

Lady Catherine responded with a curt wave of her hand, indicating that she did not want to hear anymore. Elizabeth could not understand it. They had arrived at the predetermined time and there were additional guests who, in her understanding, were not supposed to be in attendance. If anything were deemed rude, it would be *their* presence and the lack of welcome and introductions. Instead, she and the Collinses were received in such a manner to make *them* feel uncomfortable for being there. It was odd behaviour indeed, which she could only ascribe to the wealthy being accustomed to having their way.

Seeming unsure of how to proceed—as not all the introductions had been made—Mr Collins alternated between merely standing there stammering, and beginning to walk towards his seat, to ultimately remaining still with a blank look on his face.

In response to seeing his awkwardness, Lady Catherine gave what sounded like an exaggerated sigh and in a bothered manner, said, "My nephews, Mr Darcy and Colonel Fitzwilliam, are visiting for an extended period."

Though no one had asked him to, Mr Collins took his turn introducing Elizabeth to everyone in the room. Excluding Colonel Fitzwilliam, who came and assisted Charlotte and herself to their seats in a friendly manner, it was amply clear that no one at the table particularly welcomed them. Elizabeth wondered why they were invited at all if they were to be treated thus. It was inexplicable behaviour, but because it was so nonsensical, she found it that much more diverting. She hardly knew which of the unusual characters to study first. *Perhaps this evening shall be more enjoyable than I expected.*

It was scarcely a quarter of an hour later that Elizabeth found herself returning to her original estimation of the evening. The dinner progressed in an unusually quiet and cold manner. *Too quiet,* Elizabeth thought as she heard one guest slurp on their soup and another's silver clink. Any question to any person was answered by Lady Catherine in a manner which discouraged further discourse. Miss de Bourgh, Mrs Jenkinson, and Mr Darcy spoke not at all, and the colonel's attempts to be genial were overcome by his aunt's overbearingness. Elizabeth had never been to a family affair that was so formal or tedious. There was only minimal discussion about dull affairs such as the weather and Lady Catherine's age-related health ailments, but nothing of interest or consequence.

When the conversation turned to travel plans, Lady

Catherine questioned her nephews on how they had spent less time in London than they planned, thereby arriving at her home two full days earlier than expected.

"I apologise, Aunt. We found ourselves eager to see you," Colonel Fitzwilliam offered with a charming grin.

Mr Darcy gave the colonel a barely perceptible smirk but Lady Catherine appeared flattered. She maintained a stern demeanour as she said, "Nice as that is, Nephew, you might have sent word. You are always welcome here, but I would have resisted making our party as large tonight had I realised you might be joining us."

Elizabeth nearly choked on her drink and looked to Charlotte with raised eyebrows at the rudeness of their host. But Charlotte, evidently used to such treatment from the imperious woman, focused excessively on her soup.

To Elizabeth's satisfaction, neither nephew responded; instead they looked ashamed at their aunt's ill-breeding. This invited her to feel more comfortable with the gentlemen, especially when Colonel Fitzwilliam leant towards her and asked, "Miss Bennet, have you enjoyed your stay in Kent?"

"Very much so. The countryside is beautiful. One cannot see enough rolling hills or lovely meadows."

"I could not agree more. Darcy and I spent many summers here as children." He grinned and added with a slightly elevated voice clearly meant for Lady Catherine's benefit, "Being back here makes me wonder why we ever leave."

Lady Catherine responded with a head tilt and a curt smile from across the table. When her attention fell away, Colonel Fitzwilliam quickly winked at Mr Darcy, unaware that Elizabeth had noticed. In response, Mr Darcy gave a small shake of his head and looked down at his food. Elizabeth continued looking at Mr Darcy to see how he might react next and was surprised to see him raise his gaze to look straight at her.

She quickly turned her attention back to the colonel and said, "I am sure that is only enhanced since you are coming from town. I find the charms of the country are more striking when you have been away. Did you enjoy your stay in London?"

"Yes, we did enjoy it very much. There is always a new person to meet, new art to see, or music to hear."

"But nothing could ever compare to the unparalleled beauty of Kent," Mr Collins interjected. "Our own lovely piece of heaven, as I often tell Lady Catherine. Even in the small time that I have been here under the patronage of your honourable aunt, its splendour has only grown." He closed his eyes and bowed his head slightly in Lady Catherine's direction.

Elizabeth, unable to set aside her love of sketching other people's characters and finding Mr Darcy particularly quiet and inscrutable throughout the dinner, was curious to see his reaction to Mr Collins' silly comment. When she looked at him this time though, she could glean from his incredulous expression that he thought her cousin as ridiculous as she did.

Colonel Fitzwilliam, who appeared to be repressing a chuckle at her cousin's expense, merely responded, "Yes, indeed." Then he turned to Charlotte. "Mrs Collins, have you enjoyed living here as much as your husband?"

"Yes, very much so."

"Wonderful." Perhaps because of his pleasant nature, he seemed eager to continue the conversation. "And you are from Hertfordshire, are you not? How did you and Mr Collins meet?"

Elizabeth appreciated the gentleman's kindness, but regretted his subject choice. She knew Mr Collins would take it upon himself to recount their 'love story'. She had already heard the tale at least three times since she arrived, and it seemed as though Mr Collins had memorised his speech about it.

Mr Collins cleared his throat and began to answer for Charlotte. "I went to Hertfordshire to see my cousin, who is also Miss Bennet's father, about a family matter. He and my father had a long-standing grudge, you see. After my father died, I wished to bury the hatchet, as they say."

Elizabeth shuddered a little, wishing he had not made a private family matter public, but held her tongue.

"Upon my arrival, I was shocked to find all of the Bennets were abed with illness. Happily for me, Sir William Lucas, dear Charlotte's father, graciously offered to shelter me at a moment's notice. Initially, I scarce took notice of Charlotte, being preoccupied with the consideration of other eligible ladies in the vicinity."

Awful as his insult was to his now-wife, Elizabeth was thankful and surprised he did not mention that she and her sisters were the targets of his original designs.

"When my attention did alight upon Charlotte, my interest was not immediately piqued. However, she persistently inserted herself into my presence, and in due course, her pragmatic disposition could not be disregarded. A clergyman, indeed, necessitates a judicious and sensible companion. Gradually, she captivated my regard. It did not require an excessive span of time before I could confidently assert that it seemed as though we were divinely fashioned for one another."

Elizabeth made every effort to not roll her eyes and sigh, and somehow succeeded. Surprisingly, Charlotte only looked on gracefully, and remained silent. *How is she not infuriated when he speaks of her so? In portraying her as a second option, he fails to recognise her worth.*

Then again Mr Collins had surely not been any great romantic conquest for Charlotte, but a practical choice. Mr Collins was a man who could provide for her and would not be overtly cruel to her—merely embarrassing at times—and she felt she could not ask for more.

Elizabeth did not approve of looking at marriage in such a wholly prudent way as her friend did; she felt there must surely be affection between a man and wife. In this, however, it seemed that Charlotte was content and so would she be satisfied on her friend's behalf.

She looked at Mr Darcy to see how he might be looking at her cousin now but almost jumped when she saw that he was staring at her, again. Once their eyes met, his darted away quickly. *Am I imagining it or does he seem to look in my direction often? Is it to criticise? Or is it an absence of mind?* She diverted her gaze away and almost shrugged as she took a bite of her soup. *I suppose it matters very little either way. I doubt we shall ever see each other again after tonight.*

CHAPTER FOUR

Darcy lifted the fork to his mouth and took another bite of the roast. He was usually pleased with the food at Rosings during his visits, but for some reason tonight everything was flavourless. After chewing and swallowing the dry, bland morsel with the aid of his drink, he set his fork down and craned his neck to look down the table at Miss Bennet again. His interest in her had only grown as the dinner had progressed, and he found himself unable to resist stealing glances whenever he could. His aunt's continuous chatter beside him faded into background noise but still prevented him from hearing the specifics of the conversation farther down the table, much to his frustration.

Though he could not hear what was being said, he saw Miss Bennet's face darken. *She appears quite frustrated with her cousin. I wonder what he did, though I can imagine any number of reasons she might be upset with him. The man is a narrow-minded, bumbling idiot. He surely has made some pig-headed comment.*

Darcy took another bite of his food, more for appearances

than hunger. As he chewed the tasteless morsel, he sensed his aunt pause in the conversation next to him, as if waiting for his response.

"Yes, indeed," he said absently, his attention still focused on Miss Bennet. This appeased Lady Catherine enough, and she continued prattling next to him.

He wished to speak to Miss Bennet—a desire which was puzzling and intriguing—and know why she was so upset with her cousin. *Why am I so fascinated by her? I cannot understand it. She is pretty enough, but nothing exceptional. Still, there is something else that sets her apart.*

"Darcy, did you hear me?"

Pulled out of his reverie, he looked at a clearly annoyed Lady Catherine. "Forgive me, I did not. Would you be so kind as to repeat yourself?"

"I *said* how does Georgiana fare in her studies?"

"Very well, she excels in all her subjects and displays a diligent work ethic," he answered quickly before looking again at Miss Bennet.

Now, she was smirking enigmatically at his aunt. *She seems to do that often. It is as if she has a secret she knows about everyone. Does she deem herself superior to us? It is as if she mocks us, it is unheard of.*

His thoughts were interrupted again by Lady Catherine, but this time she spoke to the object of his fascination instead of himself.

"Miss Bennet," Lady Catherine called to her guest across the long dining table. "Was that you I saw walking out in the countryside from my carriage this morning?"

"Yes, your ladyship, it was. I must say I am enjoying the scenery in Kent. It is truly magnificent."

Ignoring her comment, Lady Catherine continued her interrogation, "Do you play and sing, Miss Bennet?"

The lady smiled modestly. "A little."

"Only a little? You shall try our instrument someday. You must not neglect to practise while you are here."

Miss Bennet opened her mouth to speak, but Lady Catherine interrupted her response. "Do you draw? Or know the modern languages?"

"No, not at all."

"Do you do anything besides walk around the countryside unattended?"

Darcy watched as Miss Bennet seemed to sense the rudeness of his aunt's insolent queries and the ridiculousness of her inference. Yet she reacted in the most surprising of ways, which was to poorly conceal a smile at his aunt's expense.

"I assure you, I enjoy a great number of things," she answered before she took a small bite of potatoes.

"Well, you shall never find a husband scampering about the countryside. Am I correct, Nephews? A gentleman desires a lady who is accomplished, and walking is an unproductive way to spend your time. You should be focusing your time on improving yourself in learning languages, music, drawing, and cultivating a certain degree of intelligence. There will be more time for things such as walking once you have found a husband."

Two of the gentlemen had the intelligence to stay silent, but Mr Collins, evidently feeling the need to contribute his support to his patroness, called out, "Indeed, Lady Catherine."

Miss Bennet looked down, and Darcy knew she must be nursing her wounds after receiving such a set-down. He was shocked when she looked up and was again masking amusement.

"Yes, perhaps. Although it could be argued that for a married lady, household duties would reduce the time available for favoured pastimes. I also would think it rather odd to spend so much time in the usual accomplishments only to abandon them once the prize had been won to pursue my true interests and hobbies. Surely one's husband must feel betrayed for having committed himself to a lady who becomes a very different version of herself as a wife than who she was before they married. It seems wiser to reveal my genuine interests to a man rather than putting up an artifice."

Lady Catherine reacted to this speech in a particularly singular manner: she fell silent. It was surely unprecedented to find any lady, young or old, who did not immediately accept her advice. Darcy did not know whether he should be appalled at Miss Bennet's defiance or impressed at her honesty. She was the first creature he had ever seen who dared to trifle with his formidable aunt—himself and his cousin included.

Before Lady Catherine could respond, Miss Bennet continued by smoothing things over in the most curious of ways. "But I must thank you for your condescension, Lady Catherine. Perhaps you are correct. Your depth of insight into significant matters is truly remarkable, and I will take into account what you have said. I must admit, your tendency to involve yourself in the affairs of acquaintances, even those as unfamiliar as myself, feels similar to receiving a gift."

Lady Catherine nodded curtly at Miss Bennet's concession even if Darcy understood differently. He marvelled at her cleverness. How had she managed to hold her own and appease Lady Catherine at the same time?

Miss Bennet looked up just then, catching his eye upon her. There was an impish gleam in her own eyes that he responded to with a wry half smile. She quirked the corner of her lips upwards in reply and he, quite daringly, gave an expressive glance towards his aunt and then quickly rolled his eyes. She lowered her head quickly but not before he saw the smile which overtook her countenance. *She is not a classic beauty,* he decided, *but the expressiveness of her eyes and her smile make her quite astonishing.*

Dinner continued on in this manner, and she continued to puzzle Darcy. Lady Catherine had given a report of the dinner guests before they arrived, and somehow knew, probably through Mr Collins, that though she was a part of the gentry class, she had little beyond her charms to recommend her.

She has no fortune of her own and has poor connexions with relations involved in trade and law. Darcy practically scoffed aloud at this thought as he looked out the nearest window.

By all accounts she should be trying to earn our approval, but she does not appear eager to impress us. How unusual.

He began rhythmically tapping his fingers on the polished wood of the table, resisting the urge to look at her again. *Why can I not stop staring at her? At first I was simply intrigued, but now I cannot stop wondering what she might do or say next. What is this feeling I have for her?* He furrowed his brows. *Is this...admiration? Yes, that seems close. I truly believe that if she had more to recommend her, I could very well be tempted to pursue her.* Darcy froze at this shocking realisation. She was gently born but in every way inferior to him! She was not the kind of woman who should capture his heart. *Yet why does she have this effect on me?*

Frowning, he looked down the table again, hoping to find fault in her and chase these feelings away. He watched as she conversed with the colonel. *Look at him, lucky man. He has never looked half so entertained in this dining room.* He then felt a smile begin to tug on the corners of his mouth as he watched her giggling and speaking animatedly. *Her eyes practically dance as she speaks. She certainly smiles too often, but still, it is as if the whole room has come alive merely because she is in it. Who could not be drawn in?*

"Darcy could only support my side, as naturally he is a most loyal cousin."

Hearing his name spoken startled Darcy from his musings, during which he had again fixed his gaze on Miss Bennet without fully realising it. As she glanced in his direction and found him staring, she gave him a curious look. She had noticed him looking at her again! Mortified, his mind went blank and he had no idea what his cousin had said of him. Thankfully, Fitzwilliam came to his rescue by interrupting the silence and continuing the conversation. "He is a staunch supporter of my profession."

Miss Bennet tilted her head. "Is that so, Mr Darcy?"

He was mortified at how much it affected him to hear her say his name and prayed she did not notice his flush.

"Darcy is an intelligent man, and he knows that there is more than meets the eye in the art of war," asserted Fitzwilliam. "Only one unacquainted with battle strategy would argue that the navy has been more important in this war."

The war? They were debating whether the army or the

navy had been more valuable in the war? How had they moved to this?

"Very well, we must conclude that we are at odds. Perhaps I am a simpleton, but I cannot relent." Miss Bennet took a sip of wine. After she placed it back on the table, she returned her attention to his cousin. "I cannot concede to your suggestions, sir, namely because the very geography involved allows the navy to be more significant in preventing Napoleon's forces from invading Britain. I certainly mean no disrespect to your profession, for it is not merely a matter of having more skill. Rather, just the circumstances allow the navy to be more essential. And pray tell me, what can you argue is of more importance than controlling the trade routes?"

To Darcy's alarm, he saw that Miss Bennet's charms were not lost on Fitzwilliam, who had leant back in his chair and was smiling admiringly at her replies.

She glanced to Darcy for support in this debate. He looked at her face, and saw how uncommonly intelligent her eyes made it appear. Though he could not say what all her exact points had been, he felt safe in siding with her.

"I am sorry, Cousin, on this matter I must say I agree with Miss Bennet."

The young lady seemed satisfied. Fitzwilliam chuckled. "Mark my words, Miss Bennet, there will come a day when you will see that the army will win this war. I would wager anything I had on it."

"Very well, when that happens, you may come and find me, wherever I may be, and collect your winnings," she said with a good-natured laugh.

Lady Catherine then commanded the table's attention by engaging Mr Collins on the dangers of gambling. Darcy was thankful for the distraction. He could only think how he had been paying too much attention to Miss Bennet, and had been caught at it. A woman of the *ton* would have been shopping for her trousseau for much less. He *must* find a way to control himself. As fascinating as she was, the lady was not for him. He was no romantic; he was a Darcy. Choice in marriage was not his course in life; he had been repeatedly instructed in what type of woman he was expected to marry and what station in life she would have. It had always been about increasing his family's estate. And Miss Bennet, and her circumstances, most certainly would not do that for him. He willed his eyes to look away from her, convincing himself that he needed to avoid her for the duration of dinner.

Just then, he heard her giggle at something Fitzwilliam had said. His gaze found her immediately and with it, all resolutions were lost. He was immediately drawn in again. Maybe he could not marry her, but it could not be so bad to enjoy her companionship these next few weeks, could it?

CHAPTER FIVE

Elizabeth furrowed her brow as she delicately pulled her needle upwards through her fabric. She sat comfortably in an armchair as she worked on her embroidery, basking in the warmth of the afternoon sunlight streaming through the windows of the parsonage's small back parlour. Charlotte, sitting nearby, provided pleasant accompaniment with her quiet humming as she worked on her own embroidery design. With each stitch, Elizabeth felt more and more content as her floral design gradually began to take shape.

This satisfaction was likely due, in no small part, to Mr Collins having excused himself an hour earlier to indulge in his bee-keeping. Elizabeth was thankful for it. Having already endured the sight of him shovelling in his breakfast in a most unappealing manner and hearing his repetitive prattle about the splendours of Kent, Elizabeth had reached her fill of his antics for the day. While she greatly enjoyed Charlotte's company, she found that she had little tolerance for her cousin's.

Elizabeth paused in her needlework, allowing her fingers to rest for a moment. Memories of Mr Collins's behaviour the previous night flooded her mind and interrupted her ease. *I cannot fathom how he acted at Rosings last night.* Her cheeks flushed with embarrassment. *Between his sycophantic treatment of Lady Catherine and his complete misunderstanding of social cues, it was almost painful to be around him. It is one thing to tolerate his antics in private, but to witness them in the company of others is truly mortifying. My connexion to him is an embarrassment in itself.*

She almost shook her head as she picked up her needle again.

Beside her, Charlotte let out a contented sigh as she worked diligently on her own embroidery. Elizabeth smiled. *At least Charlotte seems happy with her lot in life. Even if I am becoming less and less equal to the task of staying in the same room as her husband.*

They continued their work in comfortable silence and Elizabeth found herself thinking of her family. It was the longest she had been away from home without any close family members. She was enjoying the independence and peace that it gave her, but the tedium of life in Kent had begun to wear on her. There were no sisterly fights to squash, no mother's nerves to calm, and no father with whom to exchange knowing glances whenever the liveliness in their home worsened too quickly. She felt a slight ache for that familiar environment.

Ah well, the visit will pass quickly enough and then I shall be back at Longbourn, likely desiring I could escape to the peace of Kent again!

Why wish away this lovely sojourn when I have no notion of when or if I shall enjoy it again?

There was much to enjoy in Kent. Rosings Park was lovely, and becoming lovelier by the day as the spring progressed.

But I doubt very much that I should ever like to dine again with Lady Catherine. Her behaviour was abysmal. I would be just as embarrassed to be connected to her as to Mr Collins.

"Charlotte?" Elizabeth asked as she held up her fabric and tilted it to examine her handiwork.

"Yes?"

"Does Lady Catherine often behave as she did last night?"

"What do you mean?" Charlotte asked absently as she snipped a red thread.

"Did you not notice? She seemed displeased that we attended the dinner to which she had invited us."

"Perhaps a little. But she has every right to treat us as she wishes."

Placing her embroidery in her lap, Elizabeth looked at her friend. "I hardly think her wealth justifies such behaviour."

"Lady Catherine has been very good to us, Lizzy," Charlotte said firmly, ensuring Elizabeth would drop the subject.

Elizabeth took the hint and fell silent as Charlotte unsuccessfully tried to rethread her needle. After a few moments, Charlotte peered up with a knowing glance. "Her nephews seemed to take a fancy to you."

Elizabeth let out a laugh. "I can assure you, one of them did not."

"Whatever do you mean?" Charlotte asked as she finally pulled the red thread through the eye of the needle.

Rather surprised that her usually observant friend had

not noticed, Elizabeth replied, "Mr Darcy was so quiet the entire dinner. At times I even wondered whether he disapproved of me."

"You cannot be certain he felt that way."

"Why else would he remain silent or look intently at me throughout the dinner?"

"Perhaps he is just a little shy."

"Well, I suppose that is fair. I do not really know him after all." Elizabeth picked up her needlework and inserted her needle back into the fabric. "What do you know about him?" She had hoped to sound more off-handed about it, but she worried her slightly elevated pitch betrayed her. She regulated her tone before continuing, "Do you take his character to be proud or shy?"

"Probably a little of both," Charlotte said with a chuckle. "I must confess, I do not know much about him, but from what I do know, he has ample reason to be more than a little proud. His estate is said to be magnificent, even bigger than Rosings."

"No," Elizabeth said in shock. "How is that possible?"

Charlotte looked up at her. "Mr Collins says his father has ten thousand a year."

Elizabeth's jaw dropped. "Are you in earnest? That is an astonishing figure."

"Indeed, such a match would surely bring happiness to any woman," Charlotte responded with raised eyebrows.

Elizabeth began laughing. "You are so desperate to see me married that you are now imagining things."

Charlotte shrugged. "Very well. What then can you say to dissuade me from believing that her *other* nephew fancied you?"

"That leap of imagination is at least more believable than Mr Darcy."

"Well, what do you think?"

"I do not know him at all! My goodness, Charlotte, we had one animated conversation, and you are already picturing me married."

"You are not married, Elizabeth and that is the trouble," Charlotte said, her voice as serious as her gaze. "It would be wise to continue with your charming banter and secure his interest while the chance is still present. Even if you are not completely certain of your own feelings, opportunities such as this are rare."

"Charlotte! You are quite amusing. While I appreciate the colourful advice, I highly doubt we shall even see him again. It is doubtful Lady Catherine will want our company again while her nephews are still at Rosings."

She began to say something else when she heard the sound of a door opening and closing down the corridor. A feeling of dread overcame her as she heard Mr Collins's heavy footsteps approaching from the vestibule; he was far earlier than expected. She hurriedly placed her embroidery aside on the mahogany table next to her.

"Charlotte, if you do not need me, I think I shall go for a walk in the grove."

"Of course, but pray do not tarry long—it looks like rain."

Elizabeth nodded and stood quickly. She briskly walked out the back door just as Mr Collins opened the door into the parlour.

After making her narrow escape, she used all her self-control to avoid throwing her arms up in victory. As she walked, she felt her heart rate slow and return to a regular pace after her energetic escape, and took in the lovely landscape around her. She walked along the leaf-covered path for a few minutes, and stopped when she saw a hawk soaring above. It sailed above the trees as it weaved around the sky. Elizabeth closed her eyes, and drew in a deep breath. The fresh scent of the outdoors filled her lungs and enveloped her with tranquillity. As she exhaled, all the tension in her shoulders dissipated, leaving her feeling completely serene.

She opened her eyes and began walking again. She was enjoying the sound of last autumn's leaves rustling beneath her feet when she recognised Colonel Fitzwilliam and Mr Darcy coming towards her. As the two parties drew abreast of one another, Mr Darcy stood back in his stoic manner, seeming aloof, while Colonel Fitzwilliam beamed happily in the same agreeable manner she had noticed the night prior.

"How pleasant it is to run into you here," she greeted them.

"The pleasure is ours, Miss Bennet. And what brings you to this side of the park this afternoon?" Colonel Fitzwilliam said in a cheerful tone.

"I am enjoying a bit of a ramble. The peacefulness of nature always calls to me."

"A respite from the more bustling energy of the parsonage?" Colonel Fitzwilliam asked with a quirk of his brow, and Elizabeth laughed.

"I am not averse to conversation, but there is sometimes a surfeit of it at the parsonage house," she admitted.

"Much as we hate to further cut up your peace, would you do us the honour of allowing us to accompany you? As some means of enticement, we will show you some of the favourite spots of our childhood summers past, eh Darcy?" The colonel nudged his cousin who had, as yet, scarcely uttered a syllable.

Elizabeth wondered whether the scheme was agreeable to him or whether he had hoped they would be soon on their way. "The pleasure would be all mine."

Mr Darcy only nodded at her.

CHAPTER SIX

They walked on together with Elizabeth between them. As they strolled along the path, Colonel Fitzwilliam and Elizabeth carried most of the conversation, with Mr Darcy offering only a rare phrase or two. They spoke of the advantages and disadvantages of being in the countryside versus being in town, some of the travelling the colonel had done recently, and his family. Colonel Fitzwilliam was a good conversationalist and could match Elizabeth's wit. He was jovial and open.

Mr Darcy, by contrast, was the trio's silent, almost forgotten presence. He offered occasional smiles and even fewer laughs at Colonel Fitzwilliam's musings. It ought to have put her off the gentleman and yet in spite of, or perhaps because of his reserve, she sensed great depth to him. What words he did offer hinted at intelligence and, on one rare instance, humour. She found herself increasingly curious about him.

The conversation as they walked meant that Elizabeth's head was mostly turned towards the colonel. Yet whenever she turned her head in the opposite direction, she often caught Mr Darcy looking at her. Each time their eyes met, she would feel her stomach leap, and he would quickly look away. Although she later regretted not saying something witty about catching him staring, she remained silent during those moments. As they continued walking, she could not help but be aware of his every movement and glance over to see whether he was watching her again.

As Colonel Fitzwilliam had earlier teased Mr Darcy for walking silently in a stupid manner, Elizabeth concluded that he usually was a bit more talkative and perhaps felt inhibited by her presence. In an attempt to provoke his liveliness, she followed the colonel's course and teased him a little.

"Mr Darcy, I must beg of you, please cease speaking incessantly at once. I cannot hear your cousin's stories adequately."

It worked, somewhat. He smiled at her, not seeming offended in the least. "Forgive me, Miss Bennet. I had not realised how quiet I was."

"You should have done," the colonel inserted warmly. "Have I not tasked you for your reticence three times already?"

Mr Darcy's gaze was still intent upon her. "Would it please you if I relayed some childhood stories of my cousin here that would cause him to blush? I have an interesting one involving bees that occurred over there in that very tree." He gestured towards a small copse nearby.

"Perhaps I preferred when he was silent!" Colonel Fitzwilliam said with a mocking frown. "There are too many secrets in that brainbox of his!"

Elizabeth covered her mouth and laughed as Mr Darcy began his own round of tales based on the landscape surrounding them. Each tree seemed to have been a scene of some childhood escapade and though many of them were amusing, she also found the evident closeness between the cousins particularly charming.

Colonel Fitzwilliam interrupted one such tale, stopping their progress and gesturing at a path that had appeared to their right. "Darcy, let us go off here and take in the view at Holly Hill."

"I do not believe Miss Bennet desired to go that far, and while the scenery is beautiful, the terrain is difficult."

The colonel gave her an assessing look. "Miss Bennet, you seem like a lady who enjoys the out of doors, and is ready for an adventure. Would you like to take in the sight? It is amazingly beautiful this time of year. Makes one proud to serve and live in such a country."

She smiled at them both. "I cannot think of anything I should rather do."

"Richard, no," Mr Darcy interrupted. "It will not do."

"Whyever not? You surely cannot talk of childhood memories and not show her Holly Hill in all its glory?"

Mr Darcy stared at the colonel, his face unreadable to her but apparently not to his cousin.

"If Miss Bennet says she is equal to it—"

"It is quite a steep, dirty climb," Mr Darcy explained to her.

Elizabeth laughed. "Mr Darcy, I assure you that I am more than prepared to get my hem a little dirty. I would be more worried about yourself. I have never seen a cravat so white or boots with so few scratches. I should say your attire will suffer far more than mine."

Colonel Fitzwilliam barked out a laugh, and Mr Darcy gave her a quizzical look that she could not decipher. She wondered whether she had offended him.

"Very well," Mr Darcy said eventually. He pulled back a large tree branch, and gestured to her to go ahead into the thick wooded area off the beaten path.

Mr Darcy had exaggerated how dirty the path would be, but she surmised that he was not used to women from the country. Ladies of the *ton* probably would have baulked at walking in such conditions, but thankfully, she was not one of those. It had always been her aim to live her life with enthusiasm, to take in whatever sights she could, and meet interesting characters along the way. A life worth living, in her estimation, was made up in its depth, not in its length or status achieved. She could not imagine denying herself such a satisfying experience because of so silly a notion as propriety or a little difficulty.

They followed the overgrown path up the hill that the men had carved out through their repeated walks as youths. She quickly realised that calling this a hill had been an understatement. It was a steep incline comparable to what seemed like a small mountain. But the path that the men had made to the top as young boys sloped gently in a zig-zag motion up to the top, so the hill was not too difficult to ascend. Occasionally, there was some terrain in which she required a hand to walk over a log or jump over a fence, and Mr Darcy would swiftly and quietly provide it.

Elizabeth was invigorated that they were in unconstrained nature. She could see God's goodness and wisdom reflected in His design of every forest animal she saw, built to thrive in its environment. She took in the colours that He painted every tree and leaf, infinitely more beautiful than any painting she saw that tried to recapture it. It brought her immense joy, and she felt happier than she had in all of her time at Kent.

Mr Darcy, who had been walking ahead of her to clear the way such as he could, stopped suddenly—so suddenly that Elizabeth nearly ran into him. "We have been gone quite a long time now. I worry we shall not get you back to your hosts by dinner."

Elizabeth had not realised how much time had passed, but the sun was no longer directly overhead, suggesting they were likely nearer to the dinner hour than she had realised.

"We can go the steeper way, and get there faster. It is just ahead." Colonel Fitzwilliam gestured straight in front of them.

Elizabeth looked to where he pointed and saw there was a steep incline just past the curving path if they went straight instead. When Mr Darcy seemed as if he was about to object, she assured him, "If you are worried about me, please do not. I am equal to a climb."

"I do not think you realise how steep the climb might be," he replied.

"Perhaps not, but I would like to at least make the attempt."

He regarded her for a moment, with what she hoped was begrudging respect in his eyes. "Very well."

And so the trio went ahead. The dirt was not as compact and felt more slippery as they climbed. A few times Elizabeth needed to use her hands to catch her balance on the rocks in front of her. She could sense Mr Darcy directly behind her with his arms out, ready to catch her if she slipped. It was reassuring and made her feel protected. Although she almost slipped a few times, she managed to keep her balance the whole way and avoid falling into his arms.

When they reached the top, she saw immediately that it had been well worth the exertion it took to get there. Elizabeth looked at the scene in wonderment. As far as the eye could see, there were green rolling hills and to the east she believed she might see a glimpse of the sea.

"Darcy and I spent many a day here escaping Lady Catherine's interrogations," Colonel Fitzwilliam offered.

Elizabeth chuckled. Looking down she let out a gasp. All around their feet, bluebells blanketed the ground, enhancing the majestic scene. "This is positively dream-like! Almost heaven."

"On a clear day, I have always fancied I may see London," stated Mr Darcy quietly.

"Perhaps you can." Then with a contented sigh, she added, "Does it not feel as if time slows in moments such as these?"

Her eyes moved to look at him. As before, he was looking intently at her, and she was certain she must look wild with her hair half falling out, and her dress smeared with mud. She attempted to make a joke of it as she usually did when she felt uncomfortable. "I must look ridiculous. I am certain you are wholly unaccustomed to women with dirty dresses and unkempt hair."

He did not reply. She perceived a small headshake from him as he suddenly turned from her and briskly walked to a different part of the hilltop. She tried not to feel affronted, but her quizzical glances at his back were clearly seen by the colonel, who approached her with a conciliatory grin.

"I think Darcy feels responsible for your safety being up here."

"I hardly know Mr Darcy and am surely not his responsibility."

"You are, at least temporarily, under the protection of us both and we have absconded with you on a dangerous journey," the colonel chuckled. "Darcy always tries to behave in a way that is dignified. He is the most honourable and upright of men you will ever meet. A disciplined one too. I have seen him numerous times fulfil what he believes are his duties and responsibilities despite great personal cost to himself."

Elizabeth glanced over to where Mr Darcy still stood motionless and silent. "He is very serious."

"Try not to be offended by his reserve, he is merely uncomfortable with those he does not know well." He paused a moment before continuing. "Or he might behave like this when he is attempting to become master of his emotions."

Elizabeth contemplated this for a moment, and shrugged, unsure what to make of that. Did Mr Darcy think her a hoyden for following them up here? He had surely tried to dissuade them. She discovered she did not mind if he disapproved, for the sights had been well worth the effort and the mud, and she did not have to answer for her behaviour to someone so wholly unconnected to her.

Though perhaps the colonel was correct, and his cousin's seemingly proud and unfriendly manners could be attributed to a reserved nature and excessive dignity. She resolved to withhold judgment until she better understood him.

Mr Darcy turned and returned briskly to them. "Miss Bennet, we should be getting you back to the parsonage. Likely Mr and Mrs Collins will dine soon."

She reluctantly agreed, and they turned and headed back the way they came. They walked quietly through the woods for some time; it seemed even the colonel's capacity for easy banter had been exhausted.

"These woods remind me greatly of some in Hertfordshire," Elizabeth said eventually, breaking the silence and gesturing in Colonel Fitzwilliam's direction. "They remind me of a dreadful time when I was lost as a child."

"What happened?" he asked.

"It was late afternoon, and I was following my older cousin. I adored him, but he was trying to desert me, as to him I was just an irritation." Looking towards Colonel Fitzwilliam, she continued her story of how she had almost had to spend the night in the woods. Suddenly Elizabeth felt a hand touch her arm and gently pull her away from the colonel. Startled, she glanced to her left and realised Mr Darcy was subtly shifting her away from tripping on a large branch directly in front of her. It happened so quickly that the colonel had not noticed it. When she turned to look at Mr Darcy, his arms were again behind his back. He was looking towards the ground on the path in front of them, but she saw the corners of his mouth pulling tight for a slight moment. She quietly murmured her appreciation.

She felt a violent blush take over her whole body and was so distracted by her momentary interaction with Mr Darcy that she stopped telling her story.

"You have left us in suspense, Miss Bennet!" said the colonel. "What happened next?"

"I am sorry, I was, um…momentarily distracted," she stammered. "My parents enlisted the help of all of our neighbours and tenants. Finally, just after nightfall, our neighbour, Sir William Lucas—who is Mrs Collins's father—found me hiding up in a tree. He helped me get down and carried me home. I was quite young and a little emotional about the whole ordeal. It was very kind of him."

The gentlemen agreed and said they were thankful she did not have to spend the night in the woods. They continued in good conversation with each other as they accompanied her back to the parsonage.

CHAPTER SEVEN

As they stood just inside the parsonage gate, having finally reached their destination, Elizabeth asked the gentlemen, "Will you be attending the assembly in Westerham tomorrow night?"

"No, I do not believe so. We do not usually attend the local assemblies while we are here," the colonel replied.

"And what say you, Mr Darcy? Or does Colonel Fitzwilliam always proceed to do all the talking and negotiating for you?" She looked him full in the face while she teased him and was pleased when he smiled in reply to her jibe.

"I daresay I am able to make my own decisions. But, in this case my cousin is correct. We had not planned on attending."

"I would not mind attending in the least. My cousin here" —the colonel gestured towards Mr Darcy—"would find it almost impossible, however."

Elizabeth felt more keenly disappointed—and equally

piqued—than she had imagined she would. Did Mr Darcy imagine dancing to be beneath his dignity? Or did he think that every lady there would fall in love with him if he looked her way? Forcing herself to continue speaking lightly, she said, "And why is that, Mr Darcy?"

"I find crowds to be a bit…overwhelming."

"Overwhelming?" She raised one brow dubiously.

"I do not have your easy, sociable nature."

Seeing that Elizabeth was not completely convinced, Colonel Fitzwilliam interjected himself to help his cousin's cause. "What he is not telling you is that he is usually the centre of attention at any gathering he goes to because of his…circumstances. Attending something like a local assembly would garner him the crowd's attention, which he despises."

So, as I suspected, he imagines that every lady in the room will fall in love with him merely because he appears. "I see."

"Will you be there, Miss Bennet?"

She nodded at the colonel's question. "Yes, I am looking forward to it. I find assemblies so diverting. We do not have them often enough in Hertfordshire, and I own to my sociable nature that I find it quite agreeable to be in new places meeting new people."

"Perhaps I will try to draw Darcy out of Rosings for it, although I cannot promise he will be great company if I do bring him. If he can help it, he will not dance a single dance."

Feigning shock, Elizabeth cried, "Mr Darcy! Why, I thought you were the perfect gentleman. I cannot believe that you would ever dare to leave any ladies without a partner?"

He smiled slowly. "Indeed, I could not dare."

She laughed at this, then continued. "How I wish you

both would be there. I will not know a single soul, and I dread that my first introductions will be made in connexion to Mr Collins." Abashed, she covered her mouth after she said so, realising she had spoken too freely.

The two men chuckled. "If you would desire our company, Miss Bennet, we could not refuse being there," said Mr Darcy, adding a small, endearing smile at the end. Colonel Fitzwilliam raised his eyebrows slightly towards his cousin.

She felt her stomach squeeze with pleasure and offered Mr Darcy a genuine grin. "Very well, I look forward to seeing you tomorrow." She bid them farewell and walked towards the parsonage door.

Darcy stood next to his cousin as they watched Miss Bennet disappear into the parsonage. A brisk wind swept through the clearing, stirring some fallen blossoms from the blooming trees to swirl at their feet. He lingered a few moments longer than usual, watching the fallen flowers dance at the spot where he had last seen her before forcing himself to turn around and begin the walk back to Rosings.

They ambled along in a silence interrupted only by the melodies of birdsongs and the gentle rustling of branches overhead. As they strolled, Fitzwilliam bent down to retrieve a large branch from the ground and fashioned it into a walking stick.

"She is a delightful, charming woman, is she not?" he remarked nonchalantly as he examined the stick.

"She is...intriguing," Darcy responded, tugging at his cravat and looking at the trees ahead as he walked.

"Intriguing? Is that all you think?"

"I find her...perplexing," he admitted, his brows furrowing as he looked down.

"Is that so? Well, I find her utterly delightful."

Darcy nodded slowly in agreement. "Indeed, her wit and spirit are unlike, well, really any woman whom we have ever encountered," he conceded.

"A breath of fresh air!" the colonel exclaimed.

"Yes, but her manners are perhaps a little too playful."

"Yet she is still ladylike. In truth, I find her lightness rather enjoyable. Have you not said yourself that you tire of the airs of women of the *ton*?"

"Yes, but I wonder if she teases more than a lady ought," Darcy countered. "And one could argue she borders on impertinence."

Fitzwilliam shrugged, prompting Darcy to engage in his own debate. "But there is a sweetness in her teasing that prevents it from being truly offensive. And she is truly intelligent." Shaking his head, he concluded, "Nevertheless, she and her circumstances are too unconventional for an advantageous marriage."

"Since when did our discourse become about marriage?" The colonel chuckled as Darcy felt himself being eyed curiously. He remained silent long enough for his cousin to continue his musings.

"But yes, she is unconventional. Surely, we have never kept company with a woman who could climb such a steep terrain as she did today. And she did not even bat an eye at getting her dress muddied!" Fitzwilliam lifted his stick to hit a nearby branch and watched the leaves shake furiously before continuing, "No lady of the first circles would be caught dead looking as Miss Bennet did this afternoon."

"But she left me charmed," Darcy countered quickly, then blushed furiously as he realised his slip of tongue.

His cousin halted in his tracks and stared at him. "Has she enchanted you?"

"No, I only meant…she looked…" he said firmly. "That is ridiculous. I will not even dignify such a question with a response."

Silence hung in the air. Darcy lowered his gaze and looked sharply at his cousin when he heard him begin to chuckle. "What are you laughing at?"

"That in spite of your greatest efforts, you simply cannot resist her. It is rather entertaining to witness."

"Enough. We are not talking about this any longer."

The colonel smiled but said no more. They resumed their journey in silence as Darcy continued wrestling with his sentiments. Miss Elizabeth Bennet inspired such contrasting emotions in himself that he could not untangle all his feelings towards her. He trudged forwards in frustration, and suspected he would spend most of the evening trying to figure them out.

CHAPTER EIGHT

December 1813, Hertfordshire

The night after the Bennets' party, Mr Bingley and Mr Darcy had been invited to dine at Longbourn. Only Elizabeth and Jane were ready to greet them when they arrived. It was torture for Elizabeth to be in such intimate company with Mr Darcy; she would have preferred meeting him more informally at dinner once the rest of the family was around. Yet Jane, in her embarrassment and anticipation of her family's tardiness, had asked her to help welcome and entertain the gentlemen until dinner. Only her love for her sister could tempt her to tolerate the man's presence.

After a brief greeting, the four made their way towards the drawing room to sit down and talk until the rest of the family arrived. Jane and Mr Bingley immediately sat down together on one sofa; Mr Darcy sat on the one across from them. Rather than sit on the sofa next to him, Elizabeth chose to pull up an empty chair.

Jane and Mr Bingley mostly carried the conversation between them all. Elizabeth was resolved to not speak often to Mr Darcy. She dared not look at him but felt his gaze upon her frequently. After waiting half an hour, and with no signs of anyone in the house stirring beyond themselves, Mr Darcy shifted in his seat, looking uncomfortable. "I apologise if we misunderstood the desired time to be here."

"Not at all, sir. Schedules are followed loosely at Longbourn," Elizabeth replied matter-of-factly. She knew he would consider it impolite for her family to conduct themselves in such a manner, and took almost perverse pleasure in their proving him correct. What could she do but find the humour in it all? Tonight would be a barrage of humiliations and she was resolved to find amusement in the ridiculousness of it instead of yielding to the mortification.

She watched Mr Darcy inhale deeply and exhale slowly. No doubt he was summoning patience for an evening amongst savages. She was not ignorant of her family's shortcomings but despite their disadvantages, the Bennets were a close and loving family. No matter what fights or traces of tension were bubbling near the surface, there was a strong bond of love between all of its members. Yes, often she did wish they behaved with greater propriety, particularly her mother and younger sisters, and naturally she wished her father had been a better steward of their fortune. But it was not how it was and one could not lament it.

As she grew older, she had seen there was greater value in being together and suffering a little nonsense than being alone with dignity as one's companion, as Mr Darcy was. As she dwelt on these matters, she eyed the man and mentally dared him to look on them with disdain.

The tardiness of the Bennets, she knew, had to be driving him mad. As a man whom she knew followed schedules rigidly, he looked distinctly uneasy. He alternated between looking at his pocket watch and rubbing his fingers together at his side. At last, her sisters began to trickle in. Lydia and Kitty entered first and were arguing about a misplaced brooch. "I know you borrowed it without asking!"

"What difference does it make? It was back in your bedchamber before you even noticed."

"You cannot merely take what you wish, Lydia! I do not care if you put it back before I noticed! And there is a bead missing!"

"It was like that when I got it from your bedchamber," Lydia replied airily.

"It was not like that before."

"Yes, it was!"

"You are never careful with my things!"

As Lydia and Kitty took their squabble to the other side of the drawing room, the Gardiner children entered the room. A toddler holding small slippers ran by Elizabeth and Mr Darcy, nearly bouncing into them as she ran by. A little girl a few years older chased behind her yelling, "I didn't *particularly* want my shoes off, Annabelle. I *particularly* wanted them on." She bumped into Mr Darcy, and he looked quite alarmed.

"Amelia! Watch out sweetheart, can you apologise for running into Mr Darcy?"

The girl glared at him for a moment before continuing to chase her sister, ignoring Elizabeth's command. Elizabeth hid a smile.

Mary and the eldest of their Gardiner cousins walked into

the room, fully engaged in a discussion of music. Seven-year-old Lillian was educating Mary about song-writing, singing a ditty she had written for her new doll. "Oh Emma, you are so great. Come let's celebrate," she sang. Then she declared, "Sometimes I make up songs and I am really good at it. Would you like me to help teach you how to do it?"

Mary replied in her most sanctimonious voice. "I think not and you should heed the scriptures which tell us that pride goeth before a fall."

Elizabeth could not help herself and glanced at Mr Darcy when Mary said the word 'pride'. He was too busy looking at his pocket watch to notice.

The Gardiners and Mrs Bennet could be heard talking in the corridor, adding to the general volume of the gathering. The last of their party to arrive was Mr Bennet who, despite knowing the desired hour for dinner, startled visibly when he saw such a large party already gathered and ready to eat. He entered with his two overgrown spaniels trailing behind him. The two dogs—one young and energetic, the other old, with arthritic hips that made him hobble more than walk—scampered about, adding even more commotion to the scene, sniffing every person in the room twice before being shooed outside again by Mrs Bennet's shrieks.

Elizabeth sighed. The entire scene was a loud and hectic domestic hurricane. The cacophony was made complete by the hearth's roaring fire, which seemed determined to be heard in spite of all the noise of the others.

Though the lack of ceremony would have suggested an informal family dinner, the table was to include some few extra from the neighbourhood as well. Mrs Bennet had gone into Meryton earlier that day to call on her sister, Mrs

Philips; true to her hospitable nature, she could not resist inviting others that she encountered to join them for dinner.

As the large group began taking their seats, Elizabeth felt a sense of relief upon seeing that Mr Darcy was seated farther down the table, away from her and next to Mary and Mr Gardiner. She was glad to be distanced from him but also reassured that his proximity to Mary and her uncle, with their quieter demeanours, would likely ensure a less offensive dinner than if he had a front-row seat to the noisy antics of her youngest sisters.

However, I am certain that since he is not seated near Mr Bingley, he will not trouble himself to talk to anyone at all.

As the food was brought out and dinner progressed, her prediction proved accurate: Mr Darcy remained silent. *He would actually enjoy conversing with my uncle, if he would only give him a chance,* Elizabeth thought as she resisted the urge to shake her head.

The conversation between the rest of the guests was energetic and disorderly. Lydia and Kitty had now made up and were laughing with the young and earnest Mr Andrews. Family anecdotes were being shared, and political debates rose and waned. Conversation was never dull and engaged all members of the table. *Everyone seems to be enjoying themselves save for one.* Elizabeth glanced at Mr Darcy and could see that he looked stricken. Though she could not be certain, as she was not sitting next to him, she had not heard a syllable from him. She had been to enough of *his* family dinners that she knew they were nothing like this.

Elizabeth was distracted from her thoughts when she felt something tugging at her dress on her side. She looked down to see her four-year-old cousin looking up at her.

"Why are you not in the nursery, Amelia?" she enquired gently. "Have you already eaten all your dinner?"

The girl whispered, "Could you give me a chocolate biscuit?"

"A biscuit?" Elizabeth exclaimed softly. "I am afraid I do not have any biscuits but I should imagine that once I eat my dinner, I may have some dessert later. Do you think you ate enough so that you could have a biscuit later, too?"

"Um…" Amelia twirled a strand of her hair. "Maybe I ate three?"

"Three bites?"

"Mm-hm."

"I think you should go and have three more bites, and then I shall see that Mrs Hill brings some biscuits to the nursery. Will you do that for me?"

With that Amelia nodded and ran off, hopefully back to the nursery. Glancing up she saw that Mr Darcy had observed the exchange. No doubt he was appalled that the children were roaming about as they were. With that in mind, Elizabeth sent her mother an expressive look which Mrs Gardiner noticed. Blushing lightly, her aunt rose and left the room, no doubt wishing to speak to the maid acting as nurse for the evening, and urge her to keep better control of her charges.

"She is quite like you were as a child," said Mr Bennet.

"Strong-willed and refusing to cede to anyone's notions of what she should or should not be doing. Giving anyone who tried to rein you in a downright difficult time," added her mother.

Mr Darcy was within earshot and his interest appeared piqued for the first time. Looking curious, he turned towards Mrs Bennet.

A SHARED HISTORY

Feeling acutely aware of Mr Darcy's judgment, Elizabeth spoke first. "Well, yes. In any case...Uncle Gardiner, have you had any word from—"

She was interrupted by her father, who had a mischievous smile on his face. "Amelia particularly reminds me of when Lizzy yelled at the Finke family."

"I told you specifically not to talk to them that day, yet you went ahead and did it regardless. No one could know how much your escapades have threatened my nerves all these years," Mrs Bennet said, giving her daughter a look and a small shake of her head. Mr Darcy's eyes followed her mother's, landing on her.

"I forget how that one goes. Do tell it, Papa," cried Lydia.

Elizabeth kept a smile on her face even as she hoped her eyes shot daggers at her youngest sister. "No, I do not think anyone wants to hear that story and in any case, it was a long time ago."

Mr Darcy cleared his throat. "I think I would like to hear it."

Elizabeth looked at him, slightly shocked and wholly mortified. It was one of the first things she had heard him say all night and she was loath to give him more reasons to think ill of her, even if the event occurred when she was a child.

"Well, it appears I have no choice. Mr Darcy is the type of man to whom I could refuse nothing." Mr Bennet smiled. "When Elizabeth was eight years old—"

"It appears I have lost an ally in my father." Elizabeth laughed weakly and moved her gaze to her plate. She could not face Mr Darcy's satiric eye, and it appeared he was determined to stare at her.

"The Finkes, our neighbours to the east, had two fearsome hunting dogs. They were not responsible with them, and they were frightful beasts."

Only a desperate need to defend herself could prompt her to address Mr Darcy directly, and she interrupted her father. "Mr Darcy, before my father continues, you should know that the Bennet family has a practice: truth matters very little in pursuit of a good story."

Mr Darcy smiled briefly.

Waving her off, Mr Bennet continued. "As I was saying, these dogs frequently went to various neighbours' properties and killed chickens or scared children and the like. We had an old, loyal dog called Shep. He had been a hunter in his younger days but by this time he was more of a pet. Our children loved him and he was good to them. One day, the Finkes' dogs came over to our property while the children were outside playing. It so happened that Shep protected the children from their violent dogs, and ended up with the bottom half of his ear bit off. After we bandaged him up, when all the excitement had died down, we discovered our little Lizzy was gone from the house. Later we found out she had marched the three miles over to their property with the bloodied piece of skin from Shep's ear and gave Mr Finke a piece of her mind. She yelled at him that he had not trained his dogs well enough, that they were a menace to the neighbours, and that he needed to do something about it. He was a gentleman, mind you."

Elizabeth was covering her face in embarrassment.

"Mr Finke was outraged that Elizabeth had the audacity to address him in such a manner," her father said, "but those dogs never again troubled anyone in the neighbourhood."

"And Mr Bennet did not punish her for what she had done," Mrs Bennet added.

"Why would I?" he said, smiling at Elizabeth. "She was right—Mr Finke was a fool, and those dogs were dangerous. I admired her for her bravery in standing up to him."

"And so, she has been a little impertinent thing ever since," said her mother. "Headstrong and speaking her mind, scaring off any men who would have her."

Before Elizabeth could feel embarrassed, Mr Darcy quietly said, with a small smile, "I would like to think so."

Elizabeth met his gaze and returned the smile, feeling unable to tear herself away from his dark eyes. After a moment longer than deemed appropriate, their smiles began to fade but their eyes remained on each other. Remembering herself, Elizabeth dropped hers away first.

CHAPTER NINE

Long after all their guests had left, the five sisters and their aunt Gardiner were gathered in Jane and Elizabeth's room, dressed in their night-rails and reminiscing on the evening. Elizabeth sat on her bed behind Kitty as she plaited her hair, her thoughts busy replaying every moment she could remember about Mr Darcy. As her fingers moved deftly through her sister's hair, she wondered how he felt being there and if it was as difficult for him as it was for her. Beyond the long wait for dinner, it certainly did not seem so. He was his usual taciturn self, very likely disgusted with all of them and their unruly, undignified household. Only hearing her name spoken could draw her attention back to the present conversation.

"Lizzy, I cannot believe Papa told that story about you and Shep's ear!" Lydia exclaimed as she sifted through the ribbons laid out on Jane's dressing table.

"If I were you, I would be dead from embarrassment," Kitty said without turning around to look at Elizabeth.

"I daresay, with the company there tonight I shall survive."

"Yes, because Mr Royce was not there!" Lydia teased as she held a red ribbon against her hair and peered in the mirror.

Elizabeth only smiled and looked down.

Lydia continued as she tilted her head, still studying her reflection, "What is going on between the two of you? I daresay, he is handsome, kind, rich enough, and loves you. What more could you ask for?"

In the past, Elizabeth would have asked for a great deal more. She would have wanted love and passion above all else, and would not have married without it. However, faced with her family's imminent transitions—Jane's impending marriage and the likelihood of her other sisters following suit—she faced the possibility of being left behind. She had experienced a shift in her feelings, she realised, and knew she would rather run her own home and life than be forever dependent on others to care for her. Now, her wishes for a husband were more practical; a good, dependable man capable of providing for her would be enough. She desired a respectable man, confident that with time, she could cultivate affection and perhaps love. Where he probably would not have been a possibility before, her old friend Royce could very well be that man now.

From her seat in an armchair, Jane hushed their younger sisters. "Do not tease Lizzy." Aunt Gardiner stayed silent as she stood behind Jane and gently brushed her hair, but let a subtle smile grow across her face at the exchange.

Elizabeth laughed. "Do not worry yourself, Jane. I do not mind. To be honest, I am not sure. It would be a lie to say that I have not noticed his finer qualities. I shall only say that I am interested to know him better as an adult."

"But what do you really think? Does he make your pulse race?" Lydia enquired, clasping the ribbon close to her chest with both hands and looking up dramatically towards the ceiling.

"Lydia!" Jane exclaimed, and the sisters began laughing. Even Mary, perched comfortably on Jane's bed, lowered her book to surrender a smile. Lydia continued to chuckle as she casually tossed the ribbon back onto the table. She made her way to sit next to Mary, settling in with her legs folded beneath her.

Elizabeth lightly patted Kitty's shoulders after she finished her last plait to indicate she was finished. Kitty turned around to face her and said earnestly, "Mr Royce would doubtless make any woman happy enough. There would be no troubles there."

"Last I remember, Lizzy, you hardly gave him a second glance. Has he really altered so much in four years that he could affect you?" Mary asked, chiming in for the first time during the conversation.

"A great deal can change in four years. Not only in him but myself too," Elizabeth answered.

"Well, he would certainly have you if that's what you wanted," Lydia stated with a snicker. "He has made it a tradition to propose to you every summer he has spent here since you were twelve, regardless of how many times you have denied him."

"His proposals all were made in jest," Elizabeth responded. "Usually," she added when she saw all of her sisters looking at her with raised eyebrows.

Kitty changed the subject and looked dreamily towards the window. "Pray, I will find a man who makes my pulse race, keeps me up at night, keeps me from eating, and inspires flutterings."

Hoping to impart wisdom to her younger sister, Elizabeth responded thoughtfully and with uncharacteristic frankness. "I do not know, Kitty. As I grow older, I become increasingly convinced that true love is primarily built on mutual respect and the ability to persevere through challenges. While some may speak of flutterings and yearnings, this often only leads to disillusionment and disappointment. It is better to keep your head about you. You will see as you get older."

Mrs Gardiner stopped brushing Jane's hair and studied Elizabeth curiously at this statement. Elizabeth's eyes shifted away from her aunt and by chance glanced over at Lydia, whom she knew understood more than most the consequences of not controlling one's emotions. Her youngest sister looked down, seeming shamed, which had not been Elizabeth's intention. She was speaking of her own experiences, but she could understand how Lydia might think otherwise.

Therefore, she changed the subject quickly and brightened her voice. "Except for our dear Jane. She has appeared to catch the most desirable things of all, affection and respect for her partner."

Jane smiled demurely.

"Perhaps I could settle for that logical approach with Mr Darcy," Kitty stated nonchalantly. "In truth, I do not think it would be only logical. I daresay my heart skips a beat whenever he utters a syllable."

"Yes, he is mysterious," Lydia added with a mocking leer.

"He only looks upon us to judge us. Pray do not give him a second thought," said Elizabeth.

Kitty continued, saying, "You did not tell us he would be so handsome, Lizzy. How like you, to withhold information you knew we would be interested in!"

Elizabeth shook her head, "He is not worth our time as he considers us not worth his. Did you not notice his taciturn nature?"

"He seemed quiet, yes. But perhaps more reticent than rude," Aunt Gardiner said diplomatically as she returned to tending to Jane's tresses.

Elizabeth protested, "Did you not see him? He hardly uttered a syllable."

"You know what they say, still waters run deep!" Lydia interjected with a laugh, which grew louder when Elizabeth threw a pillow at her.

"Perhaps he is only shy. Charles says he is quite uncomfortable around people he doesn't know," Jane opined.

Elizabeth snorted. "Someone who has ten thousand a year and has an estate larger than all of Meryton put together should be shy around us? No, I am certain it is his excessive pride that silences him."

"I could endure a little disdain to be wife of a man with ten thousand a year," Kitty said with a giggle.

"There are more important things than wealth," Elizabeth said seriously. "A life spent joined with his disadvantages would only give one unhappiness. He is rude, conceited, arrogant—"

All of her sisters and Mrs Gardiner looked at her questioningly.

"I thought you said you hardly knew him," Lydia said.

A SHARED HISTORY

"That is correct, I do not really know him," Elizabeth said quickly. "But his feelings were plain for anyone to see."

Wishing that the subject of Mr Darcy might be left behind, Elizabeth turned to her older sister. "Did you say you needed some help thinking of how you wish to dress your hair for the wedding?"

CHAPTER TEN

April 1810, Kent

The assembly hall in Westerham was filled with the local gentry and nobility. Elizabeth took a deep breath as she stood between Charlotte and Mr Collins at the room's periphery, but she found little respite from the thick, stifling air. For what seemed like the tenth time that evening, another attendant bumped into her as they walked by. Gasping, Elizabeth remarked quietly to Charlotte, "What a crush!"

Charlotte nodded in agreement before turning back towards Mr Collins and an older couple, the Spencers, with whom they were engaged in conversation. As they spoke, Mr Spencer turned towards Elizabeth with slow deliberation. His crinkled eyes met hers, and he asked, "Are you enjoying the gathering tonight, Miss Bennet?"

"Indeed, it is delightful. And the music is so lively."

With some effort, Mrs Spencer straightened from her

stooped posture to look up at Elizabeth. "It is. It reminds me of our younger days when we used to attend many assemblies similar to this."

"I know you would not believe it now, but we used to be quite spry and could dance most of the night away," Mr Spencer added with a nostalgic smile.

Mrs Spencer chuckled, and Elizabeth smiled at the thought of the elderly couple dancing energetically.

"Well, I hope you will find much enjoyment in our assembly and during your stay in general," Mr Spencer said before turning back towards Mr Collins and enquiring, "Did you have the opportunity to talk to Mr Matthews tonight?"

"I have not sir, but I thank you extensively for informing me of his attendance. I must go and find him at the first possibility. It is essential that I speak to him, for I believe he has invaluable insight into solving our challenges with the church ceiling."

As the topic shifted, Elizabeth gazed around the room and her smile began to fade. *I hope Charlotte and Mr Collins will introduce me to some younger acquaintances who might want to engage in dancing, else I might not have the pleasure this evening.* Due to the dimly lit surroundings, it was difficult to make out from afar all who were in attendance. It mattered very little however, as Elizabeth did not know most of the people there regardless.

As the Spencers and Collinses continued speaking about local matters, Elizabeth stifled a yawn and edged closer to a nearby window, hoping to get a reprieve from the heat generated in the overpopulated room while remaining close enough to engage in the conversation when necessary. She spent her time there alternating between gazing out at the darkening sky and watching the behaviours of the people in the room.

"Cousin Elizabeth," Mr Collins's voice boomed, startling her from her reverie. Turning, she was surprised to find a genial middle-aged gentleman now standing with their group and gazing at her intently. *Oh lovely, perhaps Mr Collins shall introduce me to someone who might ask me to dance.*

"I am pleased to introduce Mr Douglas."

Elizabeth smiled as the introductions were made, and Mr Douglas wasted no time in asking her to dance. After an enjoyable turn with him, Elizabeth found herself being asked to dance again, this time by Mr Hamilton, a stout young man she had met a few days prior when he called on Mr Collins. After both dances, she was returned by her partner to stand with the Collinses. As she took a few deep breaths to recover from all her physical activity, her thoughts began to wander. *I have danced with two capable and agreeable gentlemen. Usually I would deem this an enjoyable evening. Nevertheless, I find myself feeling melancholy.* She gazed round the room at all the people she did not know. *Perhaps it is more of who is not in attendance. I must admit, I was truly looking forward to Mr Darcy and Colonel Fitzwilliam being here. But alas, it does not appear that they will be coming after all.*

Just as Elizabeth had given up hope on their attendance, she saw the two men enter the hall. As word spread of their arrival, she observed several older ladies look in their direction and, undoubtedly eager to initiate some matchmaking, begin whispering to presumably single young women.

The gentlemen stood quietly at the door as most of the room took in the sight of them. Colonel Fitzwilliam looked at ease, but Mr Darcy shifted uncomfortably. *I see now how very awkward it is being the centre of attention, especially for someone of his disposition.*

Elizabeth continued watching as the gentlemen fully entered the room and engaged in conversation with some men. After a few minutes, Colonel Fitzwilliam caught Elizabeth's eye across the room. He nudged Mr Darcy and the pair made their way towards her and the Collinses.

Upon reaching them, the group exchanged greetings. While Mr Darcy maintained his usual reserve, Colonel Fitzwilliam wore a big smile.

"Miss Bennet, are you enjoying the assembly as much as you anticipated?" he enquired.

"I am, sir. The music is splendid, and the decorations are lovely."

"Indeed! Are you as well, Mr and Mrs Collins?"

"Yes, very much so," answered Charlotte.

"I am certain there are few assemblies that could rival its energy and pleasantness," responded Mr Collins.

The conversation paused briefly. Just as Colonel Fitzwilliam seemed about to continue, Mr Darcy looked at Elizabeth, and somewhat abruptly asked, "Miss Bennet, would you do me the honour of the next dance?"

Surprised by his request, her heart skipped a beat. Smiling at him, she said, "I should be happy to."

As he guided her to the dance floor, a subtle excitement sailed through her, amplified by their close proximity. Towering over her, he exuded a striking, inescapable magnetism. Her stomach fluttered when she hooked her arm into his, and her anticipation grew as she thought of the impending intimate conversation that they would be allowed in their dance. She craved to understand him, delve into his opinions, and discover what made him tick.

At first, they did not talk but Elizabeth could not let it stand. Teasingly, she said, "Mr Darcy, it is a curious thing to ask a lady to dance and then not speak to her at all."

Happily, he did not appear to take offence. "I shall admit that engaging in inconsequential conversations is not my strength. I believe that you, on the other hand, would find pleasure in any topic."

"Is that so?"

"Yes, you seem to enjoy any conversation in which you participate with great energy and intelligence."

She laughed merrily at his idea of her. "I see you understand me well, sir. Remarkable given the brief time of our acquaintance! Alas, I cannot pay you the same compliment. I do not feel I know much about you at all."

"I believe you know the usual things of me."

"But nothing of your character."

Their conversation was becoming increasingly intimate; if it troubled him, he gave no sign of it. "What can you guess?"

She thought for a moment, not wishing to say anything that would be impolitic. She sensed that beneath his solemn exterior was a man of deep and strong feeling and wondered whether his aloofness was designed to mask that. She did not, however, imagine she could say so.

He was silent but locked eyes with her, and her breath caught briefly when she observed it. "I believe, sir, that you likely have a slyer sense of humour than is immediately apparent."

"And what makes you think so?"

"I have seen the way you smirk at some of your aunt's… observations."

He chuckled. "Ah yes, you have discovered me."

The dance parted them for a brief period, and when they

rejoined, she continued, "I also see you are a man who takes his duties seriously. Maybe too seriously, at times?"

He tilted his head. "You do not feel your responsibilities towards family and society are of the utmost importance?"

"Yes, I surely do. But I am determined that I shall not permit it to decide my course in life."

He drew back a little, clearly surprised. "Truly?"

She nodded firmly. "A family and a society can only suffer if its members are miserable and bitter because they are not allowed to act on their genuine desires."

"So, do you propose making every decision with only your own happiness in mind?"

"Of course not, that would be a selfish existence. There are always other considerations, such as matters of faith, that prevent us from fulfilling every desire. But I do believe one should not make life-altering decisions based only on what would make others happy."

"Though not as exciting, I think sometimes meeting one's duties *can* lead to happiness. Happiness has the ability to develop over time with consistency and pride in a job well done."

"I am not sure I am convinced," she said with an arch smile. "And that is why you will see me end up an old maid."

"I do not take your meaning."

"I cannot marry any man based on the hope that love will blossom eventually merely because I have been obligated to him long enough. I believe a genuine attachment must first exist."

He appeared thoughtful a moment and only said, "I see."

The dance parted them again and when he returned, Mr Darcy offered, "Would it surprise you to hear that I agree with you?" He quickly added, "Concerning the marriage part at least."

"It would surprise me, indeed."

"Only recently can I say my opinions on the matter have changed. But I now firmly believe that to marry without affection would be a curse indeed. When it is possible, it should be avoided."

She raised her eyebrows. "Are you a romantic, Mr Darcy? I daresay you are full of surprises."

He only chuckled, "And *you* are full of strong opinions, Miss Bennet."

She bit her lip to hide a smile.

They drew in close to each other as the movements of the dance required. They were paused in their movements face to face, and he looked at her earnestly. "It is one of the things I admire most about you."

As she felt a hot blush creep up her chest and neck, she could not deny how much she was enjoying their time together in relative solitude.

They finished their dance and at the end, he led her off the floor. As they walked, he leant towards her and asked, "May I get you some refreshments?"

Her heart fluttered, and she energetically nodded her head as she replied, "That would be lovely."

She felt a smile grow on her face as he left her and made his way towards the refreshments. As she watched him walk away, she could not help but wonder: Was it possible that Mr Darcy felt some attachment to her, as she had begun to feel for him?

CHAPTER ELEVEN

Obtaining punch from the table took Darcy longer than he had intended. When he returned to where he had left Miss Bennet, she was nowhere to be found. He walked about the hall, utilising his height to peer over others in hopes of finding her. A few of his aunt's neighbours attempted to pull him into conversation but he refused to be drawn in, preferring to continue his search. *Where could she have gone?*

He furrowed his brow as he made a second perambulation of the hall, peering into all corners of the room; the punch glasses splashed as he walked, no doubt staining his gloves. For a few minutes, he hovered about to ensure that she had not gone to the ladies' retiring room, but she did not appear. Feeling more disappointed than he would have liked to admit, he walked out to the terrace to escape the hot air of the hall.

The brisk spring air was a relief to him. He only wished its rejuvenating touch would lift his thwarted spirits more.

Despite the presence of a few people on the terrace, he kept his head lowered, not allowing his gaze to linger long enough to acknowledge any of them. He placed the two cups of punch on the balustrade and tugged at his cravat, feeling suffocated.

He looked down towards his feet. Perhaps Elizabeth Bennet was not as interested in him as he had assumed. Sighing heavily, he raised his gaze as he wearily rubbed his face. In that moment, his eyes unexpectedly met a pair of fine, dark eyes across the terrace. There she stood, adorned in a simple country dress that radiated unassuming beauty in the soft glow of the lamps. A hint of mischief played on her features. In retrospect, he would scold himself for not having previously recognised her as the most beautiful woman of his acquaintance.

True, he had met many more striking women in the *ton*. But her allure went beyond the superficial; it was a quieter beauty that took hold of him and consumed his thoughts. Her subtle allure, her sweetness and wit, had snuck into his heart, and refused to let go. It was this captivating essence that lingered, haunting his past few nights like no other sight ever had.

Only once had he witnessed beauty in a woman that could rival what he saw now, and it just so happened to have occurred the day before: Elizabeth, at the top of Holly Hill, covered in mud with her hair tousled from their vigorous hike. He could not deny his feelings for her any longer. Although he had initially rejected the notion—after all, how could he disregard her inferior birth—now it seemed far more difficult to imagine himself without her.

He looked at her affectionately. Although there were many people between them, it felt as if the terrace was empty. Their eyes locked and he manoeuvred through the crowd to reach her without ceasing eye contact. A wry smile crept over her face as they finally met, and his heart skipped a beat.

"I could not find you," he said earnestly.

Elizabeth laughed softly. "Forgive me, I needed to step outside."

"Are you unwell?"

"No," she said with a smile. "Mrs Collins was coming towards me with a gentleman she clearly wished to introduce to me. That likely would have led to a dance with him, and perhaps this is too forward to say, but I was not yet ready for *our* conversation to end. So I—"

"Hid out here?"

She laughed, the sound like a silver bell. "Yes. Am I not terrible?"

"Not in the least," he said softly. A light breeze picked up then, stirring the curls by her temples. He reached over to brush them back away from her cheek and brazen as it was, she permitted him to do it, still smiling, still meeting his gaze.

After each sipped their punch, he offered her his arm, and they strolled about the terrace and assembly hall. They continued conversing of insignificant matters that suddenly were more interesting than they had ever been with anyone else. When he saw interlopers approaching them with a clear interest in claiming Elizabeth for a dance, he froze them in their place with an icy hauteur he hoped escaped her notice.

They weaved through the crowd together arm in arm, as they walked and talked. Although they did not agree on every point, they spoke with great enthusiasm towards each other and when they disagreed, exhibited mutual respect.

Occasionally, the dense crowd demanded that he release her arm, but she would turn her head over her shoulder, seamlessly continuing their conversation, and he willingly followed her lead. Despite realising that he might look like a love-sick puppy, he found himself uncharacteristically unperturbed by appearances, content simply to be in her proximity.

Their tête-à-tête was interrupted when a stout neighbour of Mr Collins, seemingly impervious to Darcy's silent warnings, intruded to ask Elizabeth for the next dance. Dare he believe that she looked disappointed? "Go," he murmured. "I would not like to get you in trouble with your hosts."

As he stood on the edge of the set, his eyes were fixed on her as she danced. Watching her glide up and down the line with her partner, he wondered at the all-consuming tumult of emotions brewing within—feelings he could not have imagined or described before he met Elizabeth. But in this moment, he recognised the truth of what he felt with startling clarity: *I am in love.* It was like nothing he had ever expected, and yet, now that he had found it, he knew he would hold on tight and never let go.

"Darcy! I have hardly seen you all night." Fitzwilliam appeared at his side, breathless from his own exertions on the dance floor. "You have been a little preoccupied with a certain lady, eh?"

"Unlike you. Have you danced with every woman in the room yet?"

The colonel laughed. "I am having an enjoyable night in the presence of many lovely women. And you? Does your lady friend realise she is being pursued by a man who would never have serious intentions towards her?"

"That is not true," Darcy retorted softly.

"Oh-ho!" The colonel turned a gimlet eye upon his cousin, but Darcy steadfastly kept his face turned aside. "You must be joking. Tell me, how does this actually end? You are in danger. I have never seen you act this way with any woman, ever."

He did not respond.

"What would your father say?"

"I would not go against my father's wishes, but I know him. When he meets her and sees her intelligence, he will understand. We are not from different stations after all, just different circles of society."

"Yes, but I think that—"

"I will manage it," Darcy interrupted. Wishing to be rid of his cousin's company and gloomy predictions, he excused himself and walked away.

CHAPTER TWELVE

The dance Elizabeth shared with Mr Davis was pleasant, but she could give only half a mind to the conversation. She was too distracted by Mr Darcy, where he was, what he did, and how soon she could return to him. Her thoughts were interrupted when she overheard the conversation between two ladies in the dance line beside her. Amidst their hushed tones, the mention of Mr Darcy's name piqued her attention.

"And did you see Mr Darcy in attendance? He is Lady Catherine's nephew," said the lady in a pink gown.

"Indeed, I believe he was initially held with great esteem," responded a tall woman clad in blue. "Many of us were excited at the prospect of meeting him, but he has acted in such a way tonight that people feel quite the opposite now."

Despite their attempt to speak discreetly, their words carried over the music and chatter in the assembly hall.

"Indeed!" The woman in pink leant towards her friend. "He carries himself in such an aloof, haughty manner."

Elizabeth looked away from them so as not to be caught eavesdropping, but still strained to hear as the tall woman responded, "Yes! He could not be bothered to converse, and much less dance, with any local ladies. Mr Matthews, whom he has met before, said Mr Darcy hardly acknowledged him when he attempted to speak with him."

"That is appalling behaviour indeed."

The movement of the dance required the women to part to join their partners for a period. When they returned to their line, the woman in pink pointed across the room and continued in a lowered voice. "Do you see Miss Hughes over there? I was astonished she attended tonight after what happened at the last assembly."

As the women began giggling and the conversation shifted, Elizabeth found herself lost in her own thoughts again.

He has been so pleasant with me tonight. But could these women be correct? Or are these just the words of busybodies looking for fault in anyone?

Perhaps due to her distraction, her dance partner stepped on her foot during the last moves of the dance. With only a thin slipper to cushion the blow, she needed to bite her lip to conceal her cry as pain shot through her. Unaware of any injury caused to her, Mr Davis walked her off the floor. When she was free of him, she hobbled to the chairs occupied by the matrons and chaperons and sank into one, her foot throbbing.

Mr Darcy was at her side again quickly, and asked her for another dance.

"I would be honoured, sir," she said, rising from the chair only to lose her balance immediately.

He reached for her, looking alarmed. "What is the matter? Are you injured?"

"Not seriously, no," she assured him. "Alas, I do believe I must sit this dance out. Forgive me."

"Not at all. I shall remain with you."

"I would like that," she replied, feeling suddenly shy. She sat again and he took the chair next to hers. They chatted for a short while, making inconsequential observations on the room around them. After some time, she gestured over to a line of women sitting out of the dance, waiting for a partner.

"Poor dears. It is difficult to be excited to attend an assembly, but then sit out for a lack of gentlemen. It has surely happened to me before, and it is an unhappy feeling."

"That surprises me. I presumed to imagine that you would be asked to dance every set when you are at an assembly or ball."

"That is kind of you to say sir, but I assure you it is not true." With studied nonchalance she added, "It would be good of you to dance with one of them—I imagine you must know at least one or two of them."

"I usually do not dance with those outside of my party."

"You danced with me, did you not? And I flatter myself to say the experience was not wholly disagreeable else you should not have asked me a second time. Surely to dance with another could not be so wholly dreadful."

"Would it please you if I asked someone else to dance?"

"It would," she said sincerely. "I cannot abide the notion of anyone departing the night unhappily."

"Then I shall," he said. "To please you."

She smiled and then watched as Mr Darcy walked over to

the line of ladies wanting partners. She could not help but notice what a tall and entrancing image he made while moving across the room. He asked the lady who—in Elizabeth's estimation—was the plainest one of all, and he led her out to the forming set.

She watched as the woman and Mr Darcy made their way up and down the line. Her heart swelled at the sight, and she felt satisfied. Some might have thought him excessively proud, but she believed it was only because he had never been challenged to be otherwise. As evidenced by his current occupation, he was willing to hear her perspectives and opinions. That he had done as she bid him was undeniably endearing.

After dancing with two other ladies, he finally made his way back to her. They spent the rest of the evening talking animatedly over the chatter and music.

I have never been so content in all my life.

Thoughts of the evening filled Darcy's head as his carriage moved from Westerham back to Rosings Park. At some point in the night—he could not quite say when—Miss Elizabeth Bennet had irrevocably stolen his heart. He supposed it had been coming on gradually since they first met. What had started as lingering interest had grown into full-blown love.

She will be my downfall, he mused with a prickle of trepidation. *My undoing.*

He looked out the carriage window, seeing the silvery moonlight over the landscape and wondering whether she too saw it and perhaps thought of him. He never should have fallen for someone like her but he had. Undeniably he had. Perhaps she was his undoing but now she would have to be his deliverance too, setting him free from the strictures of his responsibilities and from living a life of dutiful pretence. He would marry for love. There would be consequences, but to have her at his side would be well worth whatever difficulties might arise.

All of it was done save for one thing—a formal question and announcement.

CHAPTER THIRTEEN

December 1813, Hertfordshire

Later in the week, a large party assembled at Lucas Lodge for cards, music, and conversation. Upon entering the front hall of the comfortable and familiar home, Elizabeth saw that Mr Bingley's party were already present. To her amusement, the Bingley sisters had finally arrived for their brother's approaching nuptials. *They put off having to come into Hertfordshire society as long as they possibly could.*

Elizabeth had no good opinion of the two; Mrs Hurst and Miss Bingley were silly women, better impressed by themselves than anything they saw in Hertfordshire, and their behaviour often led her to exchange an amused, knowing look with her father. However, they soon would be Jane's sisters too, so Elizabeth would be kind to them. Happily, she did not imagine she would see them often. Though Jane had made it clear that they were welcome to come to Netherfield

Park at any time, the two ladies had made it abundantly obvious they did not plan to accept the invitation often.

Elizabeth, at Jane's beckoning, walked across the room to where the Bingleys stood with Mr Darcy. Miss Bingley was the picture of high fashion, with a feather in her hair and a boldly coloured silk dress adorned with intricate lace. She was outshone only by Mr Darcy, wearing a velvet tailcoat and boots so shiny they could blind. *I would wager all I have that he polishes them with Champagne.* They were both dressed too overly fine for a neighbourhood gathering. Some would be impressed at their excessive attire but she could only scoff, certain they dressed as they did in an effort to make all of Hertfordshire society feel inferior to them.

After the usual curtseys and bows had been made, Miss Bingley drew closer to Mr Darcy. She pulled out an ornate fan and concealed her mouth as she began speaking under her breath to him. The gentleman did not reply to her but maintained his usual haughtily silent demeanour. This time Elizabeth did not stop herself from rolling her eyes even if she did turn away so they would not see her. She had never known two people who were so similar in their pretensions.

As she turned away, her eyes rested on her father engaging in conversation with Sir William. Wishing to be away from Mr Darcy and the Bingley sisters, she excused herself and gracefully glided towards them through the clusters of guests. As she joined the pair, Mr Bennet turned towards her and gently placed a hand on her shoulder.

"Elizabeth! Do join our conversation. It is riveting," he said as he gave his daughter a barely perceptible wink. "Sir William was suggesting I adopt new drainage practices for the fields."

"Ah," she said, instantly wondering if she should have found a more engaging group to talk with.

"Indeed," Sir William responded, "Mr Wesley educated me about his new drainage channels and the remarkable improvement in his soil's health. I think your father should follow suit."

As the conversation continued, Elizabeth found herself nodding and smiling absently in response to their long discussion of agricultural practices. She was vaguely aware of the topics they covered, but ultimately more grateful for the relief they provided from certain guests in attendance. As their chatter grew duller, she gazed about the room and wondered of Royce's whereabouts.

She was about to turn to Sir William and ask about her friend when a sudden burst of loud laughter diverted her gaze. Across the room, Lydia and Kitty had gathered a small group together and persuaded Mary to play music for them to dance. Kitty quickly paired off with John Lucas and per usual, Mr Andrews wasted little time in asking Lydia to dance. As Elizabeth watched Lydia and Mr Andrews glide up and down the line, giggling amidst their easy conversation, she could not help but grin. Though she knew the group was being a touch too loud, she felt reminded of herself at a younger age and the excitement she once felt at any opportunity to dance.

Her attention was drawn to the doorway closest to the dancers where a striking figure appeared. It was Royce, finally about to make his entrance, looking as handsome as ever. Elizabeth felt a small tingle of excitement at the sight. She smiled at him from across the room, watching as he navigated past dancers and mingling guests in his walk towards her. She curtseyed as he approached.

"Miss Elizabeth," he said with some exasperation after he bowed. "I regret that I am so late. Not ten minutes before the party, I was out for a ramble with Elijah when he became heavily soiled in mud and proceeded to jump on me."

Elizabeth could not stifle a giggle. "How terrible! He has always been a misbehaved dog."

Royce chuckled in agreement, rubbing behind his ear absentmindedly. "I would have to agree."

His eyes wandered across the room to where the group was dancing. "Would you do me the honour of the next dance?"

He rubbed behind his ear again as he waited for her reply; it did not escape Elizabeth's notice that a small blush came over his face.

"It would be an honour," she replied warmly.

"Wonderful!" Royce beamed, though he paused momentarily. "This is rather embarrassing, but I believe some mud remains behind my ears, and I can only imagine where else. If you will excuse me, I must go endeavour to clean up again."

Elizabeth chuckled softly. "I understand, sir. Please go do so, and I look forward to our dance when you return."

With a nod and a grateful smile, Royce excused himself, leaving Elizabeth to watch fondly as he disappeared through the doors. The room buzzed with laughter and music, and her pulse quickened as she wondered what their first dance together might portend. *Could this be it? Could he be the one with whom I share my future? Why do I feel so nervous all of a sudden? No—calm down. Enjoy the dance and becoming reacquainted with him.* She took a deep breath and turned round to seek out Jane and share the news of her impending dance.

As her eye wandered, she spotted Jane standing alone on

the far side of the room, gazing serenely out the window. Knowing her calming presence would put her at ease, she set off towards her, passing by Mr Bingley and Mr Darcy as they engaged in an animated conversation. Despite her best efforts to remain uninterested in any of Mr Darcy's affairs, she could not help but overhear snippets of their exchange as she walked by.

"Darcy, why must you always lurk in the background at these events?"

"I am not lurking. I am merely observing," Mr Darcy replied coolly.

Elizabeth quickly looked away, not wanting to seem as if she were listening, but their conversation continued to drift to her ears.

"You look miserable," Mr Bingley pressed.

"I assure you, I am not."

"Come now, let us find you a dance partner. It would lift your spirits to partake in some activity, and I am certain it would significantly improve your opinion of the evening."

"That is entirely unnecessary."

Quickening her steps to avoid further overhearing, Elizabeth had just passed them when she heard her name spoken.

"Miss Elizabeth!" Mr Bingley called out.

She sighed inwardly before turning back. "Yes?" she responded politely as she reluctantly stepped towards them.

"My good friend here," Mr Bingley said, clapping Mr Darcy on the back, "was looking about the room and expressing a desire to dance."

Mr Darcy looked sharply at his friend as all the colour drained out of his face.

"I know you enjoy the activity immensely and I know he would find pleasure in dancing with such a partner."

Mr Darcy's eyes widened as he seemed stunned into silence by his friend's strange behaviour.

Elizabeth let out a humourless laugh. "You need not force your friend to dance, sir. In any case, if he truly does desire to partake in the activity, I am certain he is perfectly capable of finding his own partner."

"I am not forcing him," Mr Bingley insisted in a jovial tone. "I am certain he was just about to ask you."

Mr Darcy's look of discomfort turned to one of puzzlement as Mr Bingley pressed on. "And how could you deny him? I know you love to dance, and not partaking now must be disappointing."

Mr Darcy's eyes remained on his friend as he tugged at his cravat.

"Mr Bingley, you are all kindness," Elizabeth said through gritted teeth, as she tucked a stray piece of hair behind her ear. "But, alas, I cannot. I am claimed for the next set with Mr Royce."

At this, Mr Darcy unexpectedly jerked his head in her direction and gave her a curious look. After taking a deep breath he said, "Bingley is correct, Miss Elizabeth. I had planned on asking you. Would you please do me the honour of dancing the following set with me?"

Her stomach dropped, and she furrowed her brow. *What? Why ever would he ask me this? I gave him a way out of this awkward situation, and he did not take it.*

She hesitated, but knowing she would have to sit out the next dance with Royce if she refused Mr Darcy, begrudgingly agreed. "I would be honoured, sir," she said coolly.

Mr Darcy nodded and responded gravely, "I look forward to it."

She excused herself to seek out Jane again, angry that she

had even come to that side of the room at all. When she reached her sister, she quickly grabbed her arm, and tugged her towards the corner of the room. "Come quickly please."

"What is it? Are you well?"

"A terrible thing has happened."

Jane gasped. "What? What is it?"

"I agreed to dance with Mr Darcy."

"Oh, Lizzy." Jane smiled at her younger sister in a half-amused, half-exasperated manner. "I daresay you will find him amiable. Charles really does insist that he is a wonderful man. He is a most loyal friend, and is kinder than he appears."

"That hardly seems possible."

"I cannot understand the way you are determined to hate him. It is not like you to take such an ardent dislike to someone so wholly unrelated to you!"

So wholly unrelated. Of course, Jane could not know how, even after all this time, such a phrase still could sting her. "I would not expect you to understand," Elizabeth mumbled, lowering her eyes.

Jane furrowed her brow. "Well, I would like to understand it, if you would tell me—"

"I beg your pardon, ladies." Royce had returned and found them in their corner. "Miss Elizabeth, do you still wish to dance? I can surely understand if sisterly—"

"I am positively mad for the dance." Elizabeth grinned up at him, secretly relieved. Jane was getting too close to home truths for her comfort.

CHAPTER FOURTEEN

For the first few minutes of her dance with Royce, Elizabeth's mind was occupied with Mr Darcy and *their* impending dance. What on earth had possessed that horrible man to ask her to dance after everything he had done to her? Realising she was using up precious time thinking about someone who did not deserve her consideration, she drew her thoughts back to the always pleasant Mr Royce.

He was an able dancer and she always liked the activity in general. Initially, it was difficult to converse because of all the commotion of the party and liveliness of the dance, but she did enjoy talking with him. As always, he could carry the conversation well, and did not leave the burden of finding a topic to her. It was a relief because in her present state, she was unequal to thinking of any subject besides the vagaries of men, and of one man in particular.

Of course, it could not help her distraction when over Royce's shoulder she observed Mr Darcy talking to her father and Mr Gardiner, and noticed that he often looked in her direction. Why was he always staring at her? And what could he mean in speaking to her father and uncle? Did he hope to discover more objectionable things about her relations so that he might congratulate himself on having avoided them?

She shook her head to help rid her mind of him. *Why am I allowing my thoughts to be consumed by him? I had been excited for this dance before Mr Darcy asked me.* She looked back to Royce. He was charming, attractive, friendly, and talkative—all qualities someone would usually want in a suitor. It was easy to be around him. Though he did not yet have her heart, she felt that with all his good qualities, he might very soon.

The object of her thoughts brought Elizabeth's attention back to the conversation when he asked, "How did you spend your day today?"

As the dance required them to circle each other, she replied energetically. "Well, I went for a walk and then planned to take up some needlework, but I confess I ended up getting lost in a book from my father's study."

"A book from your father's study? Pray, which one caught your interest?" Royce looked down at her, a charming smile spread across his face.

"A tome about ancient Greek philosophers."

"Only some light reading, then?" he teased lightly, a chuckle escaping his lips.

"Indeed," Elizabeth laughed in agreement.

"Which philosophers did you delve into?" He clasped her hands, and they moved closer to each other.

"I was reviewing the debates between the Platonists and Sophists."

"I see." The dance parted them for a moment, and she

continued to gaze at him as he began watching the other dancers with a contented expression.

When they returned to each other he looked on her warmly, but did not elaborate on the subject. Desiring some depth in their conversation, she pressed him further. "Have you heard of them?"

"Perhaps a little, but you know I am not well-versed in such matters," he admitted with an abashed smile.

He is not particularly knowledgeable in intellectual matters, but perhaps he could become so with a little guidance.

"No matter, I shall enlighten you," Elizabeth said with enthusiasm. "In essence, Plato and his followers believed there are objective and absolute truths. On the other hand, Sophists believed that truth, especially in regards to morality, is relative."

"How intriguing." He again turned his head and watched the other dancers glide next to him with evident enjoyment.

Pausing, Elizabeth waited for him to add more to his thoughts. *He is so amiable and pleasing in countless ways, but my only complaint against him is that I do not know his genuine opinions. Since we have been reacquainted, I do not know how he truly feels about anything. I wish he would share his real views.* When he remained silent, she gently prompted, "Do you lean towards one philosophy over the other?"

"I am unsure, both opinions seem to have value."

"Yes, but if you had to choose?" She tilted her head as she looked up at him earnestly. "Is there one that appeals to you more? Is truth relative or absolute?"

He looked curious at her persistence. "I am not sure. It is too hard to say. Which side do you lean towards?"

She tried to quiet the stab of annoyance she felt at his evasiveness. "Well, I find myself supporting Plato's beliefs. I find it rather absurd to deny the existence of objective truths, especially concerning morality. I could not bear to live in a world where heinous acts such as murder were not objectively wrong, but merely a rule created out of societal convention."

He nodded slowly. "Now that you say it, I believe I agree with that too."

"Indeed," Elizabeth replied, her smile a touch forced as she returned his gaze. They parted for a moment. *Would he always simply agree with my opinions? Does he even understand these concepts?*

When they met again, he promptly changed the subject. "Have you been to Oakham Mount recently?"

She imagined the disappointment on her face was showing despite her efforts to conceal it. "Not recently, have you?"

"Not since I have arrived. Perhaps we could all go soon and take in the view."

"Perhaps," she responded in an absent tone.

He continued energetically, "Do you recall the time we raced down it as children?"

She nodded, hoping her lack of interest was not evident.

As he continued reminiscing on the memory with growing enthusiasm, Elizabeth let out a gentle sigh, her thoughts wandering elsewhere. *Perhaps he will speak more of his mind and opinions once he feels secure in my affections. Do not most people have difficulty truly being themselves until they know their feelings are reciprocated? He might need a little encouragement to make him feel more confident.*

With a surge of determination to reassure him, she gave Royce an arch smile. "And as I recall, you only won that race through dishonest means."

He smiled back, clearly pleased, then chuckled.

After the dance concluded, he led her off the dance floor and asked, "May I get you some refreshments?"

"No, thank you," she answered with genuine regret. "I am to dance with Mr Darcy."

"I see," he responded. "Very well, I shall look forward to seeing you afterwards."

After escorting her to stand near her father, he walked away. Once he disappeared from view, the reality of the impending dance overcame her, and her knees suddenly became very weak. She cast her gaze down to the polished floor, took a deep breath, and resisted the urge to fidget with her dress. When she lifted her eyes again, she glimpsed Mr Darcy towering above the others as he walked in her direction. With every step that drew him closer, her pulse surged stronger within her. Her heart was beating so quickly she feared she might lose her balance if she moved. Nevertheless, she somehow managed to perform a curtsey without mishap.

"Miss Elizabeth," he said after he bowed.

"Mr Darcy," she said solemnly.

He offered his arm, and she was surprised to find herself grateful to take it and enjoy the stability which it provided as they walked to join the other dancers awaiting the first notes from the piano.

Despite the wild tempest raging within her, once the music began, she was eager to display how indifferent she was to him and to maintain civility in their interactions. Their conversation was polite enough, all formality in fact. They commented on the party, his previous and future travel plans for the wedding, and how he was enjoying Netherfield. While she hoped she appeared calm and collected as she spoke, her emotions were in tumult. It was intoxicating to be so close to him. That certain *frisson* she felt since he had come back into her life nearly overcame her when they were this near to each other. The pangs she typically felt in her stomach at the sight of him felt as though they had taken charge over her entire being. A surge of frustration ran through her and she wondered, *How can I feel this way after everything he has done to me?*

As the dance drew long, they entered into silence as they moved by rote through the moves. She studied his person as she contemplated her feelings. *He is a very handsome man, yes, but it is so much more than that. Once again I feel utterly drawn to him. This is all so strange! To be so attracted to a man I despise.* She took a deep, stabilising breath. *But, then again, given the intensity of our past connexion, it must be only natural to have some residual feelings towards him.* Without the distraction of making small talk, her pull towards him only intensified. The next time their hands touched, she wanted to let her fingers linger. *How I wish I did not feel this way!* After they parted, pausing as she waited for the next steps, she looked towards him and found he was casting a searching look over her. She averted her gaze to look up at the ceiling and gave a small shake of her head at her own silliness. *Do not overthink it. It is simply a matter of feeling an attraction, but not acting on it, which should not be too difficult for he would hardly reciprocate my feelings even if I were to express mine.* When their dance steps brought them closer to one another again his eyes gazed upon her intensely and flickered to her lips for the briefest of seconds. She felt her heart skip a beat and she longed for him to pull her in and even—dare she admit it?—kiss her.

And yet hard on the heels of those longings came another feeling entirely. Anger. How dare he come here, stare at her, and stir her up as he did? In the height of her irritation, she demanded, "Why are you here?"

"Pardon me?"

"Why did you come?"

"Sir William extended an invitation to everyone at Netherfield Park. As a guest of the house, it would have been rude of me to—"

"That is not what I meant." She resisted the urge to stamp her foot. "I mean, why did you come to Hertfordshire? To the wedding? Surely you knew I would be here. I cannot comprehend that Mr Bingley would not tell you about me and you would fail to recognise the Bennet name."

"Bingley is one of my closest friends. He asked me to stand up with him. I could not deny him."

"You could have made an excuse."

"Perhaps, but I would not do that to him. Bingley is a true friend. Plus, he needed my guidance with some issues pertaining to Netherfield." He looked off into the distance. "Trust me, it is not enjoyable for me to be here either."

She felt hurt by this, although she did not know why, and remained silent.

"Do you and Mr Royce have an understanding?" he asked abruptly.

His expression was inscrutable; hers, she imagined, was not. Annoyance commingled with disbelief joined her earlier vexation and prompted her response. "*What?*"

"Will an announcement soon be made?"

They had come to a natural stop in the figure but she moved, taking one step closer to him. Looking up she hissed, "How could you feel that you have the right to question me on any topic pertaining to matrimony?"

Realising how close they were standing, and that others

were beginning to take notice, she reluctantly stepped back again. Why did tensions soar so highly and quickly between them? Happily, it was soon time for them to move in the pattern and they quickly returned to their steps.

"I do not have a right," he said at length, "but you would honour me if you answered me regardless."

After a calming breath, she felt she could answer him. "No."

"No, I should not expect an announcement?"

She glanced up at him. "No, there is not an understanding between Mr Royce and I."

"I see." After a few moments more, Mr Darcy added, "He seems to pay a great deal of attention to you, then."

"He has made it clear that he would not mind if we… progressed in that direction. I would not be surprised if he asked me…" She trailed off, unsure whether she should say more.

"I see," he said quickly, and Elizabeth wondered if she only imagined the look of consternation upon his countenance.

Feeling a little mischievous, she added, "He is a very loyal friend. He has known our family for an age and uniformly admired them. He is not a gentleman, but has an excellent fortune. In any case, I do not mind his lack of status, for he is not as self-important as some people with more money and rank."

Mr Darcy made no reply to her not-so-veiled barb.

"It would be a wise match for me in many ways." She looked up at him and cocked her head slightly in a nonchalant way.

Mr Darcy still said nothing and stared deeply into her

eyes, his lips only thin, terse lines. "Very well," was all he said.

They did not speak anymore and the dance was soon over. As he led her away from the impromptu dance floor, she scolded herself. *Why do you do that, Lizzy? Why try to provoke him by boasting of a potential marriage prospect? You already know he does not want you.*

What was it about him that made her act this way?

CHAPTER FIFTEEN

After Elizabeth danced a short reel with John Lucas, she made her way to a nearby chair for a moment of respite. Not a moment later, Royce appeared at her side.

"May I get you some punch?" he asked enthusiastically. She forced a smile, masking the annoyance that flickered within at his incessant complaisance, and obliged with a polite nod. As she watched him bounce away with the eagerness and excitement of a puppy, she suppressed a groan thinking, *Must he always hover so closely? Would he not go spend time with others?*

Royce returned quickly with two cups of punch in hand. After settling in the chair beside her, they sipped their punch and engaged in polite, inconsequential conversation. As they neared the bottom of their cups, Elizabeth glanced across the room. Her gaze landed on Mr Darcy, who looked upon them with a piercing stare. Despite the flush she felt creeping up her neck, she determinedly looked away from him, focusing again on Royce.

"Shall we take a turn outside to get some air?" he suggested hopefully.

"Yes, I would like that very well," she answered as she began to rise.

After they made their way out of doors, Elizabeth felt the gravel crunch beneath her feet as they stepped onto the garden path. The moonlight painted subtle shadows, enhancing the beauty of the night. Inhaling the frigid winter air, she shivered slightly as it filled her lungs. After a few moments of walking side by side, Royce surprised her by taking her hand and threading it through his arm, drawing her close to himself. Her shoulders tensed at his forwardness; while they had walked this way many times before, she preferred initiating such gestures herself. *Do not be so easily bothered*, she scolded herself. *We have known each other for an age, and he merely feels comfortable is all. In any case, it is nice to be closer to another body on such a cold night.*

As they continued walking, she looked up towards him and was surprised to find him staring down at her, with a small smile playing upon his lips.

She turned her head sharply in the other direction, and saw the moon hanging low in the sky. "Oh, look!" she exclaimed, pointing upwards. "I have always loved when the moon has a crescent shape like this. It lacks the brilliancy of a full moon, but provokes me to think of what is hidden in its shadows, where the rest of the moon has gone."

"Hm," Royce responded casually.

"Does it not provoke your interest?" she asked, looking at him eagerly, hoping once again to gauge his feelings on any subject, no matter how trivial.

A SHARED HISTORY

"I like when it has a crescent shape too," he replied, seeming disinterested in the subject.

Oh, another opinion identical to my own, she thought.

He looked down at her seriously and added, "I particularly like the way the moonlight dances on your hair this evening."

Uncertain how to respond, Elizabeth quickly looked in the other direction. She remained silent as they walked past the frost-dusted plants.

When they had finished pacing in the garden, they moved towards the terrace. Royce broke the silence, speaking rapidly. "Elizabeth, I must speak candidly with you."

"Yes?" Her stomach sank. Not tonight, not with Mr Darcy just inside and too much tumult already in her mind. She prepared herself to receive the same speech that he had given her every summer for some years now. She knew what he would say although she was at a loss for what her answer should be.

He escorted her over to the terrace and placed his hand on the balustrade, looking off into the distance. "You know you have had my heart since the first summer I came here. Over the years of our acquaintance, I have spoken often to you of our future—sometimes slightly in jest, and sometimes more in earnest."

He did not wait for her to respond, and hurried through the rest of his prepared speech. "Surely you must have heard that I came into my own fortune this past year. I am now free to marry where I please, knowing I can provide a future that is comfortable for my wife."

Elizabeth, her eyes fixed on his strong hand gripping the balustrade, knew not what to say. Was this it? Was this his proposal?

"I am not going to ask you today," he said with an uncomfortable-sounding chuckle. "Pray do not alarm yourself, but I want you to understand my intentions and to think of what you might say if…nay, when…I do."

He seemed to have finished his speech and she dared look up at him, opening her mouth to speak. Before she had the chance, he continued quietly, "But pray permit me to say this: if you refuse me or ask for more time, I cannot wait for you. I am now at the age where I very much wish to be married. If you will not be my wife, I must begin to look elsewhere for my future companionship."

"Allow me to understand you. If you ask me, it would be the only time?"

"Precisely." He smiled as a light breeze ruffled his hair. He looked more assured than she had ever seen him, and she knew not if it made him more appealing or more vexing.

"I see." She lowered her gaze, looking at the ground and contemplating what he had said. "I appreciate your candour, sir."

After a few more moments of silence, he said, "Let us leave this discussion for another day, yes?"

She smiled, and indicating she was chilled, they began walking towards the terrace door. Suddenly Mr Bingley and Mr Darcy emerged from inside the house. Mr Bingley jovially greeted them, while Mr Darcy stood a small distance behind his friend, gazing off into the dark night.

"Mr Royce, you must tell me what you and Elizabeth were speaking of before we interrupted you—you looked very serious for such a cheerful gathering."

It was too dark to see the shade of Royce's countenance, but Elizabeth thought he might have flushed. Only Mr Bingley could see two people in such a private moment and think to intrude upon them! Royce seemed to flounder, so she spoke quickly. "I asked Mr Royce a peculiar question: if he had a special ability outside of the natural world, what he would wish it to be. I said I would like to be able to transport myself to any place at the merest whim."

The look he sent her was discomfiting in its tender gratefulness. "Yes, yes, and tell them where you told me you might go. Quite clever, it was."

She forced herself to smile at his accolade. "I said I would visit Paris for the morning followed by somewhere like India for the afternoon."

"Splendid idea indeed," Mr Bingley enthused. "And an interesting question to consider. For myself, I would like to be able to have excessive strength. What about you, Royce?"

"The ability to read another's heart." He said it too warmly, while looking at her a little too endearingly.

Elizabeth felt herself flush with embarrassment. With forced brightness, she turned to the silent member of the group. "And what say you, Mr Darcy?"

He seemed surprised to have been addressed. He glanced at her then returned his eyes to some point distant in the garden. "Um... Perhaps the ability to manipulate time."

"Time?" she asked.

He added quietly, "Perhaps I would go back and make different decisions."

"Interesting choice!" Mr Bingley exclaimed. "What sort of dec—"

"Oh, there is Miss Catherine," Royce exclaimed suddenly. Elizabeth saw her younger sister just inside the door to the terrace. "I promised to play lottery tickets with her."

"You had better go in, then." Elizabeth smiled at Royce, pleased at his affability towards her sisters.

"I must go in as well," Mr Bingley said, falling into step beside him. The noise of voices and laughter filled their ears as the two men opened the door to return to the party. A moment later, the door closed and peace returned.

She and Mr Darcy were left standing alone on the terrace. A few moments of silence passed.

Elizabeth was determined to appear civil after her last outburst towards him. The weather seemed an easy topic to discuss. "Is it not pleasant this time of year, when one has the ability of retreating from a warm gathering to the brisk out of doors?"

"Yes," was all the gentleman said.

Both looked towards the ground and were quiet. Mr Darcy seemed distracted by his own thoughts. Elizabeth felt the urge to be anywhere but where she was. Suddenly, both began to speak.

"I suppose I must be—"

"I daresay—"

Elizabeth forced a little laugh. "Pray do go on, sir."

He took a breath and looked as if he contemplated whether he should continue or not. "He is not what I expected. Um…what I mean is…I had imagined you would marry someone different."

She looked at him, at a loss for words. What could he possibly mean by that?

Mr Darcy seemed to read her thoughts. "His attachment to you is greater than yours is to him. I have been watching. I always believed only love would induce you into matrimony."

How dare he? Fury threatened to consume her but she held her composure. "I know what you are about."

He looked surprised by her sudden anger. "Excuse me? I do not understand."

A SHARED HISTORY

"You are the type of man who discards a lady yet feels discomfort when she has nearly secured another one—even if you no longer have any interest in her. You believe that her failure to secure you means she ought to remain alone forever."

"No, that is not what I meant." He rubbed his hand through his hair and turned to the side. Straightening his posture, he faced her again, and said in a more composed manner, "That is not what is happening here, I am merely expressing an opinion and relaying what I objectively see."

She narrowed her eyes.

"We have always spoken our minds freely to each other, and at one time we were great friends," he said. "I know you would think less of me if I did not speak what I truly believed."

Elizabeth stared into his eyes, and he met her gaze with equal intensity.

"Elizabeth? You have been out here for an age… Oh, excuse me, is something amiss?"

At the sound of Jane's voice, Elizabeth whipped her head around and quickly stepped away from Mr Darcy. The interruption made her realise how close she and Mr Darcy were standing and how heavily she was breathing.

"Yes, Jane, I was just returning." She looked back at Mr Darcy. In a low voice only he could hear, she said, "There is not much you could do to make me think any less of you than I already do."

She turned around and walked quickly to her sister and into the house.

CHAPTER SIXTEEN

April 1810, Kent

Mr Darcy and Elizabeth continued to be in each other's company at dinner parties, morning calls, church services, and impromptu meetings during walks in the woods around Rosings Park. Alas—to the chagrin of both—they were always in the company of others. However, Elizabeth cherished the rare moments when they could exchange meaningful glances, share whispered conversations, or steal brief laughs in the corners of the room. With every encounter, her esteem for him only deepened.

Charlotte continued to show curiosity about the nature of the relationship, and one morning, as they sat together enjoying refreshments in the parsonage's parlour, Elizabeth suspected she would face further interrogation. As Charlotte poured their tea, Elizabeth remained still in her chair beside the tea table watching her friend's precise movements. Charlotte set down the teapot and gave her a probing gaze. *Please do not ask me about Mr Darcy again*, Elizabeth thought, though she concealed her feelings behind a polite smile.

Charlotte looked down towards the tea as she stirred sugar and milk into their drinks. The gentle clink of her spoon against the cups carried across the room as she worked meticulously. Then, setting the spoon aside, she finally broke the silence. "Lizzy, is there some sort of an understanding between you and Mr Darcy?"

Elizabeth laughed uncomfortably through the blush that heated her cheeks at the mere mention of him. "I assure you there is not."

"He stares at you so much…I thought he surely must be ready to make you his wife," Charlotte teased.

Elizabeth's shrug elicited incredulity from her friend, whose eyes widened. "You must not be coy, not with me! Am I not one of your oldest friends?"

"Of course you are, you know you are," Elizabeth said quickly, "but I do not know what it is you wish me to say. There is nothing for me to confide."

Charlotte gave her a searching look before she gently handed her the cup of tea. Elizabeth accepted it with a small smile, then averted her gaze to the morning sunlight streaming through the windows, observing the shadows it cast on the settee across the room.

Charlotte drew Elizabeth's attention when she finally responded. "You have always been like this, keeping matters so close to your heart. I suppose I shall not find out anything until there is an announcement."

Some birds chirped happily from somewhere far away outside, and Elizabeth desperately wished she could be out of this room and wherever they were. She glanced back at her friend again and took a sip of tea. "Nothing has happened.

He has not declared any intentions, or...or really said anything," Elizabeth said, giving voice to concerns which had, in truth, plagued her. She believed his attentions were too marked to be anything but true regard and yet...yet he said nothing of true meaning to her. She flashed a brief insincere smile at her friend, trying to hide her dejection.

Charlotte pursed her lips a moment before asking, "Are you in love with him?"

Elizabeth inhaled sharply before admitting, "I enjoy his company very much." It was an inadequate answer. In truth, she felt a connexion between their souls, and could not imagine spending her life with anyone less worthy, but she could not say so, not when she felt so uncertain of his feelings and whether he would speak them.

Charlotte took a small sip of her tea before placing it gently back on the saucer. "Perhaps his stares signify nothing more than absence of thought, then. He is a bit difficult to comprehend and has a stiffness in his manner that makes him difficult to approach. But all of these things could be overlooked if one was in love with him."

Elizabeth knew what her friend was doing. How often had they provoked spirited debates between themselves by expressing ideas not their own! Charlotte wished her to leap to his defence, and in so doing, provide clues to what truly lay between them but she would not give in to that. She looked at her placidly. "Perhaps you are correct, Charlotte."

Though tempted to defend him, Elizabeth was not provoked to divulge more. She was not one to discuss her feelings, especially those of such vulnerability. Besides, it was still early in their acquaintance. Was it so surprising she had not received an offer of marriage from him? He had never explicitly stated his feelings towards her...much to her disappointment. *He is reserved,* she often reminded herself. *And we are rarely, if ever, given privacy that would allow either of us to speak freely of matters of the heart.*

However logical such notions were, love did not always make one the most rational, and she was disappointed that the status of their connexion was not more certain and that she could not have reasonable expectations of him.

Tired of being interrogated, she took one more sip of tea before hurriedly excusing herself, glad that Charlotte had duties to the parish that would keep her and Mr Collins occupied for the rest of the day. She squeezed her friend's shoulder, grabbed an apple from the bowl on the sideboard in the dining room, and set out before Charlotte could reply.

Elizabeth set out on a favoured path, surprised by the wind that sent the ribbons of her bonnet dancing. The air was chillier than she had expected it to be. As she looked for the ideal tree to lean against to enjoy her apple, she thought of the last few weeks with Mr Darcy. She was certain of her feelings for him, but now rather wondered whether they were reciprocated. He did stare at her frequently; even Charlotte had noticed and pointed it out. He also made every attempt to be in close proximity to her. Nevertheless, she could not help but wonder whether she had let her heart create more in her mind than was truly there. How would she recover if that were the case?

She continued walking, her mind still fixed on such thoughts, when a figure appeared ahead in the distance: a man pacing back and forth in an agitated manner. It took her only a moment to realise it was none other than the man who had been lately occupying her thoughts.

Mr Darcy seemed to recognise her too, and so ceased his pacing, and walked in her direction. She could not help but hope and wonder if he had been waiting for her. As he came closer, she noticed that he seemed perturbed. "I was just taking some enjoyment in the lovely day, and was about to walk this path for the afternoon."

"May I join you?" Every concern she had about his affections melted away when she saw the tender, earnest way he looked at her.

"Of course," she replied.

Initially, they walked in silence. She stared up at him and admired his form and person, her pulse racing at the realisation that they would finally have privacy. "I could make some observations about the weather, but I will spare you of small talk that you have so ruthlessly told me you despised," Elizabeth teased him lightly. Her effort was rewarded with a faint smile and a question.

"Well then, of what should we speak?"

Her mind was unusually slow, and she was thankful he did not seem to notice her clenching her hands at her side. She thought quickly of different topics before saying, "Please tell me of your childhood. What was it like in Derbyshire?"

As they walked, he described his upbringing, and his family's estate, Pemberley. She began to relax as he talked. By his own stories, Elizabeth could tell Lady Catherine had not exaggerated the Darcys' wealth; Pemberley was a grand and beautiful estate. Noting he spoke more of his studies and schooling than of typical youthful antics, Elizabeth wondered at what sort of happiness could be found in a childhood that was so structured and rigid. Mr Darcy mentioned that his mother had died a number of years ago and described his close bond with his younger sister, Georgiana. He spoke in great detail of his relationship with his father, asserting he was an excellent man who had shaped his character and understanding of the world. Then he added, "He will be here. Tomorrow. In the morning."

"Indeed?" She looked at him with amazement. "I shall look forward to meeting him."

"Yes, I would like the two of you to know each other."

She nodded and looked away before he could see how she blushed.

Instead of continuing on the footpath, he stopped walking and touched her arm to get her attention. "May I take you on a different path to show you a place that is special to me?"

Looking down where his hand was touching her arm, she could only nod.

They turned onto the new trail. She looked up at Mr Darcy as they walked and considered how quickly life could change course in a few weeks. She had come to Kent expecting it to be very dull, and had quickly met the only man she could say that she had ever loved. Though initially tempted to categorise him as a proud, pompous man, the more time she spent with him she saw that this was not so. He was reserved and guarded, yes, but she had peeled back his layers and now saw the intelligent, humble, and kind-hearted man underneath. His aloofness and awkwardness were endearing, and she appreciated the things that made him imperfect instead of desiring him to be something else. Although the two of them were quite different in their approaches to life, never had she felt such excitement in speaking with another person. Her soul had met its intellectual equal, its other half.

He led her along the unfamiliar path. It was less domesticated than even the walk to Holly Hill and they were forced to tread slowly, which Elizabeth did not mind. It felt as though they were moving leisurely as they quietly walked under a canopy of trees. Other than the occasions they had danced together, their bodies had never been so near. She wondered what he would do if she brushed his fingertips when they were close to hers.

The terrain was a little different now as they walked, and they found themselves trudging through thick grass. He stopped without warning and looked at her seriously.

"Is this acceptable? We are very close to our destination, but I apologise I did not remember how wild it was out here."

She smiled at his gentlemanly concern. "Yes, I assure you, it is no trouble."

He nodded and they continued on as their path narrowed, and they were required to walk even closer. A large broken tree laid in front of them, blocking their narrow path. He walked ahead of her, and offered her his hand for assistance. She felt that familiar thrill inside when she took it. She lifted her leg to take the big step on top of the log and lowered it to step down again. Once on the other side, their hands remained clasped and their eyes locked. She inhaled sharply to collect herself as she quickly looked away and dropped her hand, even though she was not quite ready to let go.

CHAPTER SEVENTEEN

Finally, they arrived at an idyllic river. The current was slow and calm. The bank was lined by oak trees with branches that elongated over the water, and the water reflected the colours of the skies above. Wildflowers and untamed shrubbery lined the embankment, adding colour and tranquillity to the scene. Elizabeth walked directly over to the water, took off her gloves, and dipped her fingers in it. The coolness was immediately refreshing. She looked to where Mr Darcy stood, gazing warmly at her.

"It is lovely," she said.

She walked back over towards him, and he assisted her to a weathered bench facing the scene. He gestured towards the largest tree in the area, which shouldered the bank. A frayed, broken rope hung from a high branch. "Colonel Fitzwilliam and I used to swing on this rope when we spent summers here. We carved notches into the tree that you can still see. We would climb up to the top and jump off. It was a way for us to relax after spending days in Lady Catherine's home."

She laughed at this, amused by the idea of him having childhood adventures. "Oh how delightful! It is hard to imagine you as a reckless little boy."

He gave her a mockingly disapproving look. "I shall have you know I was quite the climber as a child, and when I was not working on my lessons, an adventurous explorer."

She laughed. "I only mean that, as I know you, you are usually the perfect gentleman. It is hard to imagine you with the energies of a boy."

He looked more serious. "It was a special time to come here and be liberated. It provided a nice reprieve from the responsibilities that were expected of me from a young age. It was probably one of the only places in my childhood where I felt true freedom."

She saw weariness in his eyes, and understood that his childhood had been as strict as she suspected, and its solemnity likely exacerbated by the premature death of his mother. She was tempted to reach out and touch his hand, but remembered herself and refrained.

"Of course, in the evenings I had to come back to Rosings and Lady Catherine," he added, lightening the mood.

Elizabeth laughed. "What types of activities did you do out here?"

"Some I can tell you, others I cannot. You must understand, we had a strict rule: 'no girls allowed'."

She laughed again and they continued talking. He spoke of summers past, and she watched his mouth as he spoke. She inexplicably wondered what it would be like to kiss him. She had never kissed anyone before. Would she know what to do? Would she be bad at it? She shook her head to banish these thoughts and reminded herself to attend to what he was saying. So engaged were they in the conversation, they did not notice storm clouds rolling in until the first drops landed on them.

Mr Darcy gazed up towards the sky. "I suppose we should get back before it gets much worse."

They stood and began walking towards the path, but faster than they could get out of the grove, thunder, lightning, and thick rain commenced. Alarm coursed through Elizabeth from the sudden change in weather, and she glanced towards Mr Darcy, hoping he might have some plan for them.

He had to raise his voice for her to hear him. "I fear we must wait it out. Let us take shelter under that tree." He grabbed her hand, and they ran to sit between the roots of the tree that shouldered the stream. It provided some shelter, but they were still quickly becoming drenched by the rain. Her bonnet was soaked and half off her head as the rain began falling harder and the sky lit up from lightning striking somewhere in the vicinity. Mr Darcy took off his coat and with one arm, held it over his and Elizabeth's heads. He lightly wrapped his other arm around her shoulders to bring her closer to him and better shield her from the storm.

They huddled together with her back and head against his chest as he pulled her in tightly. The storm's ferocity kept them silent but she was thrilled—and anxious—to be so close to him. She felt his nose in her hair and his breath on her head. Her own breathing became more rapid the longer she sat next to him.

The storm subsided almost as suddenly as it had come on. He gently removed his coat from above them, but his other arm remained around her waist. She turned and lifted her head up to speak to him. "That was unexpected, was it not? I thank you for shielding me, sir."

She strove to speak lightly, and yet somehow, they became locked in one another's gazes. As she stared into his eyes, she could see hues of amber that she had never before noticed. He looked back into hers as if he had never seen anything like her before and suddenly the notion of falling in love with one another seemed all too real.

They stayed like that for a few moments. He lifted his free hand up to her cheek tenderly, and she closed her eyes at his touch. Leaning towards her, he kissed her gently. After a moment he pulled back, and they opened their eyes.

"Please forgive me, I—" Their eyes locked another moment, and this time Elizabeth closed the gap between them quickly, kissing him with a passion he quickly matched.

After some time had passed in that manner, Elizabeth began to realise how long they had been gone. She reluctantly pulled away from him. "I suppose I should be getting back now," she said softly, then stood. Mr Darcy immediately stood up as well, though he appeared to be suppressing a grin.

"What? What is it?"

"I think we must first re-arrange your hair."

She touched her hair and her eyes widened as she realised how completely disordered it had become. He turned her around and they laughed as he did all he could to help her put the pins back in and retrieve her sodden bonnet. She could not believe this moment was real—the formidable, aloof, and grand Mr Darcy laughing as he redid her hair so she could go back into her cousin's house without drawing undue notice or scurrilous accusations.

As they walked back to the parsonage in comfortable silence, Elizabeth reflected on what had just transpired and what this meant for them. Was there a 'them'? As they approached the parsonage path, Mr Darcy asked, "When may I see you again?"

"I believe tomorrow we are supposed to dine at Rosings. If you remember, my mother and youngest sister will be here to retrieve me," she said. Then added solemnly, "Before I return to Hertfordshire next week."

"I shall wait with bated breath."

As she began to turn and walk away, Mr Darcy stopped her.

"Miss Elizabeth?"

"Yes?"

"When you return to Hertfordshire, may I follow in a few days so—" He paused, an interminable pause while Elizabeth's heart pounded. "So that we might further our acquaintance?"

Her spirits soared and she had to fight to keep from bursting into happy song or something equally silly. "I should like that very well."

She moved to leave but he stopped her. Reaching towards her, he removed a hair pin that was barely hanging onto a fallen lock by her face. As he looked down at the unique piece in his hands, he rubbed over where the initials 'EB' made out of metal were placed near the top. He then lifted the hair to pin it again, and she touched his hand to stop him.

She placed the pin into the palm of his hand, "Um…you may, you may keep it," she said, feeling a little embarrassed. "As you know…"

His hands closed tightly around the pin. "I would love that."

He drew closer to her and gently tucked the uncooperative hair behind her ear. Looking into her eyes, he squeezed her hand one last time as she gazed warmly at him. Reluctantly, she turned around, swinging her wet bonnet as she walked back towards the parsonage.

"Elizabeth?"

She stopped walking and turned back towards him, attempting to hide her surprise that he called her by her Christian name. "Yes?"

"I am *very* excited to see what the future holds for us."

If she had not been worried about Charlotte or Mr Collins possibly seeing, she would have run back into his arms and kissed him again. All she could muster was a heartfelt, "And I, as well."

Once inside, she was relieved to find the front rooms empty. She ran up the stairs to her bedchamber, closed her door, and fell backwards onto her bed. Sprawled there, she clutched at her heart. *My first kiss.* Her head was spinning as she replayed the scene over and over in her head. Moment by moment. It had been perfect in every way.

She tried to push away the slight guilt she felt in letting him kiss her, and that she had allowed herself to respond in equal measure. *I am nearly a grown woman,* Elizabeth told herself, and all signs suggested that she and Mr Darcy were on the road to engagement.

She could hardly believe it. She was about to become an engaged woman. Shaking her head in wonder, Elizabeth was amazed her life could turn so quickly to a new chapter. She had never imagined such a smooth and joyous path to matrimony, but here she was, on the verge of a proposal and marriage. How strange it would be! She had always imagined Jane would be the first to marry, to leave Longbourn before her. Yet, it now seemed that Elizabeth would be the one to depart first, leaving to make her home a hundred miles away to Mr Darcy's grand estate of Pemberley, where one day she would be mistress! She resolved not to dwell on the distant future, as it made her somewhat anxious, but to think only of the things which made her smile. Which she did. Over, and over again.

She was recovered by the time she heard the Collinses returning home. Determined to conceal her giddiness, Elizabeth rose from her bed and stepped to the mirror, where she promptly burst into laughter at the sight of her dishevelled appearance. Recalling Mr Darcy's attempts to re-pin her hair made her blush, but she strove to fix her appearance and adopt a calm expression before joining her friend downstairs to help prepare for the arrival of her mother and sister the following day.

CHAPTER EIGHTEEN

When Elizabeth set out from the parsonage two days later, she took solace in the near-perfect weather. It was a lovely afternoon, neither too cold, nor too hot, and the blue sky was dotted with fluffy white clouds. It was the kind of day that offered endless possibilities for enjoyable meanderings, but for now, Elizabeth walked purposely towards the point where the path away from the parsonage met with one of Rosings' smaller lanes. It was here that she was to meet Mr Darcy at the appointed time and place they had agreed on the previous evening.

Ah, the previous evening, she thought to herself, unable to dispel the embarrassment she felt from dinner at Rosings the night before.

She cringed as she remembered her mother and sister's behaviour. Mrs Bennet had been vulgar and overly talkative, as she usually was. Lydia, only thirteen and lacking the manners to be amongst even a country society, spoke as though she were in the same circle as Lady Catherine—with no attempt at deference and no acknowledgement of the fact that she was still a child. Lydia should not have even been at the table!

Lydia spoke incessantly about the news that the officers from a regiment were coming to be stationed in Meryton, was disrespectful to her mother, and managed to throw a few coquettish looks and comments at Colonel Fitzwilliam and even Mr Darcy. They both appeared more amused than horrified but Elizabeth was mortified. Lydia's behaviour was abhorrent and yet their mother did nothing to check her.

Though she had always known her family's faults—and they were many—her time away from Longbourn had made them seem less severe. Being reacquainted with their obvious shortcomings at Rosings, in the presence of Mr Darcy and his aunt, had been humiliating. Lady Catherine made no effort to conceal her disdain, but her mother and Lydia were too oblivious to notice—and perhaps too ignorant to understand—her belittling comments.

Elizabeth could take solace that Mr Darcy's father was delayed in his travels, and thus did not witness her family's embarrassing behaviour. She was certain that whatever terrible things Lady Catherine might report to him would be smoothed over by Mr Darcy.

At least she had been fortunate enough to be seated next to Mr Darcy at dinner. His proximity to her not only kept him farther away from her mother—sparing him from Mrs Bennet's drunken chatter—but also allowed Elizabeth to more easily savour the intensity of his gaze throughout the evening, a pleasure she relished. His closeness to her became even more reassuring during her humiliation, when as her mother had more wine, she told Lady Catherine that she could not be sure what sort of fellow Elizabeth would bring home to marry one day. She cited Elizabeth's unchecked tongue and stubbornness as reasons for her doubt, and that it would take a certain kind of man, if any, to put up with *that*.

Just as Elizabeth had thought she could nearly shrink under the table, she felt Mr Darcy's hand grasp her own and give it a gentle, reassuring squeeze. He looked upon her mother with narrowed eyes; when he drew breath as if to speak some insult or deserved set-down, Elizabeth tugged his arm and shook her head. He had heeded her warning, but pursed his lips and sent a menacing stare towards the offender. Although uneasy with his behaviour, she had been flattered that he wished to defend her honour against her mother's insult. She felt equal parts embarrassed and pleased as she dwelt on the memory.

Elizabeth arrived at the spot where she was to meet Mr Darcy. He had startled her at the end of the evening, pulling her into a side room when no one was looking and asking her to meet him privately the following afternoon. When she agreed, he gave her a swift kiss on the cheek. She had been a little surprised by his brazenness, but was thrilled nevertheless. Was this to be it? Would he speak the very words she so longed to hear?

As she waited for him, she closed her eyes and lifted her head towards the sky, feeling the sun sink in on her face and listening to the songbirds in the distance. How pleased she felt to escape the parsonage today, where her mother was questioning poor Charlotte about the quality of her linens and Lydia was arguing with Mr Collins about the wisdom of his bee-keeping. She opened her eyes again and walked over to the nearest tree, tracing her fingers along the bark.

A SHARED HISTORY

Looking past the tree on whose trunk she was absentmindedly drawing shapes, she saw Mr Darcy's tall, elegant figure approaching from afar. Her heart fluttered in her chest as she imagined returning to the parsonage with him by her side and telling her mother that Mr Darcy would require a private audience with Mr Bennet. She frowned. One could not imagine how her mother's raptures at such news might be expressed.

As Mr Darcy came closer, she became less certain of the happy outcomes. His face was pale and held neither delight nor trepidation; his expression was serious, almost detached, and in her brief experience knowing him, it did not bode well. He marched determinedly towards her, and in a crisp voice said, "Let us walk." He moved past her and she hurried to keep apace. They had not walked far when he broke the silence abruptly.

"We cannot do this."

"Cannot do what?" she asked, her heart hammering in her chest.

"I cannot do this."

She tilted her head. "Do *what*?"

He stopped walking forwards and began pacing back and forth as he continued. "Do this. You and I. We cannot be together."

Had he been followed? Turning her head to glance behind her, Elizabeth said, "I do not understand. Do you mean at this moment? We cannot be seen together?"

Mr Darcy ceased pacing and took a deep breath. "We cannot have a future together. We are too different."

CHAPTER NINETEEN

Her stomach fell at his shocking declaration. Too stunned to say anything, Elizabeth stared at him as she coloured. Doubt filled her and attempting to comprehend his meaning, she finally whispered, "Why?"

His voice remained as strong and as cutting as his words. "My family will not approve. I cannot go against their wishes."

"Why would they not approve?"

"They would think your family is beneath mine. Unworthy to be connected to us."

Feeling his words almost as a physical blow, Elizabeth put her hand against a tree for support as the realisation of what was happening overtook her. "You are a gentleman and I am a gentleman's daughter."

Mr Darcy sighed in what sounded like frustration before glancing heavenward for a moment and muttering, "It would not be the same to them."

"Do you agree?" she demanded.

He clenched his jaw and stared off into distance, making no reply.

She blinked away the tears which rose suddenly. "Might I ask why this matters today when it did not matter any of the other days we trod these paths? You knew of my want of connexion before, and it did not give you pause on making advances towards me. I created no false pretences."

"I struggled with it and decided I was willing to overlook the inferiority of your circumstances until—" He broke off his explanation and looked at the ground.

Elizabeth moved towards him, determined to have an answer. Her shock remained but now her anger was fuelled. "Until what?"

"Surely you must understand," he said, finally looking at her fully.

She hoped her expression showed him every bit of the betrayal she felt. "I am afraid I do not."

Mr Darcy resumed pacing, his face showing his mind's consternation. At length, he burst out, "It is your family's vulgar behaviour. Your sister is disrespectful to her elders and her betters, speaks out of turn, and flirts with every male she sees. Your mother does nothing to correct her and instead speaks and displays herself inelegantly. They lack manners or social graces. Such conduct would disgrace the Darcy name and be a poor influence on Georgiana."

As was her custom, sorrow was overtaken by anger. "Social graces? Do you consider yourself the epitome of social grace, scowling at everyone the moment you enter the room? What of your family? They are ridiculous too. Your aunt is the rudest and most condescending woman I have yet to meet, and her daughter cowers in fear. What kind of influence are they on your sister?" Elizabeth felt herself shaking in anger. "Based on how you and Lady Catherine behave, I can only guess at the behaviour of your father and sister."

"That is enough," he said sharply.

Her voice heightened as she replied, "Oh? It is enough now when we speak of *your* family's flaws?"

"It is different, and you know that."

"No, I do not! Or are your family's faults and comportment excused by birthright and wealth?"

He covered one hand to his eyes and was silent for a brief time. Finally, he took a deep breath and exhaled slowly. "It is more than station and fortune, Elizabeth. Your mother and sister—their words and manners lacked any restraint. Your family's reputation will be harmed if they continue to act with such abandon. Truly, do you not see them for what they are?"

"Of course, I do," she said softly. "They frustrate me to no end, but I have long ago learnt to accept that people are not pawns to be controlled and manipulated. There is not anything I would not do for them."

Mr Darcy's reply, when it came a moment later, was less harsh but equally firm. "It is admirable that you feel so and yet, part of my deliberations as well. You would not wish to abstain from visiting Longbourn. You would want your family at Pemberley."

"Of course I would."

"Forgive me, I do not wish to insult you, but I cannot be tied to them. Such a connexion could only hurt and bring dishonour to my loved ones, and even my ancestors. I owe them everything I have, Elizabeth. I am bound in my duty to them."

Her eyes narrowed. How dare he look at her with a pitiful expression, demanding her understanding for his insult!

"This is utterly ridiculous. I understood we were of different dispositions, but I never imagined you would be so fastidious that you could not bear to tolerate a little absurdity. Surely you must know that to join with another in marriage requires tolerating the quirks of those they call family?"

He remained silent. She thought she detected the slightest softening in his resolve, and stepped closer to him. Furious though she was with the gentleman, Elizabeth would not give up when she saw something still worth fighting for. Conquering her anger, she pleaded softly, "Please do not do this."

"I must. Forgive me," was all he could say, though he seemed less determined than he had previously.

She ventured a step even closer and took hold of his hands, saying earnestly, "Do you love me?"

He turned his head and looked away, but he did not take his hands out of hers. "Yes," he admitted. He turned his head back towards her. For the first time that day, she could see the eyes of the man she had kissed by the river. Their gazes locked in mutual recognition that it was the first time they had spoken aloud the depth of their feelings.

"Then that should conquer everything," she implored.

His admission and her pleading seemed to weaken his resolve. In a soft voice, he asked, "Would you...would you give them up for me?"

Her hope gone, Elizabeth's thoughts turned from sadness to fury again. She dropped his hands. "Absolutely not! Have you heard anything I have said? *I do not love with conditions.* I do not love my family only on days when they behave themselves ,and I would not abandon them because they do not act appropriately to your standards."

He stared at her with a disappointed expression.

"Everyone must live and behave by certain standards, Elizabeth. In my position, I must uphold many, and cannot shirk my duties and responsibilities simply because I fell in love."

She looked at him incredulously and shook her head. "For all this talk of responsibility, all I see is a man who thinks meanly of those outside his family and social circle. I see a man who is a gentleman by reputation and inheritance only, not in his heart."

Mr Darcy listened without interrupting her, though he appeared to catch her words with resentment and surprise.

"You believe you are honourable because you fulfil what you think are your duties," she went on, "but you have disregarded the weightier matters of morality, kindness, and compassion."

His expression darkened. "I never asked for any of this. I never asked to fall in love."

"Love? How can you speak of love in such a way?" she asked in disbelief.

"You have no idea what it is like!" he nearly shouted, causing her to jump slightly at his sudden display of emotion. "I am to be master of Pemberley, with countless people who depend upon me for their livelihoods and their families' welfare. It is a life of duty and responsibility. I was never meant to marry for love!"

She backed away farther from him. He rubbed his hands through his hair and over his mouth as he attempted to regain composure. A terrible thought came to her and she asked, "Was I just a dalliance? A distraction while in Kent?"

His eyes widened and his reply was as quick as it was strong. "No, never."

She let out a relieved breath. "I hardly know what to think or believe." After a moment's pause, she added, "Are you really so capricious and unfeeling to treat someone you say you love in this manner?"

Once again he rubbed at his hair, then his hands fell into fists at his side. "I fell in love with you against my better judgment. The strength of my attachment had become impossible to overcome so I let myself believe that we could conquer all the obstacles. Only last evening, I realised I was wrong." His voice shook as he added, "I can only apologise for allowing you to believe that there was a possibility that we could get married."

Her heart sank within her chest, as she looked down at her hands, wringing them together. "I do not know why I am surprised," she said softly, more towards herself than to him. "I have seen you treat others as beneath you, neglecting to give them common decency and kindness." A tear escaped her as she added with a thick voice, "I foolishly allowed myself to be blinded to it."

He could only look towards the ground at such a statement.

Looking at him again, she choked back tears as she spoke. "If you do this, you cannot undo it. You will have to live with this for the rest of your life."

"I am sorry," he said coolly, as if he was building his walls again. His eyes looked away vacantly, but his jaw was clenched.

Elizabeth began to sob. "I cannot forsake my family."

Rather than answering her or acknowledging her pain, he said, "I wish you good health and happiness all of your days."

Then he turned and walked away from her.

CHAPTER TWENTY

How she made her way to the parsonage and to her room, Elizabeth knew not. But eventually she found herself there. She sat with her back against the closed door, sobbing quietly as she clutched her knees to her chest. Was it possible to feel so much pain and survive? It felt as though she was dying, save for the fact that she did not get the relief of knowing the agony would soon end.

Eventually, having cried all the tears she had, she crawled into her bed. She lay there, insensible, until the maid knocked on the door alerting her that dinner was at hand. She called out a reply, declining the meal and feigning illness. It was not wholly untrue; her body and head ached, and she felt as though she might cast up her accounts at any given moment.

Elizabeth lay that way for the rest of the evening until, long after the countryside had descended into darkness, she drifted into a fitful, restless sleep.

A SHARED HISTORY

She woke with the dawn and for a few moments her mind was blessedly blank, if somewhat confused as to why she was dressed in yesterday's gown. Too soon, the memory of Mr Darcy and what he had said rushed into her mind. Reminded of her grief, Elizabeth declined the maid's services to ready for the day, instead choosing to remain in bed. She marked the hours watching the shadows from the sunlight move slowly through her room, relieved the day was slowly passing her by.

At some point in the afternoon, she heard a faint knock on the door. Instead of answering, she turned on her side to face the window. She heard the door creak open, followed by her mother calling, "Lizzy, my dear? Are you awake?"

Elizabeth remained silent, prompting her mother to walk around the bed and peer at her.

"Oh dear, you look dreadful," Mrs Bennet said softly. "Is there something..." She ceased speaking and wrung her hands together nervously. Elizabeth suspected her mother realised her second-born daughter likely suffered from something more than a headache or her monthly pains. And yet, seemingly disinterested in learning more, she stopped twisting her hands and lay her arms firmly at her side as she quickly changed the subject. "You have not even touched your soup. Here, let me feed you."

In her younger years, Elizabeth would have resented her mother's inability to offer the sort of maternal succour needed by a daughter, but she had learnt to not expect more from her. Mrs Bennet gave what she was able, a well-meant but limited sort of love and caring. At this moment, Elizabeth welcomed her mother's limitations; she preferred not to communicate the depths of her anguish to anyone.

After feeding her a few bites, Mrs Bennet asked, "Are you well?"

"I am well enough, Mama," she whispered weakly, before taking another bite.

"Well, I certainly hope so. You know we are to return to Longbourn in two days. You must get well else I do not know what we will do."

Elizabeth lay back on the pillows as her mother began lecturing her about the inconvenience of falling ill so close to their travel day. "There is still so much to do before we leave. And look at you, so terribly pale. You must rest, and get better quickly, my dear."

"I shall."

"Have you had enough soup?"

She nodded weakly.

"Very well, let us lay you down again."

Once Elizabeth was again situated under the counterpane, her mother began dabbing her forehead with a wet cloth and stroking her hair. The irony was not lost on Elizabeth that the woman whose mortifying behaviour had helped ruin her happiness now was nursing her through her heartbreak.

It is of no use to be angry with her, even if she had a hand in ruining my future, she thought. *I have pleaded with her in the past to change, but to no avail. Her character is set. I cannot change her and have made peace with that.*

She inhaled deeply, suddenly overcome with grief. *How will I ever recover from this heartbreak?*

In time, she would reflect on it and try to reconcile Mr Darcy's unexpected withdrawal and harsh words with the kind man with whom she had fallen in love. Examining all of his behaviours under a magnifying glass, she would attempt to deduce how he could have treated her so coldly. Eventually she would scold herself for not recognising the patterns that revealed his true nature.

Chastising herself for excusing his pride, arrogance, and reticence towards others by calling it shyness at best or traits she could improve or manage at worst, Elizabeth would conclude that her judgment had been clouded. She had been flattered that a man who was not easily impressed had been charmed by her, and thus she had overlooked his flaws. Ultimately she would blame herself for trusting her heart to another so easily and recklessly.

But those realisations would come later. For now, a day after her heart was broken, her mind was centred only on the loss of the happy future she had envisioned so easily. Gone were the lazy days spent together at Pemberley, laughing, talking, and debating everything and nothing at the same time. Gone were the experiences and memories they would make as they travelled together. Gone were her imaginings of dark-haired boys and girls romping around them like puppies as she and he exchanged loving looks. Gone was the life she could see perfectly and clearly even though it was not real.

Even more than this, she mourned the man she had lost. A man whose companionship she had somehow come to depend on and desire in a few short weeks.

Elizabeth had long feared that her family might hinder her reputation and future happiness. Mr Darcy had said nothing of them that was untrue, but it only compounded her sorrow that the very fears she held deep in her heart were used to reject her by the one she cherished most. And she had defended her family without acknowledging that her own fears matched his concerns. Could she have been more honest?

As her mother dipped the cloth in the bowl of water again, there was another knock on the door. Elizabeth recognised Charlotte's light footsteps nearing her bedside. Her friend gently touched Elizabeth's arm and asked, "Lizzy, you look very unwell. How are you feeling? What are your symptoms?"

Instead of answering, Elizabeth just whispered, "Charlotte…" as her eyes fluttered shut.

She heard the women continue the conversation around her as Mrs Bennet informed Charlotte that Elizabeth had no fever and had managed to eat a little soup.

Elizabeth took a deep breath and opened her eyes one more time. She slowly looked from her friend to her mother staring down at her from both sides of the bed, concern etched on their faces. She turned her head into the pillow, closed her eyes, and drifted off to sleep.

Late the following morning, Elizabeth abruptly sat up in her bed. She looked around the room, feeling slightly lightheaded, and caught a glimpse of herself in the mirror. She touched her face and hair as she took in her reflection. Her complexion was pale, her eyes ringed with dark circles, and her hair a frizzled mess of uncombed curls and disarrayed plaits. She could hardly recognise herself.

He did this to me when he stripped away his affections.

How could he profess to love her, yet treat her so callously? Why had he pursued her if his disdain for her connexions could threaten their relationship? She was in disbelief that the man she loved, after winning her heart, had used her vulnerabilities to destroy it. It seemed unlikely that Mr Darcy ever truly loved her, for how could someone profess devotion while acting with such selfishness and carelessness towards the one they claimed to cherish? What sort of horrible person treated another this way?

She gripped the sheets around her tightly, and for the first time she felt a new emotion surge within. What had been sadness and regret was overtaken by anger and loathing towards the proudest, most arrogant man of her acquaintance. "You wanted to marry him?" she enquired of the bereft creature in the mirror. "He is positively the last man in the world you should ever have wished to marry."

As she vowed that she would never let anyone hurt her in this way again, her mother entered the room and gently touched her shoulder.

"How fare you today, my dear?"

Elizabeth could only reply, "Mama, let us return home. I do not belong here."

CHAPTER TWENTY-ONE

December 1813, Hertfordshire

Between dinners at Longbourn and Netherfield, as well as Mr Bingley's calls on Jane during the day, Mr Darcy and Elizabeth were constantly in the same society. Outwardly, there was no obvious renewal of feelings from the past, but at times Elizabeth could not help but wonder: Had he ever thought of her? Regretted her, even a little? Before the party at Lucas Lodge, she never would have believed so, considering how ruthlessly he had ended their relationship. But his words during their last conversation—'I had imagined you would marry someone different'—seemed to indicate that he had at least thought of her during their time apart. It was astonishing, considering how coldly he had treated her on their final meeting in Kent, that she occupied his thoughts at all. She had always assumed he sought to erase her from his memory completely and felt only grateful to have escaped such a marriage.

No matter how shocking it was that he thought of her during their time apart, she reminded herself that mere remembrance did not imply regret; that seemed implausible. How could he possibly feel remorse? He had ended their relationship based on her family's behaviour, and the Bennets were still the same as they ever were.

After their exchange at the Lucases, she was reminded of why she could never again harbour any true feelings for such a horrible man, despite the intense attraction she felt for him at times. Days later, anger still coursed through her whenever she recalled his presumption in saying, 'I always believed only love would induce you into matrimony'. How dare he conjecture on whom she should marry? How could he possess such pride? To believe his opinion mattered enough to suggest whom she should choose was nothing short of outrageous. He had rejected her and shattered her heart in the process, yet now he acted as if he had the right to lecture her. Every time she returned to the memory, she felt her body tremble with fury.

Such audacity had led her to utter the impolite words, 'There is not much you could do to make me think any less of you than I already do'. Though she regretted their cutting nature, she stood firm in their sentiment. From the depths of her heart, she had tried to treat him with civility since he came into her company again; yet, between his arrogant nature and the haunting memories of their past connexion, her resolve was tested at every turn. Thus, they carried on as hardly more than acquaintances, and certainly not very friendly ones at that.

When in company, she met him with every intention of being composed but indifferent. However, as intentions and deeds often vary, they frequently argued, engaging in spirited debates on any and every topic that arose. No observer—not even Mr Bingley or Jane—would have ever suspected them of once being in love; they appeared as adversaries. Such was the occasion during dinner one night at Netherfield when the conversation turned to Royce having spent time in the navy.

"Jane tells me that we have a common acquaintance, Mr Royce. Are you familiar with Captain Peeler?" asked Mr Bingley between courses.

"Yes, most certainly," Royce replied. "He was my captain during my time in the navy. He is an admirable soul. Tell me, how do you know him?"

Mr Bingley looked pleased by the connexion. "He is my cousin. Next time I write to him I shall tell him we have met."

"What a coincidence! Please pass on my regards to him." Royce leant back in his chair and eyed his host keenly. "That is truly remarkable." He shook his head in disbelief before continuing. "I spent my formative years at sea with your cousin. Following in my father's path and joining the Royal Navy had been my course since I was a boy. It was a critical time in my life that I would not trade for anything. I was able to see and experience much of the world."

Mr Bingley took a bite of potatoes before responding politely, "I have always admired a gentleman who spends time in the military or navy."

"Yes, he did it at the risk of losing his inheritance too," Elizabeth said proudly as she took a small bite of roast. Her eyes flickered down the table to where Mr Darcy sat. He was staring down absently at his plate as he idly pushed peas into the shape of a circle. *How desperately I wish he were not here. How cruel of him to have come to Hertfordshire nearly three weeks before the wedding!*

"Is that so?" Mr Bingley asked as he dabbed at his mouth with a napkin.

"Yes, Miss Elizabeth is correct," Royce replied. "The aunt from whom I was set to inherit preferred that I become a clergyman and often tried convincing me to leave the navy. She even threatened to pass my inheritance on to a different relation if I did not. I assured her that although I respected her and still hoped for the inheritance and property, I could not abandon the navy."

Mr Bingley tilted his head as he studied Royce. "Strong man you are. What did she do?"

"Her threats were not permanent. She was angry for a time, but then came around. She gave me the inheritance, and that is how I came into my living."

"Yes, and this is one of the things I do admire about you, Mr Royce," Elizabeth said as she placed her glass down and looked at him with a tender smile. "Your steadiness of character. I have known you many years and once you have made a decision, you adhere to it. I have known you to continue to be persistent even when the odds are against you."

"Thank you, Miss Elizabeth." Royce gazed steadily into her eyes.

She looked away and continued, "I think it is a grievous blemish on a man's character indeed to be too yielding to others' influences. If you wish to be happy in life, I do believe you should be resolved. We cannot let others dictate our happiness. After all, they will not have to live out our decisions." Her eyes wandered the room, pausing for a moment on Mr Darcy as she spoke.

"Indeed," replied Mr Royce as he straightened his back. A subtle smile grew on his face.

Down the table, Elizabeth heard Mr Darcy clearing his

throat. "Is it your opinion that we should not owe any respect or duty to the elders of our family lines?" he asked in a grave voice. "That we should give their opinions little regard even if they mean to grant us an inheritance? Care very little if they disagree with our vital life decisions?"

Elizabeth was startled; up until this point he had been mostly silent. She took a sip of wine before she looked at him and said calmly, "I believe there should be respect, but we must resolve to make our own decisions. Do you think we should be as dolls in a child's dollhouse, bending to our elders' every inclination?"

Pleased with her analogy, she picked up her fork and jabbed at a bit of roast as she waited for his response. She noticed Lydia and Kitty rolling their eyes at each other as they prepared themselves for another 'bout of verbal fisticuffs between Lizzy and Mr Darcy'. At least they were amused; Elizabeth saw Jane stiffen in her chair and Mr Bingley let out a long exhale.

Mr Darcy looked down and rubbed the polished wood of the table with one finger as he began, "You may have misunderstood me. I do not encourage mindless compliance." His hand stilled and he looked up at her again before continuing. "However, it is undeniable that wisdom often comes with age, and our elder generations possess invaluable insights and experiences to guide us. It is not wrong to consider such things when making important decisions which affect more lives than our own."

How could he be so callous, defending a position so painfully similar to the one that tore us apart? And to do it here, in front of everyone. Is this his idea of gentlemanly conduct?

She set her fork down firmly before she answered. "Although wisdom can come with age, it is not a universal truth. There are those older than me who lack understanding. Placing blind trust in someone solely based on their age seems imprudent to say the least. We risk sacrificing our own happiness to conform to another person's notions of our life." She spoke in a civil manner, but a slight sharpness to her words could be detected.

"Happiness, though desirable, cannot be the only purpose for life. There are other things to consider." Mr Darcy's dark eyes were intent upon her.

"Such as?"

"Duty to others and familial obligations," he replied calmly. "For example, I owe everything I possess to my ancestors. I am merely a steward, not truly an owner, of the Darcy fortune and land. That alone I should say obliges me to heed their good counsel."

She looked around the room and gave a humourless laugh. "I should say one risks finding oneself *too* reliant on the guidance of elders, simply because experience or practice in independent thought has not occurred. I shudder to think of the future of estates left to such people."

Miss Bingley let out a small gasp and Jane whispered, "Oh, Lizzy," under her breath. Elizabeth quickly realised she had gone too far with her public insult of Mr Darcy. Before this point, she had always implied her low opinion of him, but she had not been directly and openly derisive towards him. Glancing at him now, she saw he wore a small smile but Elizabeth thought she could perceive that he was offended.

After a few moments of silence, Mr Darcy spoke. "You have mistaken my point, or perhaps I made it poorly. I meant only that taking into consideration the advice of our elders is important. There is of course a balance between seeking counsel from a wiser generation with your best interest at heart and letting yourself become a mere puppet." He placed his napkin on top of his uneaten meal and continued, "Now if you will excuse me, Miss Bingley, I have an urgent matter of business I must attend to right away."

Miss Bingley nodded, and Mr Darcy rose from the table, then left the room.

Elizabeth, mortified and angry with herself, could not bear to look around the table and see the censure in others' eyes. She had the uncommon experience of expressing exactly what she wished to convey at the precise moment she wanted to say it. Yet, instead of feeling victorious over Mr Darcy, she felt humiliated. When the ladies rose to separate, she apologised to Miss Bingley and then sat in the corner of the room for the remainder of the gathering.

She was silent in the carriage back to Longbourn. Maintaining her composure was difficult, but she succeeded until arriving in her bedchamber, where she allowed her tears to fall freely, tears of mortification, humiliation, and regret. She knew she had not acquitted herself well; indeed, she had conducted herself as a shrew.

How could she have been so cruel to him? She had often been praised for her intelligence, but it was not usually coupled with the loss of self-control. She had previously prided herself on maintaining a certain detachment from her family's absurdity; yet even if she never displayed their impoliteness and incivility before, now she found herself behaving no better than they did at their worst.

Three years ago, she had accused Mr Darcy of lacking kindness and compassion, yet here she was today committing the same offences. She had never been so disappointed with herself in all her life.

Elizabeth had grown weary of carrying the burden of

anger within her; it was not in her nature and clinging to such resentment was transforming her into someone she neither liked nor recognised. No matter how poorly he had treated her, she vowed she would never again display such a lack of basic social graces, insulting another person in front of friends and family. Her behaviour had led only to her own degradation.

I must bury this bitterness and apologise to him as soon as possible. It is time to establish some sort of truce between us.

CHAPTER TWENTY-TWO

The next afternoon, Elizabeth discreetly tapped her toes beneath her gown as she sat next to Royce on the sofa in Longbourn's drawing room. In her subtle display of anxiety, she offered a sharp contrast to the serenity around her. Mary and Jane were quietly completing needlework, while Kitty and Royce carried on a jovial conversation. Elizabeth's nervous foot-tapping was unladylike behaviour, but she could not find it in her to stop as she anticipated Mr Darcy's arrival with Mr Bingley. She planned to quickly find a reason to be alone with him, and apologise. The mantel clock ticked loudly behind her as she awaited their appearance, each tick seeming an eternity from the last. Finally, Mr Bingley, noticeably alone, entered the room and greeted everyone. His behaviour was all that was easy and friendly, but Elizabeth thought she saw a shadow pass behind his eyes when she asked, "Do you come alone today?"

"I do."

She smiled at him, but felt a rush of disappointment greater than she expected.

"Darcy came ahead of me with the purpose of calling on your father," he added.

"Indeed?" Elizabeth furrowed her brow. "He already is here?"

"I saw him go into Papa's study a while ago," said Kitty.

Elizabeth clenched her jaw, restraining her frustration. How long had she heard Kitty prattle this morning about pointless topics when she could have provided useful information ages ago? She must have missed him enter when she and Jane had been walking with Royce around the cutting garden.

She had to wait a half an hour longer to find out Mr Darcy's purpose in calling, when he and her father approached the drawing room with an air of easiness and smiles on their faces. In his hands, Mr Darcy held one of her father's books.

"Thank you for indulging an old man in describing the works in your library," Mr Bennet was saying. "If ever I journey north, you may be assured I will take advantage of your invitation and stop at Pemberley to admire your bookshelves."

"You are welcome at any time, sir. And I thank you for showing me yours and lending this title to me." Under his breath, he added, "My friend's collection is an absolute shame. I will relish the stimulation this will provide."

Elizabeth stared dumbfounded as the two men laughed together and Mr Bennet clapped Mr Darcy on the back. "You are welcome to Longbourn at any time. Please come back once you have finished that one and we can find another interesting book for you."

My father is lending books to Mr Darcy? Are they forming something of a friendship? How could this be?

When Mr Bennet left to return to his book-room, Mr Darcy entered the room fully. He did not look at her or insert himself into the general conversation, instead choosing to sit in one of the chairs off to the side. Flustered, Elizabeth struggled to think of some excuse to go sit by him so she could undertake her apology. She found the opportunity when he suddenly stood and headed towards the door. She overheard him tell Mr Bingley that he was going out of doors for some fresh air.

As Mr Darcy reached the door, Elizabeth knew she would need to follow him out. She rose on suddenly shaking legs and announced, "Please excuse me, I think I will go for a quick stroll out of doors."

"I will join you," Royce said suddenly. "I would like to stretch my legs as well."

She attempted to push away her displeasure with Royce at foiling her plan. Much as she wished to, she could not deny his offer and, with a forced smile, politely acquiesced that he should join her.

As they exited Longbourn together, he stopped and held out his arm; Elizabeth exhaled sharply as she reluctantly took it. Her hopes of finding Mr Darcy and shaking off Royce dimmed. As they walked along, she heard her little cousins' laughing voices as they played in the distance, but there was no sign of Mr Darcy.

They rounded to the side of the house and, to her surprise, discovered him in company with Amelia and Lillian in a clearing on the other side of some shrubbery. Elizabeth and Royce remained unnoticed; she crept up as closely as she could without being seen, beckoning Royce to join her.

Lillian was yelling, "No! Do not go that way, if you do they will see you!"

"Well, what do you propose then?" Mr Darcy asked in a livelier manner than he usually displayed.

"That is where the pirates sleep! We need to go round to the other side of the house."

Amelia ran up to them, pretending to ride a broom as a horse. "Come on everybody, get on a horse like me, and we will get away."

Elizabeth was surprised to see him engaging with children of such humble birth—their father was involved in trade! Perhaps his disdain and superciliousness towards those he deemed inferior only manifested towards adults. She scolded herself. If she was determined to apologise to him, she could not dwell on such musings.

"But we do not have horses as you do," Mr Darcy said to the little girl. "I believe we should hide behind the bushes instead."

Amelia paused and with a shrug, announced, "You will probably die then." She happily galloped away around the corner of the house.

"Hurry!" shouted Lillian. "They shall be back any moment so we must hide quickly."

Elizabeth felt a grin spread across her face. Sensing Royce looking at her, she pressed her finger to her lips to remind him to stay quiet so they could remain undiscovered.

Mr Darcy and Lillian made their way towards the hedges, close to where Elizabeth and Royce were concealed, to hide from the pirates.

"Oh very well, I shall come too!" exclaimed Amelia as she abandoned her broom horse. The three sat behind some hedges where Elizabeth and Royce could still hear them without being discovered. They were silent for a few moments while they all hid.

"I have a joke for you, Mr Darcy," Lillian announced.

"What is it?" he whispered back, then urged her to speak in a whisper as well.

"The breakfast we had today was egg-cellent!"

"That is clever!"

"I have one too!" cried Amelia.

"Tell us, Amelia."

"This grass is a house!"

Mr Darcy chuckled, loudly and exaggeratedly.

"Shh! Quiet Mr Darcy. They will hear us," Lillian exclaimed. "Amelia, that is not a joke. That does not even make sense."

"Yes, it does!" argued Amelia.

Mr Darcy was more encouraging. "I thought it was very amusing, Amelia. I look forward to any and all jokes you have for me."

"Mr Darcy?"

"Yes, Amelia?"

"Will you get us more chocolate biscuits?"

"I have given you two biscuits," he said in an amused voice. "Your mother would be displeased if I were to give you more."

"Please?" added Lillian. "We will not tell her."

Deciding Mr Darcy deserved a reprieve, Elizabeth stepped into their view. Behind her Royce also revealed himself.

"That is enough, girls," Elizabeth called out. "Unhand Mr Darcy."

He looked over at her, clearly surprised by her presence. A chorus of little groans went up and Amelia explained earnestly, "But he is helping us with the pirates!"

"I see." Elizabeth smiled at him.

Suddenly Royce took it upon himself to join in the fun. He put on a wide smile and crouched down to the children. "May I have a turn helping catch the pirates?" he asked in an overly excited manner while nodding his head energetically. He turned his head a little too often towards Elizabeth, as if to make sure she saw him.

"Come, I think they are over there," he said in a spirited voice, pointing towards an opposite direction. He commenced running, and with some encouragement from Elizabeth, the girls followed.

After they ran off, she looked to Mr Darcy, standing quietly and gazing away from her. The wind gently lifted his hair away from his forehead, and her breath caught in her chest. He was so strikingly handsome when she was not arguing with him. It was unfortunate that such good looks were wasted on a terrible man.

She looked towards the children and saw Royce staring eagerly in her direction again. *Yes, that is wonderful. We all see you playing with my cousins.* She bid herself to be polite. She knew such behaviour bothered her more than it should. He only wanted her approval after all.

She turned back to Mr Darcy, impatient to say the words she needed to now that they were alone. "I apologise for interrupting you and my cousins," she said awkwardly. "I appreciate you spending time with them and giving their day some joy."

"It was easy. They are wonderful children," he said quietly, looking at the ground.

"They have just come through a particularly trying time."

He tilted his head, and looked at her inquisitively.

"My aunt was gravely ill recently," she said quietly as she

gazed at the lawn. "It came on suddenly, and for a time, we thought we would lose her. The doctor could not explain how she recovered, but her health seemed to return as mysteriously as it had declined."

"I am terribly sorry. That must have been distressing for all of you."

She glanced at him and saw him looking at her with more feeling and compassion than he usually showed. "It was. And in some ways, it still is."

They both said nothing for some time.

"My parents care a great deal for the girls. During my aunt's illness they took turns coming to Longbourn for weeks at a time. My aunt and uncle tried to be strong during the whole ordeal, but they needed much support."

She hoped to make him understand that in spite of how short they fell of fashionable society's standards, her parents were kind-hearted and loving. They deserved his respect.

"If things had taken a turn for the worse, I am sure they would have helped my uncle for the rest of their days."

He looked serious, and said with all sincerity, "That is very admirable. And how does your aunt fare now?"

"She is no longer ill, as you have seen. She made the journey here to deliver the children before returning to Cheapside to assist my uncle with some business matters. And she will make the journey back again for the wedding without exhausting herself, which is far more than we could have said just a few months ago. However, the mental anguish of coming so close to death—of leaving her children motherless and her husband without a wife—left a mark on her. It has left a mark on all of us, really."

Her eyes flickered to Mr Darcy for a moment before gazing back out into the countryside again.

"We recognise that she has triumphed, but the sudden brush with death has left a lingering unease. Even though the danger has passed, an undercurrent of anxiety remains."

Tears began to sting her eyes as she recalled the ordeal, and she was reminded of how easy and natural it once was for her to talk to him. To her surprise, he reached as if to touch her arm to comfort her before quickly stopping himself. Then he shook his head and rubbed his hand across his chin. "I am deeply sorry for what you had to endure. After losing my mother at a young age, I can understand more than most how the thought of your small cousins losing a parent is a heavy burden to carry. I can imagine how it can haunt you, even in your case, long after the danger has passed. Were there anything that I could do to lessen your and your family's fears."

Everything that had just passed between them—from his genuine understanding to acknowledging that her family had commendable qualities—provided far more comfort than whatever physical touch of condolence he might have given.

Elizabeth nodded again. "Thank you."

After another reflective pause in the conversation listening to the laughter of Amelia and Lillian as they dashed about with Royce, she cleared her throat and said in a lighter tone, "I must say, I was rather surprised to see you frolicking with the children."

"There is no need to be shocked. However, I imagine with your current opinion of me, you might think that I would prefer dragging children behind my carriage rather than play with them." After a pause, Mr Darcy added quietly, "I usually save that for Sundays."

Surprised, Elizabeth giggled. Mr Darcy joined her with a chuckle.

At his mention of her negative regard for him, however, she knew she must do what she had set out to do. She inhaled deeply before continuing. "Mr Darcy, I must speak to you about something."

He turned to her with a surprised expression, but nodded to indicate that she should continue.

"I wish to say, well, I wish to apologise for yesterday. My words were cutting and I regret speaking them to you."

His eyes widened in apparent consternation. The intensity of his gaze almost compelled her to step back from him. After a moment, he blinked rapidly and shook his head before finally saying gravely, "Consider your apology accepted."

He was silent for a long moment before continuing, "The manner in which I treated you upon our last day together in Kent may have merited some enmity on your end towards me. It is understandable that you do not hold me in the highest esteem. Nevertheless, I appreciate you offering words of contrition. It is a testament to your character that you are willing to seek amends."

His brow furrowed and he added, "I must argue for my own share of the blame. The peculiar coldness that has existed between us since my arrival here has not sat well upon me. It felt more desirable to debate with you than behave as hardly more than acquaintances."

"Our shared history does make for an awkward and emotional reunion," Elizabeth agreed. "But I am quite tired of being angry with you and hating you. It is not in my nature to dwell on pain and regret, and I hope that henceforth we might conduct ourselves as friends."

"I would like that very much," he said, almost eagerly.

"Very well, then. Friends?" She held out her hand and smiled at him.

He took her hand into his and returned her smile. "Friends."

She dropped his hand abruptly when she saw Royce and her cousins walking towards them.

"We escaped the pirates!" cried Lillian.

Royce looked from Elizabeth to Mr Darcy and seeming eager to interrupt their private conversation, said, "Well, this has been delightful. Should we go back inside? I am sure everyone wonders where we have disappeared to."

"Uh, yes. I am sure you are right," Elizabeth responded, and they all walked back inside together.

CHAPTER TWENTY-THREE

Elizabeth awoke with a jolt; the feeling of a restless night clung to her. Her thoughts, consumed by the events of the previous day, had haunted her sleep. As Jane slumbered beside her, Elizabeth stared at the ceiling and in the faint morning light, studied the cracks in the plaster, seeking familiar images in the lines as she had as a child. She quickly found the rabbit shape that always appeared to her first, but then her mind began to wander.

What a strange predicament she had found herself in! She had gone from being in love with Mr Darcy to despising him with every fibre of her being—and now they were friends! How was she to navigate this new, unexpected state?

He is prideful, yet showed warmth to my father. He is ill-mannered and belittled my family, yet played sweetly with my cousins and showed compassion to me and for my family. He is a conundrum!

She turned on her side, pulled the blankets over her shoulders, and tried to warm herself from the draughty room. It was much too early to be awake; even the servants were likely still abed. Yet despite her attempts to will her eyes shut, her thoughts persisted, circling in relentless repetition. After much tossing and turning, she recognised the futility of her efforts.

With sunlight now faintly streaming in through the window, Elizabeth slipped from the bed and went to her dressing table to start readying herself for church.

She looked in the mirror and gasped at her unruly hair. Her loose plait had come undone, and now her dark tresses were in such disorder that she resembled one of her father's hounds. And on a Sunday, when she was bound for church services and thus fated to see Mr Darcy—her suitor turned enemy turned friend. She could not help but laugh at herself, knowing he likely would be thanking his lucky stars that he did not marry such a lady. Using some water, brush and comb, she somehow managed her hair into something more tolerable.

Deciding not to summon their maid, Elizabeth opened her wardrobe and stared at her gowns. She pulled out two of her favourites and held them up to the light before putting them back and shaking her head in frustration. Typically she did not put so much thought into what she would wear for Sunday services, but this morning she desired to make a greater effort. She chose not to question the reason for it.

Unsatisfied with her own closet, she recalled a green dress of Kitty's that had looked particularly flattering on her and made her eyes stand out. Kitty's height and figure was closest to her own, and Elizabeth was certain the gown would fit her. *She will not mind. I have certainly lent her enough of my gowns and bonnets, and she owes me five shillings besides!*

Opening the door to her sisters' room, she found them all deeply asleep. She tiptoed in and rummaged through their closet to find the desired gown. Once she found it, she stealthily grabbed it and made her escape back to her own chamber.

Elizabeth pulled on the dress and evaluated herself in the mirror. She looked quite pretty, if she did say so herself. It made her wonder if it was a common feeling, this desire to look one's best to a past suitor, whether or not he was an enemy or friend. It seemed a natural desire to present oneself well when meeting an old love and meant nothing more, she assured herself, reasoning that no lady would wish a former beau to find validation for withdrawing his affections based on her looks.

It mattered little though, she told herself, for he had been utterly confident in ending their relationship all those years ago. He may have thought her pretty then, but now she doubted he noticed her appearance at all.

Jane stirred, bringing Elizabeth back to the present. As always, her sister looked angelic in repose. Elizabeth was happy for Jane and her impending marriage to a worthy man, but she felt a touch of melancholy that this would be the last time they would leave for church from the same house. Their family circle was about to change completely. Jane would be settled at Netherfield, only three miles from Longbourn but nevertheless, things would never quite be the same.

Elizabeth sat on the foot of her bed and smiled fondly at her sister, who looked at her with tired eyes. "You look lovely, Lizzy," Jane said gently.

"Thank you. Come let us get you ready, sit up and I will brush your hair. You must let me help you dress for one of our last mornings in the same room together." She gave her elder sister a sly look. "I cannot think that Mr Bingley will do as good a job as me, but I will try to teach him what I can."

A SHARED HISTORY

Jane laughed and sat up to comply with Elizabeth's request.

An hour or so later, breakfast eaten and Kitty's annoyance assuaged, Elizabeth and her family spilled from the house for the short walk to the church. A light layer of snow crunched softly underfoot as she walked past the familiar bare-branched trees that lined the path. Gazing ahead, the old stone building came into view; carriages and curricles were still drawing near when she saw Mr Bingley and Mr Darcy standing in the churchyard. A flutter shot through her stomach and she only dimly heard Lydia teasing Jane, "Your Prince Charming awaits."

CHAPTER TWENTY-FOUR

Darcy's heart raced, his footsteps crunching in the snow as he paced across the church lawn. He flinched at every noise, hoping and fearing that it was the Bennets arriving at last. Sleep had eluded him once more, much like every restless night since his arrival nearly a fortnight ago in Hertfordshire. When Bingley had invited him to his wedding, the mere thought of being in Elizabeth's presence was torturous. Yet the idea of refusing, of not seizing this chance haunted him. He would forever wonder 'what if' and live with regrets if he did not at least see her and try.

Despite his fatigue, excitement surged through him. Their conversation yesterday had altered his doubts. Today, he would see Elizabeth, not as a stranger or an adversary, but as a friend. The abruptness of this change, and the new opportunity it allowed, quite happily bewildered him.

Remorse had settled in swiftly after leaving Kent three years ago. Soon after their last conversation, in which he had broken her heart as well as his own, Darcy had realised the depth of his foolishness. Only the awful, life-altering news that had pulled him from his bed the previous night could have led him to such a terrible misstep with Elizabeth hours later. It was an error born from the deepest levels of grief and shock. A mistake that would plague him the rest of his life, wronging the only woman he had ever truly loved.

The anticipation of seeing her again always lingered in his thoughts. Sometimes he would wonder whether he had idealised her, perhaps as means to protect himself against the ache of living without her. Yet, the last few days had proved that reality far surpassed his memories. The idea of her paled in comparison to the truth of her, and his love for the woman he had always held dear was reaffirmed.

Love. It seemed such a shallow word to describe what he felt for Elizabeth. Love and admiration barely skimmed the surface of his profound sentiments. She was so much more than the woman he loved; she had been an extension of himself, the complement that made him whole. She was everything to him and he had spurned her. Giving up Elizabeth Bennet had been the hardest thing he had ever done but at the time, it seemed the only possible choice.

Efforts to erase her from his memory had long been abandoned. Once, driven only by the sheer need to produce an heir, Darcy had attempted to find another to replace her. But every Season he spent in town amongst eligible ladies only confirmed for him that none could compare. The graceful, beautiful statues of the *ton* had nothing on his living, breathing, vivacious Elizabeth.

It had been folly to even try; she was unforgettable, incomparable. His upbringing had fostered a sense of superiority, but she, a good woman, had been the impetus for a transformative shift in his character. She was his reckoning, the force that humbled him and taught him the failures of his ways. For that, he owed her everything.

How her words during their last conversation had haunted him! To hear that he was 'a gentleman in appearances only' and that he had disregarded morality, kindness and compassion! He had always believed himself to be an honourable man, and it was devastating to receive such censure from the woman he loved. It took him some time to realise how right she had been and to use her words to change his course, to care for others regardless of their position in society. He had endeavoured to become a generous, compassionate, and thoughtful landlord, brother, friend, and peer. How many lives were affected just by Elizabeth speaking truth to him where others had failed?

Thus, when Bingley had told him of his impending nuptials and requested that he be there, Darcy set aside his fears and hesitation because he owed his support to his friend, no matter how difficult his reunion with Elizabeth might be. He knew she would despise him for how he had treated her, and rightly so—she deserved far better than his callous behaviour. He swore to himself that he would do nothing to upset her during his stay. It was enough to see her again and hope for the long-awaited chance to make amends. But as they had reunited, he found himself in awe as she deftly dismantled him with her sharp, clever wit. He attempted to rekindle their past dynamic by engaging in banter, only to realise his mistake when he pushed her too far in arguments, unmasking the true depth of her anger.

Her apology, though unnecessary, stunned him. And then she had given him an olive branch, offering him her friendship. She was far more generous than he deserved, and he was anxious to take advantage of this new opportunity. Beginning a friendship with her was more than he could have hoped for, and yet only halfway to what he truly wanted. She had given him hope where there previously had not been an inkling, and he would be a fool to let a chance like this be squandered.

Bingley's wedding was in mere days and afterwards, Darcy would have no choice but to leave Netherfield, to leave Elizabeth. There was not much time but he would make the most of it. He paced in front of Longbourn's small church, awaiting her with no little anxiety. His tension was so great he felt as though he might jump at the slightest provocation.

He froze by the church steps as the Bennet family finally came into view on the lane. As they drew closer, his quickened breath made clouds in the cold winter air. Mr Bennet and Mrs Bennet led the group slowly. Behind them, the five sisters followed. Miss Bennet and Elizabeth walked together, their faces pink and energetic from the cold and their lively conversation, while the younger three trailed behind, chatting and laughing. Elizabeth's merry laugh reached his ear and bewitched, he stood motionless, his eyes fixed on her.

As the family neared, Mr Bennet fell back to speak to Miss Lydia, leaving his wife to lead the way. When they reached the courtyard, Bingley stepped forwards to assist Mrs Bennet up the steps.

"Mr Bingley! How very gallant you are! Such a gentleman. Our Jane is a lucky woman. In fact, our whole family is so very lucky to have you."

Bingley took her compliments in good stride, as he maintained a warm smile. "It is I who am the lucky one."

Miss Bennet remained at the bottom of the steps, smiling fondly at the actions of her soon-to-be husband. Once

Bingley had finished his duty with Mrs Bennet, he returned quickly to help his betrothed up the steps. Darcy bit back a smile seeing Bingley gazing adoringly at the lady; his focus on her was so intent that he barely acknowledged the rest of the Bennets before guiding her into the church.

Suddenly he heard Elizabeth's voice.

"Good morning, Mr Darcy."

He moved quickly to her side and instinctively extended his arm to assist her. As she placed her hand gently on his arm, he felt a familiar thrill race through him, eventually taking hold of his chest and stealing his breath away. All too soon though, the moment was over as she ascended the last step. She quickly withdrew her hand and gave him a small smile. As they stood together on the top step, their eyes met, and he allowed his gaze to linger longer than necessary. Her eyes were brightened from her walk, and her face was flushed from the cold. She was a vision. There had never been a woman so beautiful anywhere.

Although wishing with all his might that he could walk with her into the church, he refrained, fearing it might be too forward. Instead, he gave her a brief nod, his gaze reluctantly shifting to the bottom of the steps where Miss Mary Bennet stood. As he descended the stairs to escort her, he could still feel the warmth of where Elizabeth's hand had rested on his arm, as if imprinted on him.

Once all the Bennets had entered the chapel, he followed with haste, looking for Elizabeth. He spotted her seated next to her elder sister and Bingley in the Bennet family pew. There was somehow still an open seat next to her and he began walking towards her, shuffling and nudging impatiently through the parishioners, all in high spirits wishing felicity towards the happy couple as it was the last service before their wedding. He met their greetings politely while wishing he could run towards the seat that was still vacant.

As he finally reached the pew, he found Mr Royce had emerged seemingly from nowhere and slipped in next to Elizabeth. Did that man ever leave her alone? Disappointed, Darcy clenched his jaw and slipped into the row behind her.

He watched her longingly throughout the service, admiring the attentive way she listened to the sermon. Some paid little attention and others listened passively, but she was different. It was as if she and the vicar were having a conversation. Her dark, beautiful eyes were filled with emotion as she silently took in his every word.

When the final hymn began, Darcy was surprised the service was almost over. He had been lost in his thoughts, staring at Elizabeth and thinking of her the entire time. Feeling a little embarrassed, he was determined to look away, lest the other church-goers notice. His resolve proved to be weak, however, as the hymn seemed to be a favourite of Elizabeth's. She knew it well and though her voice was not trained, its warmth and emotion were captivating. When he had dwelt on memories of her in the past, he would frequently and fondly think of a time she had sung for their party in Kent. The reality again proved itself to be at the least every bit as beautiful as the memory.

Soon the parishioners made their way out of doors, some awaiting carriages to be brought round, while others talked amiably before walking home. Elizabeth had been standing with Miss Bennet, but slowly was being edged out by family and friends wishing to express their last congratulations towards her eldest sister. To his delight, Darcy soon found himself standing with her. He glanced towards the stairs and was relieved to see Mr Royce engaging in what appeared to be an illuminating conversation with a Meryton neighbour. Heartened he could speak to Elizabeth without his rival lingering about, he asked,

"Do you still plan to attend Netherfield for dinner tomorrow evening?"

"We are very much looking forward to it."

They were silent again.

She broke the silence this time with her own question. "Did you enjoy the service?"

"Exceptionally. I quite enjoyed…Your, um…I could hear you sing. You sang beautifully." He waved his hands out to the sides in a circular motion repeatedly to emphasise his point. "You have a wonderful voice."

Feeling awkward and foolish, he flushed. Why was he using his hands so much? He had never been proficient talking to women. Elizabeth had been the exception, until now.

She glanced down, seeming discomfited by his compliment. "Thank you."

Concerned he had overstepped, Darcy said, "I hope such praise does not embarrass you."

"I am not embarrassed. If I seem so, it is only that, well… to be frank…I am unsure how to act with you. I am so accustomed to arguing with you that it is difficult to accept a compliment. My mind usually prepares for a heated exchange. I must admit this sudden shift is a little strange."

He nodded in understanding. "You can say what you desire to say."

She grinned but did not say anything.

"Come now, say it," he teased. "Your frankness of character is one of my favourite things about you."

Her smile grew and she looked at him with a playful

expression. "Well, simply put, of course I sang with emotion. The hymn is about a subject dear to us all, our salvation."

He grinned a larger smile than he typically allowed himself.

Mr Bennet had begun to gather up his ladies for the walk back to Longbourn. Miss Catherine suddenly appeared at Elizabeth's side. "Lizzy, my gown does look very pretty on you, but please do not go off on one of your walks in it. I would rather it remain free of tears and mud—I wish to wear it for Jane's wedding."

Darcy thought he saw her blushing at her sister's admonishment as she bid him farewell and fell in beside Miss Bennet to begin the walk back to Longbourn. He watched as the family walked away and felt satisfied. They had conquered their first conversation as friends, and she had teased him good-naturedly as she used to. It was the best he had felt in years.

CHAPTER TWENTY-FIVE

The following day, Elizabeth peered through the side-glass from her seat in the Bennets' carriage as they drew closer to Netherfield Park. She admired the scene before her as frost adorned the trees along the lane and a light snowfall dusted the ground.

As the house finally came into view, her sisters conversed energetically around her. Their parents, who originally intended to join the dinner, had been forced to stay home. Mrs Bennet had caught the cold suffered by Amelia and Lillian and needed to rest in hopes of recovering before the wedding on Saturday morning. Mr Bennet, perhaps keener to avoid the social event than out of true devotion, had opted to remain behind as well, claiming he must be at Longbourn to welcome Mr and Mrs Gardiner and Annabelle back from their short trip to London. Thus, only the five Bennet sisters would be attending the evening's gathering. Elizabeth, anticipating her hours in Mr Darcy's company, could only hope the youngest three would comport themselves well. At the moment, she feared the worst. Mary and Lydia were heatedly arguing. Elizabeth rolled her eyes; she had heard this dispute in one form or another a hundred times. She put her hands to her temples, feeling every bump of the carriage wheels as her head began to throb.

At long last, the carriage stopped in front of the entry steps to Netherfield. Elizabeth exited as quickly as she could, taking a few deep breaths before walking up the steps to enter the house. They were met at the door by a servant, who led them into the drawing room. The throbbing lessened but she remained a little unsteady and stared at one spot on the carpet as they were announced. *Pray dinner will begin soon*, she thought; she had eaten little and hunger often brought on headaches.

Happily, they were not too long in the drawing room. Within half an hour, the guests were led into the dining room. Elizabeth took slow bites of her soup, and gradually felt the pain in her head abate. As conversation swirled round her, she observed the dining room. It was beautifully furnished; everything about Netherfield was grand and opulent. Of the houses she had visited, it was second only to Rosings in its lavishness. Elizabeth reflected in disbelief that in a few days, it would be her sister's home. She could not imagine living in a house as grand as Netherfield, having always pictured herself living in a home similar to Longbourn—which was, admittedly, a large home but not terribly grand. *Likely for the best that things went off between Mr Darcy and I, as Pemberley is no doubt ten times as grand as Netherfield.*

Her heart clenched, and she gave a big sigh. *How things have changed!* It was hard to believe she and Mr Darcy had once been so close to an understanding. She could not but shake her head at the thought, now certain it was for the best that he had been exposed to all of her family before it was too late. It would have been terrible for both parties if they had married, and he had learnt to despise them after the engagement or wedding. His own family would have scorned her, and perhaps him as well. Their marriage would have been filled with strife and unhappiness.

She gazed down the table at him thoughtfully. As if her mind had been read, the man himself was staring back at her. She averted her eyes away quickly towards the window. The sight of snow falling peacefully calmed her spirits, but she remained subdued throughout dinner. She felt unsure of how to act towards Mr Darcy. She had been heartened by his friendliness at church but now, only a day later, he seemed to have returned to his usual quiet manner. *With my headache, I am scarcely better, but it remains all very awkward.* Had he come to her side when they first entered Netherfield or offered his arm to escort her to dinner, she might have known how to act. *He is difficult to understand. It seems too forward to suddenly seek his company or act overtly friendly.* Drawing a deep breath, she comforted herself that the situation would end in a few days. *This is the last gathering we will attend together before the wedding, and afterwards we can part as indifferent acquaintances.*

Stricken by the thought, she turned her attention to the view outside of the window and watched as the snow began to blanket the trees outside. It was majestic; she wished she could go out and enjoy the brisk air. She wondered whether Mr Darcy enjoyed being outside in the snow, and imagined them taking a walk in it together. Wind began scratching on the windows, alerting her to the strange path her thoughts had wandered down.

Soon thereafter, Elizabeth realised that what had been a beautiful scene of flakes descending from the sky had taken a fierce turn. The wind was howling and she could hardly see out the window. A violent snowstorm was upon them.

Across from her, Mr Hurst shifted in his seat to look out the window. "This storm has come out of nowhere."

"I agree," answered Mrs Hurst. "I never expected to see such snow in this part of the country."

"It is quite unusual," Mary added.

Jane nodded in agreement and clearly concerned, looked at Mr Bingley. His eyes widened before he exchanged a knowing glance with Mr Darcy and abruptly turned and whispered to his sister. Miss Bingley rolled her eyes and took a sip of wine. Finally, she sighed, cleared her throat, and addressed the table.

"It appears as though the storm has only increased in its severity. I must request that you ladies stay here for the night. The roads would be too dangerous to attempt to return home. We shall wish for better weather so you may depart in the morning."

Elizabeth groaned inwardly before looking around the room. Jane's face appeared to relax at the invitation, as Mary and Kitty nodded in relief. Lydia, however, wore an absent expression as she held her hand close to her face and fidgeted with her nails. Elizabeth heard a screech of wind against the window and sighed. *Perhaps it is better to stay. We cannot risk our safety because of my discomfort with Mr Darcy, about which none of my family is aware.*

"We have rooms to accommodate everyone." Miss Bingley paused, clearly wanting to stop her charity here, but upon her brother's encouraging nods continued with a twinge of disgust. "And clothing to spare for those of you who will need them."

Elizabeth masked her unease with an insincere smile. "Thank you for your gracious offer, Miss Bingley."

CHAPTER TWENTY-SIX

After dinner, the women stood to withdraw, while the gentlemen stayed behind to enjoy some port. Darcy watched longingly as Elizabeth left the room. The port was poured, and Darcy whirled the drink around in his glass. His custom was to have only a few sips of the drink, mostly for appearance's sake, but tonight he could not deny that he felt tempted to have more.

The conversation had turned to a hunt Bingley had recently attended. Darcy was uninterested and hardly listened to the story. He had little regard for hunting when he was in a decent state of mind, and much less patience to discuss it in the one he was in now. Most of his thoughts were focused on the spot in the drawing room where Elizabeth resided, wherever that might be.

He finally took a sip from his port and resisted the urge to down it all in one gulp. Why were things so uncomfortable between them again? After their conversation yesterday, he had had high hopes for tonight. Alas, since she had arrived at

Netherfield, she had hardly given him a second glance. She had seemed forlorn since her first step into the home, and she did not have an inviting air about her. It had almost been easier to be around her when she viewed him as an adversary, for she had surely paid more attention to him when she hated him! At this thought, he slammed his glass down on the table harder than he meant to.

"Darcy?" Bingley enquired. "Forgive me, it seems I have rather monopolised the conversation."

"Not at all." Darcy forced a conciliatory smile. "I suppose I am distracted."

"Shall we join the ladies?"

It was evident Bingley was as eager as he to rejoin the ladies, and after an amused glance at Hurst, nearly snoring into his port, Darcy was quick to push his chair back and stand, hoping there would be some improvement between himself and Elizabeth.

Any gathering where Royce is absent is a gathering to be cherished, he thought as the men moved down the hall. Upon entering the drawing room, his eyes first fell on Mrs Hurst, Miss Bennet, and Miss Bingley seated together on a settee. Mrs Hurst was absentmindedly fiddling with her necklace, while Miss Bennet wore a calm smile. Next to her, Miss Bingley tapped her fingers lightly on the arm of the settee, her lips pursed in a slight pout.

Across from them, he noticed Miss Lydia, seated in an armchair, her hands gesturing energetically as she spoke to Miss Catherine. Next to her on the settee was Miss Mary, who had a book open in her lap. A flutter stirred in his stomach as soon as he saw Elizabeth seated beside her. She looked lovely, wearing an amused smile as she listened to her youngest sister.

A SHARED HISTORY

Elizabeth turned her head towards him for the briefest moment before frowning and quickly looking away, affording him no exceptional interest. His heart sank and he took a seat near the chaise longue where Hurst had sprawled.

Apparently heedless of her husband's lethargy, Mrs Hurst glanced hopefully around the room and proposed, "Who would like to play a game of charades?"

Miss Bingley glared at her sister.

"It has been so long since we have last played," pleaded Mrs Hurst.

Miss Catherine giggled. "I think charades sounds splendid!"

Upon seeing the rest of the Bennet sisters nod in agreement, Miss Bingley agreed with reluctant resignation, and the game soon was underway. Darcy found himself in rare agreement with Miss Bingley. He would have much preferred quiet conversation, where he might have drawn Elizabeth aside. He rarely enjoyed games such as these and now, feeling his hopes for a future with Elizabeth were again lost, he could hardly feign interest.

Eventually, he picked up a book and returned to the sofa near where Hurst was napping, darting a few glances at Elizabeth whenever temptation could not be conquered. She never looked back at him. Unlike him, she actually enjoyed people, parties, and games, and looked quite entertained. It was the happiest he had seen her all night.

At length, Miss Bingley interrupted his thoughts. "I believe I have had enough of charades for one evening," she said, looking in Darcy's direction. "I find myself in the mood for reading. Would it be an inconvenience if I joined you?"

He shook his head, hoping his disappointment was not evident in his expression. "Not at all."

If only Elizabeth could give him a quarter of as much attention as Miss Bingley did! As she approached his side of the room, he took a deep breath to strengthen his forbearance. If anyone tested his amended character of practising the law of kindness to all creatures, it was Caroline Bingley. She slowly walked towards him, fluttering her eyelashes, and sat beside him on the sofa with a book she picked up from the side table. The longer they sat, the more Darcy resisted the urge to groan when he observed that she never turned her page. As often occurred when they were in the same party, she had feigned interest in reading in order to be close to him. He glanced at Elizabeth again, and saw her studying them briefly before looking away, seemingly indifferent.

Would she have any reaction at all, it would be preferable. She seems to hardly care that I am in the same room as her. It would be worth Miss Bingley's incessant fawning if it meant Elizabeth showed a spark of interest in me.

He looked back to his page and attempted to distract himself. Before long, Darcy was drawn from his book when he heard Elizabeth's name called out to lead the next charade. As she moved towards the front of the room, he closed his book and watched her. It proved difficult to look upon her impassively, for in contrast to some hours ago when she appeared wan, her liveliness and beauty were on full display. He nearly groaned so great was his desire to jump from his seat and kiss her.

Her hands clasped in front of her, Elizabeth said, "Very well, here is mine: 'My first doth affliction denote, which my second is destined to feel. And my whole is the best antidote that affliction to soften and heal'."

She smiled archly as she heard the murmuring throughout the room. After a few minutes, when no one was able to solve her riddle, she began looking a little smug. "Does no one have an answer?" When no response came, she said, "Well then, if no—"

"Woman," Darcy said loudly.

Everyone turned to look at him. From the looks on their faces, it seemed most had forgotten he was even there.

He cleared his throat. "The answer is 'woman'."

She smiled brilliantly at him. "Mr Darcy is correct. Good job, sir."

The room clapped at his victory. He abruptly looked down at his book again, opening to the last page he had been reading. After a few more rounds of charades, the group dispersed to individual pursuits. Elizabeth sat by the hearth, apparently content to listen to others' conversations.

He gazed upon her as she watched her sister and Bingley whisper to each other on the other side of the room. A deep, sincere smile spread across her face. She turned her head in his direction, and their eyes met. His heart jumped. Whether it was intentional or by chance that she smiled in his direction, it gave him all the encouragement he needed. Without hesitation, he crossed the room swiftly, as if beckoned, to join her. If he was being too eager, he did not care.

"May I sit with you?" he asked, his voice breathless as he approached.

She looked taken aback but answered, "Of course."

As Darcy sat down next to her, he could not help but feel very alert to how close she was sitting, and every movement that she made. He cleared his throat, eager to begin some conversation between them. "You have been quiet tonight. Are you concerned about the snow?"

She smiled. "No, I am not concerned as long as no one is injured."

He nodded.

"I do feel concern for Mary, though." She tilted her head in her sister's direction. "It is her birthday tomorrow, and I know she will be disappointed not to be at Longbourn. My mother has a big breakfast made for our birthdays. It is a tradition for us."

"Ah, I see. Perhaps we should try to celebrate here."

She straightened at this suggestion and appeared a little astonished. "That would be very kind, sir."

Pleased by Elizabeth's response, he assured her he would see to the arrangements. Then, uncertain what to say next, Darcy fell silent.

She looked up at him with a gentle smile. "Are you sad to be away from Derbyshire? I know how much you adore it."

"A little," he admitted. "Though if there is a time to be away, it is now, in the thick of winter. It is quite cold."

"Yes, I imagine so. And how is Pemberley? Is it as lovely as I recall from your descriptions of it?"

"It is. Perhaps even lovelier. The library has been improved, with a new collection of volumes recently arrived, and we have added a gazebo by the lake."

"Oh really? It surprises me that your father would change anything." She paused before continuing with a teasing smile, "From the way you had always described him, it seemed as though he believed Pemberley could not ever be improved upon."

Darcy cleared his throat. "Yes, well…" He paused, not yet ready to delve into the reasons behind the changes. He knew he would tell her the whole truth soon, but not here, not as they were surrounded by all the others. Shifting the conversation, he added, "Lambton, the nearest village, has changed greatly too."

"Oh?"

"Yes, it has almost doubled in size in recent years. There is even a book shop now. You would enjoy it."

Elizabeth's smile deepened. "It sounds charming."

He paused as the image of them strolling the cobbled streets together flashed briefly in his mind. "It is," he said softly.

Their conversation continued to flow easily and naturally, and soon the Hursts rose to retire for the evening. Led by their clearly exasperated hostess, the three youngest Bennets followed to be shown to their rooms.

Darcy wished to remain with Elizabeth and continue their pleasant conversation but when Bingley and Miss Bennet stood, he knew Elizabeth would withdraw for propriety's sake. *How I wish I could simply speak candidly with her, and tell her of all my regrets. I must find a way to tell her the truth about that day.*

Just as he predicted, she soon excused herself. Disappointed, Darcy stood up with her. "Miss Elizabeth, I wanted to enquire...Would you join me in the library tomorrow after breakfast?"

She looked surprised at his request, tilting her head and looking at him curiously.

"There are...some books I thought you in particular might like to peruse as we are snowed in."

"That would be lovely. Thank you, Mr Darcy."

"I look forward to seeing you in the morning," he said before reaching out, almost impulsively, to tuck a loose strand of hair behind her ear. His hand lingered there for a moment before he pulled it down slowly and chastised himself for his actions. *Have some control, man! You cannot touch her just because you want to!* He laid his hand quickly by his side. As was his instinct when he felt nervous, he reached into his pocket, retrieving a familiar small object and fumbling with it between his fingers.

Elizabeth appeared stunned for a few moments at what had just transpired, before finally responding, "Likewise." After a slight pause, she continued, "Goodnight, Mr Darcy." Then she turned on her heel and walked out of the room.

CHAPTER TWENTY-SEVEN

Elizabeth's bedchamber, as everything at Netherfield, was decorated with an excess of adornment. While it was much grander than the room which she shared with Jane at Longbourn, its opulence made it feel less comfortable. It was odd to be sleeping in a room alone, but soon she would have to get used to such solitude; after the wedding on Saturday, Jane would no longer be at Longbourn. Elizabeth would miss her companionship dearly. Much as she was excited for her beloved sister, she could not help feeling some anxiety for Jane's impending nuptials—and those concerns begot more fretful thoughts, which brought about another subject all together.

It was a strange turn of events that had brought Mr Darcy back into her company after more than three years; even stranger was how her feelings had changed for him in the course of a few days. Had he not hurt her so badly before, she could be in real danger of again growing attached to him.

Every interaction with him left her feeling closer to falling in love with him again. And now they would have to spend the night under the same roof! *Oh! Why did I ask him to be friends? Could I not allow him to think I insulted him and do not care for him at all?*

She shook her head at her agreement to meet him in the library the following morning. Foolish girl! She must do better at guarding her heart. She would fulfil her promise and then avoid him the rest of her stay. It would not do to care for a man with whom she could have no future. Although resolved to be amiable—and inconveniently drawn to his company—Elizabeth still believed Mr Darcy to be one of the most prideful and disdainful persons of her acquaintance.

Elizabeth pulled back the bedcovers and climbed onto the mattress, her thoughts about Mr Darcy still swirling madly. Despite the battle waging within her—the temptation to fall for him again versus the conviction that he was a man she could not trust—she reminded herself that he had made it quite clear he neither regretted her nor desired her. That was the home truth, was it not? *I do not need to convince myself that he is not suitable for me if he is not even fighting for my heart. And yet,* she thought, *why had he touched my hair?* Frustration welled within her at the notion that he would so nonchalantly play with her emotions. It was exciting, yes, but highly improper. Perhaps he merely acted impulsively because of their shared history, and it was something he now regretted.

Realising that she was not going to have any sound answers this evening, Elizabeth resolved to stop thinking about it. She laid her head on a soft pillow and covered her face with another one. Closing her eyes, she attempted to calm herself and fall sleep. Her efforts would be in vain though, for these unrelenting thoughts would keep her up for most of the night.

Elizabeth's eyes stung as they fluttered open. Her head felt clouded with fog as a dull, throbbing headache made itself known. She pulled the expensive linens close to her with heavy, aching arms and squeezed her eyes tight, trying to will herself back to sleep. Within minutes, she knew it was a lost cause. Exhausted, she tossed the blankets aside and drew apart the curtains surrounding her bed. She saw that while it was still dark outside, the colours in the sky revealed that sunrise was approaching.

Rising from the bed, she walked over to the fire. She felt its warmth touch her skin and yet remained cold, seemingly unable to get warm. Sitting down on the floor in front of it, she curled her knees up to her chest as she watched the movement of the flames. There was something calming about watching a fire, and she would accept anything that would soothe her nerves today. *It is not much longer. He will be gone soon,* she told herself.

In the depths of the night, something peculiar had happened. Something she thought she had put to death a long time ago had apparently only been sleeping and was reawakened with force. Her rekindled feelings for Mr Darcy, which had taken root the previous evening, flourished with newfound intensity. She realised now that the once formidable barrier of resentment she had held against him had crumbled, leaving behind only lingering affection and a compelling attraction. She found herself both surprised and disheartened by her own vulnerability, for Mr Darcy had barely touched her and she was already thinking about being near him the very next day.

The only credit she could give herself was that she did not think she loved him but was instead intensely intrigued by and attracted to him. *This is nothing more than slipping back into old, comfortable habits. I will not love someone who can only cause me heartache. He does not even find me tempting!* Once Mr Darcy was out of her life again, she knew she would be able to move on.

She had vowed not to be so easily swayed into giving away her heart again. She had learnt from the painful lesson of the past that her head must overrule her heart. And so, during her restless hours in the quiet of the night, a solution to protect herself had unfolded. What had initially been a fleeting idea had rapidly grown into an undeniable resolution: she would agree to marry Royce when he proposed. The notion brought her tranquillity; she hoped it would quiet her yearnings, for she could not be tempted to flirt with one if she was resolved to marry another.

There was no valid reason why she should not marry Royce. Their life together promised comfort and contentment. She liked him and believed that, given time, love would surely blossom between them. Her experience with Mr Darcy had taught her that practicality and reason should guide matters of the heart. Royce possessed qualities desirable in a husband: he was amiable, charming, devoted, good-looking, and wealthy. Most importantly, he was kind to her family, and would be able to support and care for them in the event of her father's passing. Refusing such an opportunity seemed foolish. Inhaling deeply, Elizabeth saw that light had broken, and soon it would be an appropriate hour to go downstairs for breakfast.

After dressing, she made her way through the dark corridor towards the dining room. Most of the rooms she passed required candlelight due to the ominous, grey skies which threatened a resurgence of the storm. Doubtful that the roads were acceptable for travel, Elizabeth suspected she and her sisters would likely remain another night at Netherfield.

As she stepped into the dining room, her eyes widened as they fell on a sumptuous breakfast display fit for a king. The grandeur of the scene provided a lovely contrast to the melancholy skies, and she felt her spirits lift at its cheerfulness. She walked along the sideboard, her fingertips tracing the table as she took in all the culinary sights. There were cakes, fruit, eggs, meats, and even hot chocolate, all arranged with great care in a celebratory fashion.

The others began to enter; with the exception of a rather confused-looking Miss Bingley, all appeared equally impressed. Last to arrive was Mr Darcy, who entered through the door closest to Elizabeth and came to stand next to her. Feeling overwhelmed at his nearness, she removed herself from his presence by briskly walking over to the opposite side of the room as murmurings of excitement at the breakfast could be heard.

Jane's eyes sparkled as she looked warmly at Mr Bingley. "This is magnificent! I do not recall ever seeing such a splendid breakfast."

"Well, it is a very special day, is it not?" He beamed as he gestured towards Mary. "Our cook prepared this feast in honour of Miss Mary's birthday."

Jane placed her hand to her chest. "How kind of you to think of that in the midst of this storm."

Despite the great kindness that was being shown to her,

Mary seemed subdued and kept her gaze on the floor. Mr Bingley, still smiling, said, "Much as I would like to claim all of the credit, it was brought to my attention by Dar—"

He was interrupted by Mr Darcy, who seemed eager to deflect any further praise. "Happy Birthday, Miss Mary," he said with his usual formal tone. Felicitous wishes from all around were bestowed upon Mary. From across the room, Elizabeth caught Mr Darcy's eye and mouthed, "Thank you." His expression softened slightly as he nodded in return.

She drew her attention back to Mary, whose brows were furrowed as she remained oddly detached from the conversation and festivities designed to please her. Elizabeth's cheeks heated at her sister's rudeness and in a gentle, prodding voice, she said, "Mary, is there something you would also like to say?" She nodded towards Mr Darcy and Mr Bingley.

Mary looked up towards them without making eye contact. "Thank you," she said in a voice devoid of any feeling.

Elizabeth sighed. *Why is she behaving so ungraciously when Mr Darcy ensured a celebration for her? I can hardly blame him for the low opinion he holds of my family.*

Mr Bingley and Mr Darcy appeared unperturbed and soon after, the breakfast began jovially, with laughter and conversation heard all around as the group indulged in the various culinary presentations.

As the breakfast progressed, Elizabeth noticed Jane wore a worried expression. "Are you well?" she asked quietly.

"Yes, I only hope we will be able to return home soon," Jane responded softly. "I would like to know that Aunt and Uncle Gardiner are at Longbourn safely."

Elizabeth gave her sister's hand a comforting squeeze. "I am certain of it. They were supposed to arrive hours before the snow began to fall, and you know that Uncle is diligent about a timely departure."

"Yes, I am sure you are correct. But even so, Mama must be so overwhelmed with the wedding preparations without me there to assist—it is only four days away now."

"I am confident we will be able to return quickly."

Jane nodded, looking more reassured, and Elizabeth rose and went to the sideboard for another pastry. Mr Darcy came to stand beside her with his plate.

"Will you join me in the library once you have finished your breakfast?" he asked.

"I—"

He added quietly so only her ears could hear, "There is something I would like to discuss with you."

"Yes, of course," she said, and remembering her vow to avoid his close company, added, "I wonder if you would like me to bring one of my sisters who might enjoy your suggestions of books to keep us occupied while confined at Netherfield."

After what looked like a flash of disappointment, Mr Darcy quickly recovered, his expression shifting as he looked over her. "Very well. Of course, one of your sisters may accompany you."

Pleased at her 'victory', Elizabeth's response was interrupted by the clatter of a fork hitting the ground. She glanced over to find Mary in her seat, staring at her hand, where the utensil had presumably slipped from her grasp. The room fell into a hushed silence, the clinking of cutlery ceasing as all eyes turned to Mary.

"You cannot be clumsy on your birthday," laughed Lydia.

"Are you feeling well, Mary?" Elizabeth asked, concern edging her voice.

Mary took a deep breath and closed her eyes. When she opened them, she appeared stricken. Elizabeth walked quickly towards her and placed a comforting hand on her back. Mary raised her own to her mouth and all the colour drained out of her face. "Please excuse me, I am feeling quite unwell," she said abruptly, pushing her chair out, standing, and nearly running out of the room.

"Jane, come quickly!" Elizabeth cried. As she turned to ensure Jane would follow them, she saw Mr Darcy's face painted with concern.

A short time later, Elizabeth wrung her hands together as she looked down at Mary. Her sister lay curled up in the centre of her bed, gripping the counterpane, still fully clothed in her day dress. Elizabeth exchanged a concerned glance with Jane. "I cannot believe she has fallen so ill, especially on her birthday," she murmured as she leant down to stroke Mary's arm. Jane nodded in response.

Just then, Mary abruptly sat up with her hand covering her mouth. Jane acted quickly and picked up a nearby basin and placed it on the bed. Elizabeth moved swiftly to hold back her sister's hair as Jane laid a gentle hand on her back. After Mary finished retching, she continued hovering over the basin as her body trembled. Jane looked up at Elizabeth. "She is truly ill. I wish we had Hill's special tea to soothe her stomach."

"Indeed," Elizabeth responded. "Perhaps I should fetch Mrs Nicholls and see if there are any remedies available in the house. There could be some left over from previous tenants or servants. And Jane," she added, suddenly realising Mary's illness could spread, "you are to be married in a few days. You should not be too close to Mary."

"I will tend to my sister," Jane said firmly.

The two exchanged a look before Elizabeth slipped from the room. There, in the corridor, she nearly collided with Mr Darcy, who stood watching Mr Bingley as he paced anxiously.

"How does Miss Mary fare?" Mr Darcy asked, looking concerned.

"Is Jane well?" pressed Mr Bingley, his agitation evident.

"Jane is well, and attending to Mary, who is quite ill, but I am certain she will recover," Elizabeth replied as she began to walk again.

Mr Bingley sighed with relief while Mr Darcy fell into step beside her. "How may I assist?"

She gave him a small smile. "That is very kind. But you need not concern yourself, sir."

He touched her arm to stop her. "Miss Elizabeth, please?"

She stopped walking and looked down at his hand where it lay on her arm. He quickly dropped it and she drew her gaze back to his face.

"Well," she responded, hoping the surprise she felt at his compassion was not showing in her expression. "If you insist. I was on my way to find Mrs Nicholls to ask her to bring us some remedies and cold compresses. Could you locate her with our requests?"

"Certainly," he replied eagerly. "Please attend to your sister, and I will find Mrs Nicholls right away." He turned and without another word, walked briskly down the corridor.

Elizabeth tilted her head as she watched him walk away. *Confusing man.* She gave her head a small shake and returned to Mary's chamber where she found Jane still at Mary's side, stroking her back. Much sooner than she expected, there was a knock on the door. Elizabeth stood and quickly walked across the room to open it. Standing in the corridor, she saw Mr Darcy with Mrs Nicholls in tow. The housekeeper carried a basket filled with herbs in the crook of her elbow and held a basin of cool water and cloths.

"Miss Elizabeth," the old woman said kindly. "I was told your sister was ill."

"Yes. Please come in." Elizabeth shifted to make space for Mrs Nicholls to enter, while Mr Darcy remained in the corridor. Before closing the door, she caught his eye. "Thank you, your help is truly appreciated," she said.

"I am glad I could be of service," he replied as he held her gaze.

As she closed the door and turned to see Mrs Nicholls preparing compresses for Mary, Elizabeth thought of how Mr Darcy had attended to her as well. It was yet another layer to add to the complex portrait of the man. When he had unfeelingly cast her aside, she had learnt to be guarded and distrustful of men. Yet, here, witnessing his care for her sister, she could not help but think of his unexpected kindnesses. His subtle orchestration of breakfast for Mary was followed by his offering assistance while she was ill.

These opposing behaviours were at odds with each other and confounded her understanding of him. How could the man who once loathed her family to the extent of breaking off a near engagement now devote himself to her sister's well-being? *Have I misjudged him fully or simply failed to see his hidden aspects? I once knew his gentler demeanour and thought it a lie, but is this tenderness truer to his character than I believed?*

Determined to quell these thoughts, she remembered her resolution to marry Royce. Dwelling on Mr Darcy would serve no good purpose, she told herself as she picked up a dampened cloth to press to Mary's temple. It would be best not to entangle herself with any more thoughts about Mr Darcy.

But what did he want to discuss with me privately?

CHAPTER TWENTY-EIGHT

By mid-afternoon, Mary's stomach had settled and she was sleeping. Jane dozed by her bedside, seemingly—to Elizabeth's great relief—less perturbed by the snow and illness keeping her away from Longbourn and her wedding preparations. *It is likely a relief to have a respite from Mama speaking of it or worrying over every detail,* she thought, looking down to re-read the note that had been delivered to Netherfield by Longbourn's exhausted, snow-covered stableboy an hour earlier.

Lizzy,
    I write to assure you that all is well at Longbourn. We are recovered from our colds, and everyone is safe from the storm. Thankfully, my brother and sister arrived before the snowstorm to tend to the children. I am quite relieved—the little ones are so lively and loud, their antics were beginning to wear on my nerves!

The wedding arrangements are progressing, though, as you might imagine, it would be far easier if you and Jane especially were here to help. It is in four days and I worry if Cook has enough rum and almonds for the bride cake. Please, do not trouble Jane with any of this and cause her to look any less radiant on her big day! You must keep her content until she returns to Longbourn, which, your father informs me, remains too hazardous to attempt, even by sleigh. The men and horses will be out with snow-ploughs today but this weather is most worrisome. Can you imagine if something happened to Jane and her wedding had to be postponed? It would be positively dreadful! As soon as the roads are safe, please return quickly. I expect Miss Bingley and Mrs Hurst are providing you girls with night-rails and their fine gowns but I have sent a few things with Young Jimmy. Send him back to us with word of your sisters' well-being.

Your devoted Mama

Elizabeth folded up the letter and pulled on a pair of the wool stockings her mother had thoughtfully packed in the small bag Jimmy had carried. Glancing out of the window in her bedchamber, she was encouraged to see that the skies were a bright blue. Not only were the roads being cleared but Mary should be well enough that they could return to Longbourn tomorrow. And now, Elizabeth felt she could safely venture out of doors for a solitary stroll. Though unladylike, she was restless and craved such exercise more than ever right now. She pulled on yesterday's warm gown and went downstairs. As she was near the front door putting on her gloves and cloak, she heard her name called.

"Miss Elizabeth," said Mr Darcy, emerging from the drawing room.

Her insides tightened. "Mr Darcy," she said in surprise. "I was about to go for a walk. I find myself feeling restive after all the confinement of these last days."

"Would it be an inconvenience if I accompanied you? I too am feeling a bit restless."

"Not at all, sir." She tried to hide the reluctance in her voice. Her resolution to avoid him was being tested. In equal measure, she both longed for and dreaded his society.

He joined her in the vestibule and after putting on his own coat, hat, and gloves, he offered her his arm. Once outside, they walked quietly on the cleared front path. She listened to their footsteps crunch in the snow as she felt the invigorating icy air graze across her face.

Finally, he broke the silence. "How fares your sister?"

"Mary is better, sleeping peacefully and more recovered with every passing hour," she said as her breath became visible in the cold air. "She is a bit weak now, but I believe she is on the mend."

"I am thankful to hear it." He then added, "It has been a pleasure to become better acquainted with your family."

She laughed, and he looked confused. "Come now, Mr Darcy. We are friends now. You can be honest with me."

He looked at her questioningly, his cheeks flushed with a rosy hue from the brisk air.

"It is no secret that you despise my family."

"That is untrue." On her disbelieving look, he said, "I assure you, I do not despise them."

She allowed her silence to communicate her scepticism.

After another pause, he continued, "I believe what you see as disdain is more likely discomfort. Surely you remember that I do not recommend myself easily to strangers. I shall admit though, I did fear they might try my patience in coming to Hertfordshire."

She shivered as the cold air ran through her body before responding, "They are, I know, livelier in spirit than you may think dignified."

"They are livelier than what I am accustomed to, but it does not mean I dislike it," he said. "Indeed, I have come to admire them. I have felt more warmth in your family in a few short days than I have experienced with mine in my entire life."

It is a compliment born of his own deprivation, she thought with a surge of sympathy. He sighed, and she could tell he had more to say. "But?"

He glanced at her, wincing. "But, as one who cares for your circumstances…I can only say—and pray forgive me any censure for I do not mean it as such—I do wish that your father would have prepared better for the future of your family upon his departure from this world. I fear he has put you at a disadvantage."

Elizabeth looked down, unable to deny the truth of his words. And he spoke them with such gentleness that she could not fault him. A gust of wind swept through, cutting through the last remnants of warmth she felt. She drew her coat more tightly around herself.

They went along in silence once more until Mr Darcy spoke again. "Miss Lydia seems much altered since I encountered her in Kent."

"She is three years older. That can do much in a lady's maturity and countenance, particularly when the years in question take the lady from a child to a young woman."

"She seems more…"

"Proper?" she finished for him.

"Well…yes."

Elizabeth was silent for a contemplative moment, then decided she felt she could trust him. She had an idea he might have already heard parts of the tale from Mr Bingley, and preferring to take charge of the truth before Miss Bingley or anyone else could twist the narrative, she considered it prudent to disclose the story herself, just in case he had not heard it yet. Mr Darcy was not one to gossip, so it would only shape his opinion of her family, and not spread to the public.

"Not so long ago, Lydia had a hard lesson in the realities and evils of this world."

"Oh?"

Taking a breath, she said quietly, "She was deceived by the looks and charm of an older man, who promised her marriage. Alas, she allowed him some small liberties, only to be abandoned soon afterwards. We are fortunate the news did not get out. There were rumours of course, but the extent of what happened was never revealed to larger society and she was spared any public disgrace."

Mr Darcy was silent for a moment. "And what of that gentleman, Mr Andrews? I see them together often."

"Mr Andrews? He has long admired my sister for her vivaciousness. Although he knew the truth of all that happened, he did not discard her. He visited her daily, and engaged with her when she felt that there was no redemption for her. Their affection grew and they love each other very much."

"It seems there is much to admire in his constancy."

"Yes. It is regrettable they cannot marry."

"Why can they not?"

"He has not a penny to his name. Although born a gentleman, he is a second-born son who has had a prolonged feud with his older brother. He has no inheritance, and his brother is making it difficult for him to establish himself in a profession. For now, he and Lydia are great friends. They are young enough that it is not hurting her prospects to be in his company so often, but one day, possibly soon, they will have to separate. I fear for what it will do to both."

He furrowed his brows and was silent. Elizabeth wondered whether she ought to regret confiding in him as she had. "I beg you to not be too quick to judge her, sir. Lydia thought herself in love and believed wholly that a marriage proposal was imminent. Although I am not excusing her actions, I have compassion for her failings. And I find more faults with the man who fooled her so cruelly."

"Please, you are too hasty in your assessment of me," said Mr Darcy. "I do not judge her. Would it surprise you that a member of my family has a similar history?"

"Yes, that surprises me, indeed."

"You have trusted me with a difficult story. I believe I can trust you also."

Then he recounted the story of his sister, Georgiana, who at fifteen had been deceived by an older man as well, one who was a close friend of the family. Although she had not lost her virtue, the man—whose true aim was her fortune—had persuaded her into an elopement. Mr Darcy had raced to intercept the couple just in time to prevent the marriage.

Elizabeth could scarcely imagine the fear and panic of

such a situation. "How awful, I am so sorry that happened to her, and to you. How does she fare now?"

"She sometimes has happy moments, but mostly she seems a shell of her former self."

Elizabeth contemplated this and felt the extent of his grief over it, especially since she had all but gone through almost the same experience with her sister. Another gust of wind blew through; chilled, she instinctively moved closer to Mr Darcy for warmth. "I am sorry for her. I hope her spirits recover and she will marry a gentleman who adores her."

He nodded and quietly thanked her.

She wondered why his father, the elder Mr Darcy, had not taken care of the matter but left it up to his son. Politely, she said, "And your father? It must have been difficult for him."

"My father died before this occurred."

"Oh," she gasped, stopping to look at him in shock. "Mr Bingley had not said…I am so sorry, I did not know." Her grip on his arm tightened as she watched him sigh heavily.

"Yes, um, he died three years ago…before our last conversation in Kent."

"What? You never told me."

He looked away from her, then down at the ground before replying. "I received the dreadful news in the hours after dining with your family at Rosings. It was then when I learnt I was the new master of Pemberley and guardian to my sister."

Her shock—that he had heard of his father's death in the hours after the horrible dinner he endured with Lydia and Mrs Bennet—resonated deeply. Yet even as she now understood why his behaviour towards her had changed so drastically in mere hours, it was sympathy for his loss that overwhelmed her.

"I am grieved for you," Elizabeth said feelingly. "Please accept my condolences, belated though they are." She understood it now, the new solemnity in his face, his softer demeanour, the almost paternal-like concern he had shown Mary. It was as if his entire aspect had aged. He had endured much in the years since she saw him last and now shouldered a great responsibility. She felt a surge of compassion and admiration for him.

He murmured his thanks and they began walking again, both seemingly lost in thought as they turned back towards the house. Only the sound of their feet softly shuffling through the snow broke their shared silence.

"I recall you were quite close to your father," Elizabeth said. "It must have been difficult to lose him."

"Yes, it certainly was," he answered in a hoarse voice. "We were beginning to enjoy the change in our relationship from father and son to something more like equals. He was the closest friend I had."

Her heart and eyes filled with emotion. "I am sure it was difficult to learn how to manage your estate while taking on responsibility for your sister at the same time."

"Indeed. It was for a period of time, quite overwhelming." He paused for a moment before saying in a rushed manner, "To be honest, I have long wanted to speak to you about this and offer my sincerest apologies."

Elizabeth tilted her head as she looked at him, surprised by how the conversation was shifting. "An apology?"

"Yes, I owe you one." He halted and turned to her. "I learnt the news of my father's death only hours before you and I spoke, and amid such turmoil I know I cannot have behaved as I ought to have done." After a deep breath, he continued, "I have since learnt that when in the deepest stages of grief, it is unwise to make monumental decisions."

"I have heard that too," she interjected softly.

"Had I but known that advice three years ago." He shook his head as though disgusted with himself. "I wish, most sincerely, for you to know I am grieved by how I spoke that day. I regret that I caused you pain."

She was stunned by his confession and for a moment, contemplated everything he had said and the anger she had carried. There was no reason to speak of it now; in these past days, she had set aside her ire and resentment. "It does help to understand why your demeanour with me changed so much in one night. I was hurt and angry but I forgive you, Mr Darcy. And I do thank you for telling me."

They were both quiet for a few minutes, but continued walking. In the distance, Elizabeth heard the soft thud of snow hitting the ground, presumably falling from a tree, as she attempted to think of something to say to fill the silence. Mr Darcy's revelations had left her dumbfounded and her thoughts were awhirl.

He broke the silence first. "Do you ever think about that spring?"

She felt a twinge in her stomach. "Yes, I do. Do you?"

"They are some of the fondest memories I have," he responded quietly. "Have you—have you ever fallen in love with another?"

Taken aback by his question, Elizabeth's heart raced and thudded in her chest. Choosing honesty over prevarication, she said, "No." Then, feeling bold, she added, "Have you?"

"No," he said instantly.

Elizabeth could feel his eyes on her but she dared not look at him. They had arrived back to Netherfield's front courtyard and as they neared the front door, she heard his sharp intake of breath, as if he would speak, but he remained silent. Suddenly he said, "Has Mr Royce asked you to marry him, as you predicted?"

"No, the dangerous weather and our current predicament has certainly detained him. But I believe the question should occur soon after I arrive home… And I mean to say yes."

He stopped and turned to face her. "You just said you had not fallen in love with another."

"I do not love him, but I respect him," she confessed. "I believe love changes as you get older, and though you do not fall in love as powerfully as you do the first time, it does not mean it is not true. I will grow to love him in my duty to him."

"Duty? I thought you once said—"

"I know what I once said," she said sharply. Checking her tone, she continued more softly, "But that was before."

He nodded and gazed into the distance. When he looked back at her, his eyes were bleak and intense. "Will he treat you well?"

"I am certain he will."

She resumed walking and as she reached the front steps, he took her arm and gave his head a slight shake. His mouth was pulled tight as he gazed towards the ground, and his body tense. In a soft voice, he said, "Do you think if I had not ceased my attentions, we would have married?"

Her mouth dropped open, surprised by such a frank question. He murmured a quick apology but continued to look at her, clearly wishing to know her answer.

"I do not know, we are so different now, how can it signify?"

He interrupted, "But do you?"

She felt her eyes sting and looked at the ground. Sighing, she climbed the last step and looked up at him. "Yes. Yes, I do," she said quietly.

Mr Darcy closed his eyes. "I have been such a fool, Elizabeth."

Her heart dropped within her chest and she felt herself blush, unsure what to say, or think, or even feel. In that most inauspicious of moments, the door opened and Kitty appeared. Giggling, she grabbed Elizabeth's arm and began pulling her into the house.

"Lizzy, you must come inside and help us convince Miss Bingley to allow us to set up an archery pitch in the snow!"

"Um…" Elizabeth tried to tug her arm from her sister's grasp. "I do not…the snow will prevent…"

"Oh, fie on that! Come now, it would be so amusing, would it not? Mr Darcy, you would like it too, I think?"

The high colour on Mr Darcy's countenance was all the indication that something of great import had just passed between them, but Elizabeth hoped her sister would mistake it for the effect of the cold.

He did not seem to hear Kitty's pleadings. "Please excuse me," was all he said, before walking briskly past them and into the house.

CHAPTER TWENTY-NINE

Darcy did not acknowledge the servant rushing to meet him; still clad in his coat and hat, he strode past the grand stairs and turned into the corridor with determined strides. Though he could not precisely say in that moment where he was headed, his need for solitude was of the utmost importance. In the direction he was heading lay the gallery, a room he knew had been mostly unoccupied since the arrival of their unexpected guests. It was the sanctuary he sought, where he could be alone with his tumultuous thoughts.

Upon reaching the gallery, he swung open the doors with force. Inside he saw it was exactly what he needed: a quiet, elegant room, with tall ceilings, grand windows, ornate furniture, and tasteful works of art. But most importantly, there was not another soul inside. The fire was unlit, assuring him that Miss Bingley had no plans for using the room.

His gaze rested almost immediately on a settee in the middle of the room. Tossing aside his hat, Darcy walked over and collapsed into its thick cushions. His shoulders heaved as he inhaled and exhaled sharply, attempting to gather his thoughts. However, the persistent image of Elizabeth exchanging vows with Royce shattered his ability to think clearly. He buried his face into his hands and dug his fingers into his head. *What a fool I am to believe I ever had a chance.*

Moments later, he looked up and stared out of the room's large windows, attempting to find peace in the view of Hertfordshire's snowy countryside. He found little solace in the pretty landscape and realised his leg was trembling almost uncontrollably. Unable to stay still any longer, Darcy stood abruptly, clasped his hands behind his back, and began to pace the room. Maddening, it was simply maddening. There was no other way to describe it. He had come so far in just a few days, and now Elizabeth had decided she would accept another man, a man she did not even love.

His pacing slowed at the far end of the room, coming to a stop in front of a large portrait of a gentleman he assumed was a former owner of Netherfield. He fixed his gaze on the stern figure depicted in the painting, but his thoughts wandered far from the image before him.

Was this how it was to end, after all this time? After years of yearning and regret, they had been thrown together again for what purpose? That he might watch as she entered into a loveless marriage? For she was resolved to say yes, and Royce was sure to ask her again very soon. He saw how the man practically wagged his tail every time she came around. *Obsequious, wheedling nodcock.*

Releasing his hands from their tight clasp, Darcy calmed himself with several deep breaths. He knew it was not right to think so harshly of Royce. The man had done nothing wrong in taking advantage of an opportunity that *he* had foolishly thrown away. Rather than censure, Royce deserved praise for his cleverness in taking a treasure where he saw one. Not that Darcy could praise the man he so envied, of course.

Exhausted and downcast, Darcy rubbed the back of his neck. *What am I to do now? Leave? Fight?* He was so weary of this battle for Elizabeth's heart—constantly tossed about, feeling the depths of sorrow at her disdain for him, only to be lifted to the highest jubilation if she merely cast a warm look in his direction. And now, again, he was thrown back into deepest despair as he learnt he had lost the battle.

A rush of anger coursed through him. Turning around sharply, he strode across the room back towards the settee, raised his hand as he clenched it into a fist, and slammed it down into the cushioned arm. Then he did it again, and again, and again, every strike pushing him deeper into frustration. Finally, feeling as though he had allowed his pent-up emotions to escape, he sat down on the settee again. After this outpouring of anger and frustration, he found sorrow was the only emotion left. It only compounded his grief to know that this feeling would be his only companion the rest of his days.

He knew Elizabeth would scold him for such an outburst of temper. Thinking of how she would admonish him for such a display made him smile for the briefest of moments before sadness again overwhelmed him. What was he to do? It was hopeless. He had lost her.

What would he do without her the rest of his life? Without this unpredictable and lovely woman, forever keeping him on edge, making him feel alive? She pulled him in with the brilliance of her mind, only to cut him down to size and pull the rug out from under him the next moment with her wit and good humour. He was left in a daze after every interaction, every moment spent trying to match wits with her, and it was so frustratingly wonderful. A future without her seemed bleak indeed.

Perhaps he should just leave Hertfordshire and be done with it. Surrender all hope and go on with his life, doing everything he could to put it behind him. He sat in silence as thoughts continued racing through his head.

Why would she do this? Why would she enter into a marriage where she did not actively love her partner? A small voice in his head told him that he knew why. Had he not said it himself in his remarks about Mr Bennet's paternal failures? Because she had to, to secure her own future where her father had not.

She was a woman who deserved to live a life full of love; it was the only way she could thrive. She would only wither being married to a man like Mr Royce, for he would not inspire her passion or stimulate her intellect. Yes, she would be comfortable and would not want for anything with regards to material needs, but at what cost? She would have put to death her heart.

Sitting up, Darcy reached in his pocket and withdrew a small object, smoothing his thumb over it as he often did when needing to calm his thoughts or revisit a memory. His misery began subsiding as he realised Elizabeth had not yet told Royce she would marry him.

If she has not yet said 'yes', perhaps there is still time to change her mind. Perhaps I still might hope.

Something had held her back, and their own friendship had been re-established and deepened. Was it possible she still felt something for him? In the last day or two, something in her look and manner suggested it was possible.

Perhaps she is marrying Royce only because she is unsure of my feelings.

Heartened, Darcy decided to change his course, and actively pursue her. He would not allow a woman as wonderful as Elizabeth to commit to a life where she would not reach her full potential for happiness. She needed to be aware she had a choice, to know that his feelings had remained unchanged since that long-ago spring and that he would follow her to the ends of the earth if needed. This was his last chance. If he was to go down in this fight, he would go down swinging.

CHAPTER THIRTY

Elizabeth tugged at the satin dress she was wearing as she sat between Kitty and Mr Hurst at the dining table. She felt wildly uncomfortable in Miss Bingley's clothes—their garish hues, the tightness of the cut, and the thin material felt almost indecent going over her curves. To say nothing of being cold! Despite the fact that the dress chosen for her tonight was the finest satin she had ever seen, Elizabeth felt unnerved by wearing clothes she did not own. Her discomfort was only amplified at Miss Bingley's sour expression when she saw Elizabeth and all of her sisters in the borrowed garments. Elizabeth hoped to wear her own much less fashionable gown tomorrow and return home to Longbourn, where she could wear her well-worn muslins and wool without worries of staining or tearing her attire.

Nor would her own gowns give her the sickly pallor that the colour of this particular gown provided; she could not help but wonder if Miss Bingley chose this pinkish-yellow hue for her on purpose. In addition to her usual haughtiness, the lady treated Elizabeth as some sort of rival for Mr Darcy's affections. Generally, she would laugh at such a thought, for she had previously been so sure of his indifference towards her. But tonight, she could not help but wonder at him.

'*I have been such a fool, Elizabeth.*'

She could not understand the meaning of the words he had declared only hours earlier. Did he imply that he regretted ending their previous attachment? Or did he only mean he regretted speaking without tenderness on that fateful day?

She pushed her carrots to the side of her plate as she pondered his most recent disclosures, especially that he had acted so coldly to her out of shock and grief at his father's untimely death. Was he telling her these things to express remorse that they were not able to marry or was he suggesting that the outcome could have been different had his father not died so unexpectedly? Or, as seemed more likely, he would have expressed the same sentiments but in a kinder or gentler manner? Her head fairly whirled with the attempt to understand him. She was thankful she was not seated next to him at dinner, so she would not be forced to speak to him and decipher his meanings. It would be too overwhelming.

Mr Bingley interrupted her thoughts, as he asked Jane, "How does Miss Mary fare this evening?"

"Much better," Jane responded. "She remains weak, but has made much progress today."

Elizabeth glanced towards their end of the table, where Mr Darcy also sat, intending to add her own thoughts on Mary's condition. However, she was quickly distracted by Mr Darcy's unyielding stare. She almost started when she met his eyes, as there was something in his looks that was altered. There was no air of awkwardness as there usually was. Instead, he gazed at her with a look of determination.

She hoped her flush was not easily detected by the others as she looked back to her plate. "I am certain she will be fully recovered and out of her room by tomorrow morning. With Netherfield's drive cleared, perhaps some of my sisters, if not Mary, might return to Longbourn. My mother must be frantic without Jane at home to prepare for her wedding."

Mr Bingley and Jane exchanged happy smiles and as conversation about the wedding began, Elizabeth was unable to resist another glance at Mr Darcy. Not only was he still looking at her, but he also dared a charming smile. Confused, she looked away abruptly.

He continued with this behaviour throughout dinner. It was unnerving to say the least.

Others at the table began to notice his bold looks at her, but to Elizabeth's great relief, Lydia and Kitty seemed unaware. Although she did not wish illness on Mary, Elizabeth was thankful she was still absent. Her observant sister certainly would have taken notice, and likely sent disapproving looks his way.

Miss Bingley appeared the most intrigued, as she repeatedly glanced from Mr Darcy to Elizabeth, eyes narrowed and lips pursed. She attempted to distract him more than once by directing conversation back to herself, but his attentions were not swayed. Elizabeth did not dare to be caught looking at him again, and focused her attentions on her plate and the conversation—dull as it was—of Mr Hurst beside her.

After dinner, the party went into the drawing room. After no little time, Miss Bingley introduced an idea. "Why do we not all dance? We have not partaken in the activity since we were all together at Lucas Lodge," she suggested as she batted her eyes coquettishly in Mr Darcy's direction.

Before the ladies could agree, Elizabeth was surprised to hear Mr Darcy energetically speak. "That sounds splendid. Come Bingley, Hurst, let us move the rugs and furniture."

Elizabeth could not help but raise her eyebrows at him. It was so contrary to his usual reluctance for the activity. The rest of the party agreed to the idea and the men began moving the furniture, so there would be enough room to dance.

"Of course, Miss Elizabeth, you will have to play for us, for no one here plays so well as you." Miss Bingley smirked in Elizabeth's direction.

She had just opened her mouth to respond, when Mr Darcy cut in, saying, "I am sure she would oblige, but I would ask you to permit her to begin after the first set." Then, turning towards Elizabeth, he enquired respectfully, "Miss Elizabeth, will you do me the honour of the first dance?" He smiled as he looked at her, leading to giggles from Kitty and Lydia.

A simple "Yes" was all Elizabeth could muster.

After the room was situated to their liking, Mr Darcy walked determinedly towards her to retrieve her for the dance. Her heart jumped as she saw him come, looking so very tall and commanding. It was not to her credit that he disarmed her so easily merely by walking in her direction.

"May I?" He held out his hand. His demeanour and features were more relaxed than usual. She only nodded and he smiled as he led her to the improvised dance floor. At the pianoforte, Miss Bingley began playing a reel, and they commenced dancing.

"Smiling does you good," she blurted out. She shook her

head slightly as she chastised herself for speaking her thoughts aloud to him.

"What do you mean?" He chuckled softly as he looked down at her.

"Um, only that you just…look…handsome when you smile," she said, blushing wildly.

"We have only been dancing a minute, and you are already blushing and commenting on my looks," Mr Darcy whispered in her ear as their moves brought them closer together. Their hands clasped as part of the dance, and he held her hand a moment longer than would be deemed proper.

"Despise me for my lowly country manners if you dare." She gave him an arch smile, refusing to reveal any other signs of embarrassment. "You know you are a handsome man. You would have to be quite daft to not realise it, or its effect on ladies."

She could not help herself from laughing as she said it. It was bold to say such things to a man, but though it was surely an awkward conversation, she felt comfortable in his presence. It was, she knew, their shared history; no matter how much pain had been felt in it, they had been linked intimately at one time. In an odd way, speaking with him felt very similar to conversing with a close friend.

"Shall we change the subject?" she said gaily. "It is your turn to introduce a topic, for I seem unable to carry an ordinary conversation this evening."

His left eyebrow lifted. "I quite like your topic of conversation. I daresay we should keep it going. Let us discuss different settings in which you have seen me, and what degree of handsomeness I had in them."

They both laughed and Elizabeth marvelled at the alteration in his character. He seemed to be flirting with her! Deciding to change the subject herself, she said, "You have been absent most of the day. I hope nothing dreadful occupied you."

He cleared his throat. "Yes, there was a matter of business, and I had to determine how to approach it."

"I see. I hope the time alone permitted you clarity of mind."

"It did. I have decided on the course of action I will take."

"Good," she said, and from there conversation seemed to wither. He looked more uncomfortable and for a short time they said nothing, only moving through the pattern silently while Mr Bingley and Jane, Kitty and Lydia, and the Hursts danced down the line.

Elizabeth, unwilling for the dance to end without further conversation, desired to tease him more. "Are you often silent unless your dance partner carries the conversation?"

"I shall talk of whatever you request," he said. "Should we discuss all the couples dancing? Or perhaps books?"

"No—I cannot talk of books while dancing. My head is always full of something else."

They carried on in this manner and as the last notes neared, he said, "This is my third time dancing with you. I must say each dance has been different from the one preceding it."

"How so, sir?"

"The first time we were falling in love, and the second time, I believe you hated me."

"And what about this one? How would you categorise this dance?"

The music stopped, and the time had come for him to give her up again. He stopped smiling, and looking at her intently, said quietly, "And this time I am imagining what it could have been like for us had I not given you up in Kent."

She started and almost let out an audible gasp. The invisible but fraught line she had only inched towards, he had completely crossed. As if he had not just said something shocking, Mr Darcy led her towards the pianoforte where she would take her turn to play. He bowed and stepped away. Elizabeth prepared herself to play, even as his words had left her feeling discomfited and unsure of herself.

Her fingers traced over the keys, unable to think of tunes to pull from memory for her mind was too full of thoughts of Mr Darcy. The more distance she had from his advances, the more she felt vexation begin to rise in her chest. He had previously expressed regret over how things had ended between them, but not once had he suggested that regret should be turned into a different future for them. But here he was, seemingly doing just that. How could he play with her emotions so casually? Did he not know how difficult it was for her to be around him after he broke her heart? He could not flirt with her as if he had not crushed her heart all those years ago!

She dared a glance towards him when she could, and had every intention of glaring furiously at him. When her eyes found him, however, her icy heart was thawed at what she saw.

Mr Darcy had walked past Miss Bingley, Mrs Hurst, Jane, and then Lydia to stand in front of a very unassuming Kitty, who was sitting in an armchair and lightly tapping her feet to the music. Elizabeth saw him bow, and though she could not hear from where she was, could infer that he asked her for the next dance. Kitty's face filled with pleasure at being singled out, and Elizabeth wondered whether her own surprise was as evident. She had every expectation that he would not dance with any of her sisters after he danced with her, as he typically avoided dancing with those he did not know well. She had doubted that he would even dance with Miss Bingley or Mrs Hurst, given his general aversion to the activity and his tendency to avoid doing things that did not align with his own desires. Elizabeth's vexation faded into appreciation at the sight, realising that Mr Darcy had sought to make one of her sillier sisters feel more welcome during their unexpected stay at Netherfield.

The dancers stood up in their line and she began her chosen piece for the dance. As she touched each key, she attempted to think of his actions with a clear head. She did believe now that he most certainly was making advances towards her. But, she could absolutely under no circumstances take him seriously. He was more than likely caught up in the emotion of being around a former lover coupled with feeling dull while in the country. A fleeting infatuation. She would try to avoid him for the remainder of her time at Netherfield. She would marry Royce, never see Mr Darcy again, and live the rest of her life with him as simply a memory of her youth.

CHAPTER THIRTY-ONE

Hours later, Elizabeth gazed upon herself absently in the mirror as she brushed her hair to prepare for bed.

"Lizzy!"

Startled, she turned and saw Lydia standing in the doorway.

"What are you doing? I have been standing here for two minutes and you have brushed the same section of hair over and over again," exclaimed Lydia. "What in the world is wrong with you? You look absolutely mad."

"Oh...um..." Elizabeth's hand rose to her cheek as she fumbled for a reply.

"I hoped to borrow your brush, but I can tell you will need it the rest of the night to finish brushing all the hair on your head!"

"Oh goodness, you are right." She joined Lydia in laughter. "I suppose I was deep in thought about...when we shall be able to return home."

"Yes, a second night at Netherfield wearing Miss Bingley's finery." Her sister grinned.

"Are you missing your plain flannel night-rail? Mrs Hurst and Miss Bingley will soon run out of gowns to share with us."

Lydia's eyes widened. "It cannot be so long before we are able to leave!"

Elizabeth smiled reassuringly. "If there is no further snowfall, we might leave as soon as we receive word that the roads are deemed safe. I hope it is tomorrow."

"Kitty and I as well," Lydia said, nodding in agreement. "Hopefully Mr Bingley does not keep us locked in here longer than necessary. I cannot help but wonder that both he and Jane enjoy this current predicament."

"Lydia!" Elizabeth exclaimed, chuckling. She had wondered the same thing. After their laughter subsided, she added, "I am quite ready to leave, but cannot help but remember that once we return to Longbourn, Jane will be leaving it again only days later to make her home here."

Her younger sister frowned. "It will be strange, will not it?"

"Very much so."

They sat in silence for a moment before Lydia said, "Here, let me brush your hair since you seem so incapable. We would not want you to brush yourself bald, would we?"

She came to stand behind Elizabeth at the dressing table and began brushing her hair. Elizabeth watched in the mirror as her sister stifled a huge grin. "What are you laughing at? What are you doing to me?" She began touching her hair to ensure Lydia had not pulled a prank on her.

"It is nothing," Lydia said, giggling. "Do you remember

the time Mama horribly singed the top of her hair with the curling tongs?"

Elizabeth burst out laughing. "Yes! I came home from a walk to the smell of burnt hair! The entire house smelt horrid!"

"She had to wear a cap for months until her hair grew back! It looked so odd, standing straight up until the weight of it could pull it down again."

"And we were only allowed to use rag curlers from then on!"

Tears streamed from Elizabeth's eyes and Lydia was nearly doubled over.

"Papa hardly knew what to do with her nerves over it," Lydia recollected between giggles. "He came into the house, smelt the hair, heard the screaming, and turned and walked back out the door and down the lane until after sundown." She paused again, struggling to contain her merriment. "Without even trying to help or calm her! I daresay our parents are some of the most ridiculous people I have ever known."

A moment later, Jane entered the room. "I could hear your laughter echoing down the hall and had to find out what was so amusing."

"Come join us," Lydia said.

Elizabeth rose from her seat and the three sisters climbed onto her bed to recount the story to Jane.

"Poor, dear Mama! I remember that day, too," Jane said, trying to suppress a smile.

They continued sharing stories about their parents and life at Longbourn, and soon heard the door swing open. Kitty and Mary stood in the doorway. Mary appeared noticeably stronger than she had earlier that day, while

Kitty looked positively giddy, her eyes sparkling with excitement.

"Mary, how are you? You were asleep the last time we went to check on you." Elizabeth sat up straighter to get a closer look at her sister.

Mary managed a small smile, leaning slightly on the doorframe for support. "I am better. Still weak and tired but improving every hour."

Elizabeth felt relief wash over her. "How wonderful. Come join us." She patted the counterpane and moved herself closer to Jane to allow room for Mary and Kitty.

Mary stepped slowly into the room. "I was feeling well enough that I wished to leave my room and take a short stroll around the house. I came across Kitty in the corridor, and—"

Kitty interrupted, practically bouncing on her toes. "And you will never guess what we heard!"

"What?" cried Lydia.

"After I all but bumped into Kitty," Mary said, sinking slowly onto the bed, "she realised she had forgot her magazine in the drawing room. We walked there to retrieve it but stopped at the door when we overheard Mr Darcy, Mr Hurst, and the Bingley sisters talking…and our names mentioned."

"Oh dear," Elizabeth said lightly. "Dare I suppose you did not like what you heard?"

"Miss Bingley had the most to say," Kitty said, rolling her eyes. "She complains that Mama can hardly hold her tongue, and that all of us save for Jane lack basic manners. It was quite rude, particularly as we are guests under her roof."

Remembering how Miss Bingley had studied her at dinner, Elizabeth asked, with affected nonchalance, "I should imagine she shredded me very well."

"Her opinion is that you have no beauty. She thinks you have a thin face, no handsome features, your nose wants character, that your eyes are shrewish—"

"Kitty, enough!" Jane cut in sharply.

It was wounding to hear such cruelties, but Elizabeth maintained an air of indifference. "Thankfully I do not want for her good opinion. It does not bother me if people I care nothing for despise me. It only proves what I already suspected of her feelings."

Jane took Elizabeth's hand and squeezed it. "How very uncivil. I cannot believe she would speak so! I will speak to Charles about it in the morning."

"But wait! We have not yet got to the good part!" cried Kitty. "Miss Bingley said that although Mr Darcy had reported to her of your beauty before she was acquainted with you, she was quite disappointed when she finally met you. She found your manners unfashionable and said you were far too self-sufficient. She was quite underwhelmed with you."

"Kitty, we do not care to hear more," Jane said in a shocked voice.

Heedless of Jane's protest, Kitty went on, "And then *Mr Darcy* said—sounding not at all amused, I might say—'Not only do I think her beautiful, I think she is one of the handsomest women of my acquaintance, whether in the country or in town. And while *you* may consider her too self-sufficient, I consider her perfectly confident considering she is one of the most intelligent people that I know.'"

Elizabeth swallowed and, unwilling to let her sisters see how his words affected her, looked down at her toes.

"Kitty! I was there, too. You are taking over the story," protested Mary.

A SHARED HISTORY

"*Then,*" Kitty continued excitedly, "Miss Bingley said 'Perhaps without her low connexions and ill-behaved family she could marry out of her sphere.' But Mr Darcy would have none of it. He said quite sternly, 'No, that is not to be borne. Any man would consider himself blessed to be united to her. Family and all'."

Mary interjected, "Kitty, you are forgetting what he said about Mr Bingley."

"He said he even told as much to Mr Bingley when Mr Bingley suggested some members of his family objected to Jane." Kitty looked at Jane and asked her, "Did you know such a thing? Who objected to us?"

Before Jane could answer, Mary interrupted again. "That is not all of what Mr Darcy said to Miss Bingley! He told her that he had encouraged her brother's attachment to Jane because marrying anyone connected to Elizabeth could only bring honour to the Bingley name. It could only be a privilege to marry into such a family."

Elizabeth felt her eyes widen and her mouth drop open in shock before she remembered herself and closed it.

"Just then we heard someone stand, and come towards the door. So, we were forced to hurry away quickly and did not hear the rest," said Kitty. "Nor did I fetch my magazine."

"Lizzy, did you not believe Mr Darcy despised you, and all of us?" asked Lydia.

"That is what we all thought," Mary added. "But Kitty tells me he very kindly danced with all of you tonight."

Lydia nodded. "However, he insisted on Lizzy for the first dance, and did stare at her a great deal tonight."

Elizabeth looked at her sisters, all watching her curiously. She felt their surprise and carried it more deeply herself. But she could only return their gazes silently, for she had no answers to give.

CHAPTER THIRTY-TWO

Elizabeth peered into the music room. Seeing that no one was in there, she hastily entered. She had heard voices coming from within Netherfield's morning room but hoped she might slip away undetected into this quieter space. In her efforts to avoid Mr Darcy, she had not left her bedchamber for breakfast, and thus—although she had been awake since before the clock struck seven—she had not yet eaten a proper meal.

She sat down at the pianoforte, which was at least as fine an instrument as the one in the drawing room. Looking over her shoulder, she debated playing at risk of being heard. Hoping that she was far enough removed to evade detection, tedium won the day, and she began playing a melancholy tune, touching the keys gently so the notes were barely discernible to any ears but hers.

Her thoughts turned towards all that had happened in the last day. Elizabeth hardly knew what to think. Until now, she had been uncertain about what lay within Mr Darcy's heart.

While she knew he held a certain affection for her, she had never suspected the depth of his feelings. She had believed his attentions these past two weeks were merely a brief rekindling of the remnants of their former connexion, not suggestive of any genuine desire to reignite their relationship.

All of that had changed yesterday. His confession to her and his disclosures to the Bingleys had left her astonished. He openly expressed regret to her over the way things had ended between them and went so far as to praise her beauty, her intelligence, and even her family to others. With this unmistakable confirmation of his high regard for her, it was evident that his change in demeanour the previous night was not simply the impulse of the moment as she had assumed, but signified his intention to rekindle their romance.

Elizabeth grappled with her own emotions as she contemplated this newfound revelation. That she was attracted to Mr Darcy was undeniable, but was it love or simply a return to the comfort of a past love? And if it *was* love, was it a sound and true one? How could she possibly trust someone who had once utterly eviscerated her heart?

"I always loved the way you played. It was one of the first things that drew me to you and tested my resolve against falling in love with you."

Elizabeth stopped playing immediately, startled to hear Mr Darcy's voice. *Of course he would find me. He likely has been searching for me.* She turned her head and saw him leaning against the doorframe.

"How long have you been standing there?"

"A few minutes."

"Oh." She turned and looked down at her hands on the

instrument. She heard his footsteps as he walked closer to her, at length taking a seat next to her on the piano bench.

"You had not come downstairs and I worried for you. Miss Bennet assured me you are well."

"I am." She was about to resume playing, when he spoke again.

"I have always been captivated by the way you play and sing from the depths of your heart. It is apparent that your approach is not rooted in classical training, but, as with everything you do, it is filled with charm and grace."

"Do you realise that you often insult me in your compliments?" she asked with a little laugh.

"I apologise," he said earnestly. "I do not mean it as an insult. I suppose what I am trying to say is you have always fascinated me by not adhering to conventional standards but still managing to leave a lasting and extraordinary impression."

He took a deep breath before continuing, "You are unlike anyone I have ever encountered, Miss Elizabeth. I was raised with a set of expectations about what constitutes an accomplished woman, and to be honest, you do not quite fit that mould. However, in my heart, you are far more than accomplished."

She blushed, and turned her head away before he could notice. Elizabeth knew she should leave but could not bring herself to do so. Instead, she changed the subject.

"What would you like me to play? My fingers await your command."

He leant his head towards her. "May I play something for you instead?"

"I had no idea that you played, sir. You are full of

surprises of late." On his look, she shifted away from the centre of the bench and urged, "Pray, go on."

He cleared his throat, moved a few inches nearer, and began playing slowly. She immediately recognised the song as a children's tune. She giggled as he fumbled through the song, and clapped emphatically when he was done.

"My musical skills are inferior to yours, of course. This is the only song Georgiana has ever been able to teach me," he said with a mischievous half-smile. "I will offer my talents in page-turning, if you will continue to play?"

When she agreed, he slid off the bench and stood next to her at the instrument.

She resumed playing the melancholic melody she had been practising earlier, her fingers dancing over the keys while she ruminated about what had initially drawn her to him. He was a complex individual; his quiet demeanour and air of mystery had always fascinated her. He had a way of keeping her guessing about his true feelings, and she relished the challenge of deciphering him. Although he projected an air of aloofness, beneath that exterior, he was more engaged and interesting than anyone she had ever encountered. Since reuniting with him, she had rediscovered his kindness and gentleness. She thought of his compassion towards Georgiana, his caring demeanour with Mary, and his considerate treatment of her cousins and sisters.

If he was sometimes prideful and haughty, he also was strangely humble. For much as he possessed numerous talents and considerable wealth, he never flaunted them ostentatiously. He was calm, but not boring. And while he possessed wit and intelligence in abundance, he was quiet and understated about it—a gentleman of refined manners—which only made his wry humour all the more endearing.

And there was that certain something about him that remained elusive.

Even during their disagreements, she had secretly hoped he would reveal more of himself. He did not rattle off like some men of her acquaintance, but when he did speak, it was always intelligent and impressive. He genuinely listened to her when she spoke and challenged her in ways no one ever had. Deep down, she had always yearned for a partner who would push her to grow, and Mr Darcy had fulfilled that desire, both in the past and in the present.

As he stood beside her, turning the pages, she stole a glance at his profile. His striking good looks had always overwhelmed her, and her attraction to him remained as potent as ever. The way he gazed at her had a way of melting her heart. *The way he is gazing at me right now.*

Elizabeth's heart leapt as understanding hit her like a sack of heavy stones crashing onto her chest—she loved him. Perhaps she had never truly stopped, and had been lying to herself this whole time. It was not merely attraction or intrigue based on residual feelings from the past. It was genuine, profound, and undeniably alive—it was love in its purest, most authentic form. Tears welled up in her eyes, and her throat constricted as a lump formed.

The piano keys clanged loudly as she abruptly stopped playing. She stared straight ahead, drawing in deep, ragged breaths. Why was it suddenly so difficult to breathe?

He looked at her, concern in his expression. "Are you well?"

She did not know what to do or say; all she knew was that she could not remain in this room next to him.

"I am so sorry, please excuse me, I must leave."

Elizabeth stood and walked out of the room, barely

hearing his calls to her. She turned down the corridor and kept walking. Hearing voices drifting from the stairs and in the drawing room, she turned blindly down another small corridor. Grabbing a worn shawl from a peg, she slipped out through a servants' door at the side of the house and hurried outside, heedless of her bare head.

Once outside, the cold air felt clarifying. She could breathe better out of the confines of the house, and the whiteness of the new snow made her feel more at peace. She walked quickly and briskly. At first uncertain of her direction, she soon realised her feet were taking her towards Longbourn. She needed to escape Mr Darcy. She needed to be home.

CHAPTER THIRTY-THREE

Elizabeth drew her arms closer to her body, her hands clenched into fists as she braced against the cold. The longer she walked towards Longbourn, the wind, which had been initially invigorating, became increasingly harsh. A sudden gust whipped past her, through the narrow lane, blowing powdery snow with it. As it stung her cheeks, she kept her eyes on the path ahead and her tumultuous thoughts consumed her. *How could this have happened? How could I have fallen in love, despite all my best efforts to not do so?*

As shivers raced through her, she realised that in her frantic haste to escape Netherfield, she had not dressed appropriately for such frigid weather. She drew the shawl more tightly around her shoulders as she continued walking, certain she could make the few miles home if she kept a brisk pace. The snow crunched underfoot and a part of her recognised her foolishness. Three miles in only half-boots and a shawl was sheer folly. Another big gust of wind struck against her, confirming she was nonsensical, but she ignored it. Her thoughts were too full of him.

What a fool I have been, to fall in love again so easily... She had been trying to deny her feelings for him this whole time, trying to protect her heart. She only now realised she was too late. Her heart was no longer hers to give to Royce or any other man. It belonged to Mr Darcy, still and likely always. In suggesting they become friends, she had destroyed any emotional distance between them—her only defence in not falling in love with him again. As the wind whipped up the snow from the ground into swirling clouds, a surge of frustration coursed through her. *How am I here again, in love with a man who cannot offer me marriage?*

A moment later, she heard a deep voice cutting through the wind. "Elizabeth!"

Her stomach sank. She did not turn around, instead keeping her eyes straight towards Longbourn. *No, I cannot see him. Not now.*

Mr Darcy called her name again, and she felt she could no longer disregard it. Reluctantly, she turned around to face him. He was closer than she expected, only a few feet away. The sight of him rendered her frozen for a moment. As he approached, fully clothed in a greatcoat, hat, scarf, and gloves, it only highlighted her own chill and reminded her of how inadequately she was dressed.

"How quickly you walk!" he panted as he finally caught up with her, his cheeks reddened by the cold. "I came immediately after you left, and you were out of sight by the time I exited the house." Unable to meet his eye, she looked to the ground as he added, "I had to guess which direction you walked."

She did not say anything in response, worried that her voice would betray all of the emotions she felt.

After a few moments pause, she looked up to meet his gaze. In his dark eyes, she saw a mixture of relief and concern. Still unable to respond to him, she felt tears begin to sting her eyes as a lump formed in her throat.

He continued to study her face as he said, "I am so thankful I found you. The longer I have been out here the more it looks as if it might… Come, let us go back."

He reached out to take her arm and guide her back in the direction of Netherfield, but the warmth of his touch felt as needles, heightening every conflicting emotion she was enduring. She abruptly pulled away as she turned back in the direction of Longbourn, her voice trembling with desperation. "I cannot… I must go home."

Mr Darcy quickened his pace to match hers, falling into step beside her. "Did I do something to upset you?"

"No, you have done nothing wrong," she replied, her voice trembling as tears welled in her eyes.

"What troubles you so?" The concern in his voice grew more urgent. She folded her arms around herself and clenched her jaw as she continued to walk, but offered no reply. At her silence, he implored, "I insist you come back."

"No, I cannot," she said with a thick voice.

Out of her periphery, she could see that he continued to look at her. He pressed, "You cannot go all the way back to Longbourn dressed in such a way, and the weather appears to be worsening. Please, it is not safe."

Elizabeth's gaze fell to her damp boots; in spite of her woollen stockings, her feet were growing colder with each step. A chill crept up her spine as she looked up to see the clouds churning in an ominous way. With a shiver of resignation, she nodded. "How foolish I have been. Yes, let us return."

He quickly removed his coat and placed it around her before wrapping his scarf around her neck. Warmth, *his* warmth, immediately soothed and relieved her even as she tried to refuse it. "I cannot take these, what will you—"

"I insist," he shouted above the blowing winds. Once it had passed, he added in a more regulated tone, "Come, let us get to Netherfield before the weather worsens."

As they turned back towards the house, the wind intensified to such a level that visibility was diminished. Snow was chaotically whirling in every direction, obscuring the landscape around them. A fierce gust nearly knocked her over as concern surged through her.

She looked towards Mr Darcy. "I am so sorry," she cried, steeling herself to continue, "I never should have…"

He met her gaze with a look of unwavering resolve. "Keep walking," was all he had time to say before another blast of wind cut off his words.

Elizabeth pushed against the wind, trying to follow his instructions. *What have I done?* Panic made her breath come in short gasps. *Not only to myself, but to Mr Darcy too.* It seemed doubtful that they could make it all the way back to Netherfield; even finding it seemed unlikely now, as the lane had been completely obscured by blowing snow and they could not be sure which direction to take.

The recklessness of her decision to leave in inclement weather overtook her. Why had she let her emotions consume her so fully that she had not noticed that a storm was bearing down? Her insides sank as she grasped the grave danger they were in, realising that it was her own foolishness that now jeopardised both herself and the man she loved. What were they going to do?

She looked at Mr Darcy, his hat blown off and his hair in disarray as it matted against his head, and a strange calm overcame her. *Despite my foolishness, he is with me.*

He stopped suddenly, his head turning from side to side as if trying to assess their surroundings. He gazed at her with a look of determination, firmly grabbed her arm and shouted against the wind, "Come…this way!" He pointed at a copse of trees visible only momentarily between bursts of the storm.

"But Nether—"

"Trust me!" The wind was too loud to argue further, so she did.

CHAPTER THIRTY-FOUR

As they stumbled through the snow, a rush of wind almost knocked them down again. Once they steadied themselves, Mr Darcy wrapped one arm around Elizabeth's body to keep her from falling. As they drew closer, she could now see that the sycamore trees they had been walking towards stood near an outbuilding, which she recognised as one of Netherfield's old barns.

He led her to it and attempted to open the door, but the wind battered against him. He worked against the gale for a few moments, finally managing to yank it open and usher her into the barn. Following quickly, he slammed the door shut.

Once inside, Elizabeth felt instant relief from the wind that had been pushing and pulling against her. Before her eyes could adjust to the dim light, she was immediately met with the musty scents of damp wood mingled with hay. The only sound was the muffled wind scraping against the barn's exterior. As she continued to catch her breath, her vision began to clear, revealing that right in front of her, taking up nearly all the space in the small building, was a fine, enclosed carriage.

As she gazed upon it, Elizabeth wrapped her arms around herself instinctively in an effort to warm herself. Mr Darcy responded swiftly. "Please, allow me to assist you into the carriage. You must sit after such a trying experience, and the warmth will do you good," he said urgently as he gestured towards the vehicle.

She nodded, and Mr Darcy pulled down the step and opened the door, offering his hand to help her climb inside. He followed and sat down opposite her. Relief washed over her as she finally rested. She looked at Mr Darcy and her heart warmed in gratitude towards him for finding her, though not at an inconsiderable risk to himself.

His eyes immediately began to scan her person as he asked, "Are you well? Have you any injuries?"

She took a deep, steadying breath before responding. "I am well. I thank you for finding me, and for bringing me here. How…how could you tell this was here? I could hardly see anything of our surroundings, but you seemed to know exactly where we were."

"I recognised the copse of trees next to the barn. I have ridden by this area many times and suggested it to Bingley when he told me of his plan to surprise your sister with this carriage. The coach house, as you may know, is undergoing some repairs to its roof, and this barn offered a solution for his plans to keep the carriage hidden."

"How fortunate," she said just as a wave of cold overcame her and sent her teeth chattering.

"You must be freezing," Mr Darcy said immediately. "Let us cover you."

There were lap rugs and furs folded on one side of the

carriage, and he reached over to help arrange them over her. Was it her imagination or did his hand linger a moment too long? *Likely not,* she decided. *He is merely wishing that I should not catch my death.*

After he finished and sat down again across from her, she cast a glance at him. His hair was wet, and his cravat dishevelled. He rubbed his hands together briskly, as if attempting to generate warmth.

"You must cover yourself too," she said earnestly.

He nodded and pulled the remaining lap rug over himself.

They were silent for a few moments until she felt a shiver run through her, despite his coat and the rugs covering her. Her damp gown clinging to her skin offered little comfort.

"I can see you are still cold." He abruptly rose, his lap rug falling to the floor as he moved across the small space between them, and sat next to her. She looked at him in surprise as her heart raced.

"You will get warm faster if I sit next to you," he explained, picking up his fallen blanket and laying it around her shoulders.

She nodded and shifted over her heavy lap rug to cover him as well. "Why did you follow me?"

"You left the music room so hastily. I saw you leave the house and was worried about you. I came to find you."

"I am so sorry." She put her head in her hands. "I never ought to have left. How regrettable that you should be affected now as well!"

"I am only glad I found you and that you are safe. The winds are quite fierce, but they have brought no new snow, which is most fortunate."

Elizabeth looked away, feeling a sense of guilt and gratitude towards him. They sat next to each other in silence, and she realised he was correct, she was slowly becoming warmer, as well as growing tired from her exertions in the cold. She stifled a yawn and could not keep her eyes from closing.

"Perhaps you would wish to shut your eyes and rest. Once you awaken, the storm will have subsided, and we will be able to return to the house."

It was a welcome request; she was, in fact, quite sleepy. She found following his directions far easier than pulling herself from her worries and fears about their safety. Without quite meaning to, she leant against his chest and closed her eyes. He initially stiffened, perhaps in surprise, then quickly relaxed. Then, he lifted his arms to gently cradle her head with one hand and pull her in closer with the other. Even with the wind howling and tree branches scratching on the old barn's frame, drifting off to sleep in his warm embrace was easier than she had anticipated.

When Elizabeth woke, her head still comfortably ensconced on Mr Darcy's chest, memories of all that had transpired washed over her. It was brighter inside the carriage, and gazing out the side-glass, she saw sunlight peeking through the barn window. Clearly, the storm had ended. It was quiet now—so very quiet. A pang of worry struck her; she wondered how Jane and the others were faring and whether they were aware of—and anxious about—their absence. However, relief quickly took over as she thought, *But now that it is safe to return, any worry will thankfully be short-lived.*

Her gown felt mostly dry and she was not cold, bundled

as she was in lap blankets and feeling the warmth of another body so close to hers. *Mr Darcy's body.* She turned to see if he had fallen asleep as she had, and her insides jumped to see that he was quietly looking down at her.

A rush of feeling flooded through her. She considered asking him how long she had been sleeping, but she did not. Instead, she only looked at him.

Before she realised what she was doing, Elizabeth sat up, turned towards him, and put her arms around his neck. She stared into his eyes and pulled his face close to hers, looking at him for a moment before pressing her lips to his. She pulled back, letting her eyes linger on his for a moment longer.

His expression was inscrutable, but his arms remained around her body, keeping her close to him. Before she could wonder how he felt about what had transpired, he closed the gap between them and kissed her again, deeply. The intensity of it took her by surprise, but she quickly responded with equal fervour.

Nothing she had ever experienced in her life had ever felt so perfect. After everything they had been through, after all these years, they were finally here, losing themselves in this moment. Their ordeal in the storm seemed a distant memory compared to the joy she felt in his embrace; she would endure a thousand storms just to be here with him. As his arms drew her in even closer, she surrendered to everything she had been holding back since he first arrived. She allowed the depths of her feelings, far too profound and frightening to express in words, to flow through their kiss.

As if both simultaneously realising that it may not be wise to continue in such a passionate manner, they drew apart at the same time with ragged breaths. When she opened her eyes to look at him, his face was slightly flushed, but his gaze remained locked on hers. His fingertips tenderly traced her cheek before lightly grazing her neck and falling away. She looked down and gave a small, nervous chuckle. When she looked up again, she saw the eyes she knew so well still looking at her with that familiar intensity. She smiled softly and planted one final, tender kiss on his cheek.

"Shall we get back to the others now?" she asked quietly.

He nodded, and they exited the carriage together. Mr Darcy opened the barn door, and she saw a wonderland of windswept snowdrifts bathed in the gentle light of the early afternoon sun. It appeared as if the winds had blown the snow but no more had fallen, just as Mr Darcy had said. The lane and paths were visible in places, and although the ground was partly frozen, it looked much the same as it generally did, to Elizabeth's relief.

Mr Darcy took her hand as they began the walk back to Netherfield. They walked hand in hand in comfortable silence, occasionally glancing at each other and smiling. As they approached the house, they entered through a servants' door, which led directly into a dark, quiet corridor.

"Perhaps we should go different directions from here, to not attract too much attention," he said quietly.

Nodding, she returned his coat and scarf.

He pulled her to him and gave her a long kiss on her forehead. "I look forward to seeing you at dinner." Then he gave her a warm look, smiled, and squeezed her hand.

Elizabeth turned away from him and made her way to her room. Once inside, she closed the door and rested her head and back against the door. She slowly slid until she was sitting on the floor, her head in her hands, awash with dismay.

A gnawing feeling had begun to take root soon after they had left the carriage. Initially she could not quite identify it, but as they walked on, their hands clasped, she recognised it. Regret. What had she done, kissing him and encouraging such liberties? She had misled him and had made a grave mistake in so doing. Even if he had changed his mind regarding her suitability as a marriage partner, she could not trust him. Yes, she loved him and yes, she cared about his happiness, but—

But a woman surrendered a great deal when she married. The entirety of her life, her future, the lives of potential children, was placed into the hands of the man she wed. And she could not trust Mr Darcy.

He might think he loved her now, but what would happen once they married and her family continued to bring embarrassment upon them? Would his affection outlast his mortification? *No.* Theirs would become a marriage not unlike that of her parents, and she could not bear that. The pain of a husband's scorn was too much for her. He would surely come to regret marrying her; his love would grow cold. She could not imagine how it might feel to be so discarded by him. *Again.*

She so fervently wanted to be with him, but logic and wisdom must prevail. For a time, she could not move, frozen by the impossible predicament she was in. Finally, she did the only thing that could release her sorrows: she wept.

CHAPTER THIRTY-FIVE

To her great relief, once Elizabeth came downstairs for tea, it was evident no one had noticed her and Mr. Darcy's absence earlier in the day. Consequently, the rest of the afternoon passed as usual.

In the drawing room after dinner, the party debated how to occupy their time. Everyone was growing increasingly restless the longer they were forced to remain indoors and in company with those who had grown tiresome. They had played charades and were readying themselves to listen to Miss Bingley play the pianoforte…again.

It had been challenging, but Elizabeth had avoided looking at Mr Darcy throughout dinner. She did, however, frequently feel that she was being stared at during the meal, and felt it even now as she sat alone in a chair watching Miss Bingley prepare to play. She kept her eyes fixed upon the lady, willing herself not to look in the direction of the man with whom she had spent a romantic afternoon.

Just as Miss Bingley announced her musical selections, Lydia and Kitty, who had disappeared when the ladies withdrew after dinner, emerged into the room with their customary clamour. Lydia paid no attention to Miss Bingley's glare in their direction for interrupting her. "Let us not spend another dull evening listening to music," she cried. "Come, play a marvellous new game that Kitty and I created!"

"How delightful!" Mr Bingley exclaimed in wonderment, ignoring his sister's look of protestation.

Lydia preened. "In honour of our dear sister's coming marriage, where she and Mr Bingley will exchange wedding rings, we have created a game called 'Rings'. Kitty and I have made twenty of these rings." She held out her hand and displayed a few small circles made of twine.

Excitedly, Kitty added, "We have hidden them throughout the house. They are attached to small pieces of paper on which we wrote clues for how to find the next! You will search in pairs, and whichever pair finds the most in one hour shall be named the winner!"

It was evident from the stirring and chuckling heard among the group that everyone welcomed the new diversion.

"Shall we form teams?" Mr Bingley enquired.

"Kitty and I have already created the teams," Lydia informed him. "Kitty, you tell them."

"Our first pair is Jane and Mr Bingley," Kitty announced. Jane smiled in her betrothed's direction as he briskly walked to stand next to her, whispering something in her ear that made her giggle.

Kitty continued to announce the pairs. Elizabeth listened with a sinking heart as two names were not announced: hers and Mr Darcy's.

"Last but not least, Lizzy you will pair with Mr Darcy," Kitty concluded.

Elizabeth's heart skipped a beat, she then sent her younger sisters a stern look; Kitty and Lydia exchanged mischievous smiles. Unable to scold them as she might have liked, she instead glanced quickly at Mr Darcy for the first time that evening.

He smiled warmly at her as he approached. How did he even make *walking* appear attractive? When he was at her side, he murmured in her ear, "I could not have asked for a better way to get you alone tonight. Remind me to thank your sisters later."

She looked down and ignored what he said, determined to not let him affect her in *that* way. It was going to be harder than she thought.

Kitty and Lydia went about the room giving everyone their first rings along with their individual clues. Mr Darcy read their clue aloud.

"The answer of this is a room, but I guarantee it will not be caught; it is one with an open flame, sink, and even a pot."

"Kitchen," they both said in unison. He helped her rise and she preceded him as they left the drawing room and headed towards the kitchen. As soon as they gained the shadows of the candlelit hall, she saw him reaching for her hand. Before his hand could touch hers, she quickly drew hers away. His body appeared to stiffen slightly, and he shook his hand briefly. Then, he clasped his hands behind his back as they continued to walk.

Once they entered the kitchen, Elizabeth began looking intently for the ring, leaving him to stand at the door. She moved pots and pans, her eyes scanning each one, and noticed Mr Darcy approaching her. As she began manoeuvring a heavy pot, his hand appeared seemingly out of nowhere to help her lift it.

"Allow me to assist you," he offered.

"No," she answered curtly as she met his eye. He started, but he kept her gaze. She turned away as she placed the pot back down, and softened her expression as she said, "I thank you, but I do not need your help."

Out of the corner of her eye, she saw his head tilt as he continued to study her, though he said nothing further. Their search was interrupted by the sound of a shocked gasp. In the doorway stood a scullery maid, wearing a polite expression, though her eyes betrayed curiosity at them rummaging about the kitchen.

She curtseyed before asking respectfully, "Is there anything you require, sir? Ma'am?"

Mr Darcy turned as he replied, "Thank you, but I believe we have everything we need. You may return to your duties."

The maid curtseyed again and left, leaving them to their search.

Mr Darcy placed a gentle hand on the small of Elizabeth's back to guide her to a different section of the room, as he said, "Perhaps it is hidden among the spices."

She quickly stepped out of his embrace, clearing her throat as she looked down at the floor. He was quiet for a moment before finally asking, "Is something wrong?"

Elizabeth lifted her chin. "This morning was a mistake."

"Indeed?"

She continued in a voice devoid of emotion, a tone carefully contrived to keep the pain in her heart at bay. "Yes. Amidst an exceedingly trying experience, I was confused by the solicitude of someone who used to hold my heart. I allowed my emotions to get the better of me. Please forgive me for my impropriety."

She felt his eyes on her as she walked about, ostensibly seeking the next ring. The silence was painful.

"Why are you doing this?" he said finally.

"I still plan to marry Mr Royce."

The colour left his face. "Surely, you are in jest."

"I am not," she replied tersely. "Have I not already told you I intended to do so?"

After a moment, he ran his hands through his hair and shook his head. "Do not marry him, Elizabeth."

"Whyever not?"

"He is a nitwit," he responded quickly. Her frown seemed to prompt his regret at speaking ill of the man. "Forgive me, I ought not to have said that. What I should have said was, do not marry him because you do not love him."

Elizabeth remained silent, unable to deny the truth in that.

"He does not understand you. He is not clever enough for you and most importantly, he would not make you happy." In a quieter voice, he added, "Certainly not as I would."

"You think you would make me happy?" she asked. "Why?"

"Because I love you."

The effect of his words was considerable. Elizabeth felt them through every fibre of her being. Although she had suspected as much, hearing him say it aloud was unsettling. She folded her arms over her chest, abandoning the pretence of searching for the ring. "I give no credit to that statement. You are infatuated with me, perhaps, but you surely do not love me."

He looked at her incredulously. "You do not know how I

have ached for you, loved you, longed for you, these past three years."

"And what if I do not believe you? I cannot help but think you are only feeling all the dullness of country society—as it was three years ago in Kent—and your mind is playing tricks on you." Calming herself, for she had felt the need to defend her heart all too acutely, Elizabeth added, "You are caught up in sentiment. I am sure the feelings that earlier curtailed your regard for me will quickly take over and you will forget me not long after you leave. Just as it happened before."

"I could never forget you, Elizabeth," he said softly, walking across the kitchen to close the gap between them. "Pray do not try to tell me how I feel. I have loved you for three years complete."

She did all she could to avoid looking at him, but he leant in closer until she could no longer evade his gaze.

"I never stopped loving you," he said in an earnest, vulnerable voice.

She was quiet, unable to think of anything to say as she looked into his dark, beseeching eyes.

"I know you love me too."

She could not dispute him but neither could she give him what he wished for. "Love is not always enough."

"I cannot understand you. What more could anyone wish for than to love and be loved in return?"

She was silent.

"Presently you stand in front of someone who loves you, Elizabeth, and for whom you hold those same feelings. Yet, you will marry another man, one whom you do not love? What more is it that you wish for?"

"Trust," she replied finally. "I want a man whose love is certain, not tossed aside or bent by the wind. Mr Royce has had a lasting affection for me for over four years. *Yours* on the other hand…"

His face looked pained as he looked to the ground. "I cannot deny my past errors," he said in a wounded voice. "Amid the turmoil of losing my father and assuming all of my new responsibilities, I made a grave mistake. Can you not forgive me for that?"

"Whether I forgive you or not, the problem remains." Tears formed in her eyes and she blinked rapidly to keep them back. "My family is as they are. They will offend you again. Will you cast me aside the first time they embarrass you in front of your friends and family? They will do that eventually—you know it is inevitable. Would you know them among London society? Or would you rather whisk me away to Pemberley and ensure we would never see them again? That would not make me happy."

"I would not do that, Elizabeth. I have been practically a father these last three years. One cannot experience such responsibility and remain unaltered. Taking care of Georgiana and seeing her through difficult times has made me much more compassionate and understanding of the joys and trials of family."

He ventured closer to her and held her face in his hands; she looked at him through tears as he spoke. "I love you. I loved you three years ago, I love you today, and I never stopped loving you between. Do not call it infatuation. I would marry you right here and right now if you would have me. Do you not love me?"

"You abandoned me," she said. "And yes, I might forgive but I can never trust you. I have no wish to risk my heart, to take the chance that I will again feel the pain I felt back then. I waited for you every day for a *year*. Any time I heard a new young man was in town, or an unexpected knock came on our front door, I hoped that it was you. It nearly destroyed me. It took me so long to regain my spirits back. I cannot risk such agony a second time."

She could see the anguish in his countenance before he turned his back to her and walked across the room. He lifted his fist as if to hit the wall in frustration, but quickly regaining his composure, dropped his hand to his side. After a few steadying breaths, he turned back towards her.

"Would that I could undo it, but I cannot." He walked back towards her slowly, tentatively taking her into his arms. "I am so sorry I injured you as I did. I have hated myself since that day for the way I treated you. You cannot know how many times I desired to come find you here. I refrained because I thought…I thought you must surely despise me. That thought gave me unimaginable pain throughout many long, dark nights."

Leaning back a little and looking into her eyes, he said, pleadingly, "If you gave me another chance, I would not hurt you again."

"I do not think I can," she whispered.

He closed his eyes in agony. "All I desire is for you to be happy. Tell me how I can do that," he said softly. After a long moment of silence, he seemed to admit defeat. "If that means you wish me to stop pursuing you, then say so. I respect your words too much to do otherwise."

She closed her eyes a moment to gather her strength. "I do. I want you to stop pursuing me." She felt his muscles tense at her words, but he did not let her go.

Finally, he kissed the top of her head and said calmly, "I have regretted what I did to you every day for the last three years. But I wonder, will you regret today for the rest of your life?"

She stared into his eyes, with no answer to give.

Mr Darcy stepped back and took in the sight of her one last time before saying, "I shall leave you alone, Elizabeth."

Then he turned and left the room.

CHAPTER THIRTY-SIX

The following morning, the roads were deemed safe enough for the Bennet sisters to return to Longbourn, which put Elizabeth and Mr Darcy in company one last time—at breakfast. Despite her fraught emotions after their heart-breaking conversation, she somehow summoned the strength to exude an air of indifference towards him, and true to his word, he hardly uttered a syllable or cast a look towards her. Although Elizabeth was acutely aware of his movements and any contributions to discourse that he offered, it was easier than she had anticipated to avoid his gaze and conversation when he did not offer it. He had not even come to Netherfield's front hall to take leave of her and her sisters when the hosts made their goodbyes at the end of their stay. She had dared not name the feelings this had invoked in her, lest she reawaken everything she was attempting to bury.

On Saturday, two days after they returned home, the morning of the wedding had finally arrived, and Longbourn was bursting with frenzied activity. Women, both family and servant, ran back and forth in every direction getting ready for the day while the men were ushered—or ordered—round to fulfil last-minute tasks.

Elizabeth sat upon her bed, relishing some much-needed quiet amidst the chaos. She supposed she might call it *her* room now, for Jane had resigned it this morning. All her things were packed and gone to Netherfield. Elizabeth felt her chest rise and fall with her breath as she sat knowing it could not be long until her mother sent a sister or a maid to fetch her for another of the multitude of wedding tasks. Unsurprisingly, having Jane away for the days leading up to the ceremony had caused undue distress as there were many details that depended upon the bride's presence for completion.

If nothing else, sewing lace trim on Jane's gown and decorating Longbourn with garlands and ribbons had allowed Elizabeth to conceal her tumultuous emotions. She did not want her melancholy to take anything away from the day her sister had long dreamt about. Thankfully, Jane was too distracted by her own happiness and the busyness of the preparations to notice Elizabeth's desolation. Nevertheless, pretending to be in happy spirits had begun to wear on her, and she relished even a moment of respite. All her thoughts were occupied with Mr Darcy.

Today is likely the last I shall ever see him. The notion provoked both anxiety and relief. *You told him not to pursue you,* she reminded herself. *You told him you could not trust him again.*

Her thoughts were interrupted by her mother's shrill voice asking for her. Mrs Bennet was in the drawing room and somehow, even a floor away and through a closed door,

Elizabeth could hear her shouting, "Lizzy? Lizzy! Where are you? Oh, where has that girl got to?"

Elizabeth heard someone murmur something in reply and thankfully it seemed the matter was dropped. Still, she needed to join them. She must stand up with Jane, and the time to go to the church approached rapidly. She changed quickly from a morning dress into her pale yellow gown, dressing herself and pinning her own hair since summoning the maid would only alert her mother to her whereabouts. Leaving her bedchamber, she almost immediately ran into her mother and Mrs Gardiner standing in the hall.

"Did you not hear me calling you?" Mrs Bennet asked immediately. "Your hair! How is your hair not done properly yet? They are bringing up the carriages!"

Aunt Gardiner only gave her a concerned look, but Elizabeth avoided her gaze and went to find her sister.

She found Jane sitting in front of the dressing table in their mother's bedchamber. Instead of looking at herself, she was twirling one of the wedding flowers between her fingers, smiling in a dreamy, distant way. She looked ethereal with her hair pulled back and pearl combs placed delicately throughout her golden hair. Elizabeth's heart swelled even as her eyes stung with tears at the sight. How could she have been so caught up in her own feelings when this day was about Jane and Mr Bingley?

"Oh Jane," she cried. "You look so, so beautiful. But how do you feel?"

"I hardly know," Jane admitted. "Excited and thrilled…a little frightened, perhaps?"

"Exactly as you should be on such a wonderful occasion. Come now, let us make you a wife!" Elizabeth exclaimed with a laugh.

Their ceremony went off perfectly, which considering it was a Bennet affair, gave Elizabeth considerable relief. Seeing the happiness on Jane's face went a long way to making her feel happy as well. Alas, being in Mr Darcy's presence without any attention from the gentleman was harder than she had imagined. His perfect indifference was more painful than any spite could have been. When they entered the vestry to witness the lines being written and make the marriage official, she yearned for a meaningful look or stare of the kind he had before so frequently bestowed on her.

Alas, he offered nary a word or glance in the small room. He was ever true to his vow to honour her wishes, she reflected sadly. She condemned herself for even wanting to hope for his attention; had she not asked him to leave her alone? What was wrong with her?

The wedding breakfast at Longbourn progressed in the same way. Although she spoke to her family and neighbours, and managed smiles for Jane, she could not help but be completely aware of whatever part of the room Mr Darcy moved. Which, at this moment, was precisely located opposite of her as he engaged in conversation with Mr Andrews. As she watched him, she only dreaded the condition of her heart after he left. It would be far more difficult for it to heal this time, when it was entirely her decision to send him away.

"Miss Bennet? Did you hear me?" Her thoughts were interrupted by Royce, who was unexpectedly standing next to her. She felt a burst of irritation at the sight of him.

"I apologise, sir. I did not. What did you say?"

"I asked whether you and your sisters fare well after being trapped at Netherfield? Your mother told me of your unfortunate circumstances."

"Unfortunate indeed. I do not believe I could have lived another day in such a dreadful state." She smiled to show she only teased. "But I am ungenerous to my new brother and his excellent household. Other than the tedium from being indoors too long, we were very well cared for."

Royce nodded at that, then spoke of the commonplaces appropriate for the day, asking about the ceremony, complimenting her and her sisters on the arrangements and the like. Finally, he broached what it seemed had been his intention in conversing with her.

"Will you be at home on Monday? I should like to call on you."

She smiled and nodded with more energy than she felt. "Yes, I will."

"There is something of great import I should like to discuss with you."

There was an earnestness in his voice that alarmed her. For a brief moment Elizabeth wished to recant, to tell him no, she would not be at home on Monday, or any day for that matter. *This is what you wished for,* she reminded herself. *Safety. A man you can trust if not love.*

As she opened her mouth to speak, she glanced sideways and noticed Jane hovering near their conversation, her fingers fumbling with the side of her dress. Although Jane did not interrupt their conversation, her eyes flickered between herself and Royce.

Elizabeth smiled and called out, "Jane! Is there something you require?"

She shook her head, as her cheeks flushed slightly. "No, not at all. I did not intend to interrupt. But there is something I would like to show you when you are available."

Elizabeth looked up at Royce with a soft smile. He

chuckled as he gestured towards Jane. "I would never dream of standing in the way of sisterly matters. In any case, I see Miss Catherine over there. She wished to show me and Maria one of her most recent sketches."

Leaning closer, he murmured just for her ears, "I look forward to speaking with you on Monday."

With a bow, he turned and made his way towards Kitty across the room. Elizabeth returned her attention to Jane, who leant towards Elizabeth and whispered excitedly, "There is something I would like to show you outside. Charles has given me the most remarkable wedding present."

"Oh?"

Jane looked at her with sparkling eyes. "Yes, I cannot wait for you to see it."

Elizabeth nodded, and the two slipped discreetly out of the room. They moved deftly through the corridor, and into the entry hall, where Elizabeth started at the sight of Mr Darcy standing with Mr Bingley. The two men appeared to be waiting for them; Mr Bingley hopped from one foot to the other, as he clearly anticipated showing them whatever the mysterious present was.

Her eyes briefly met Mr Darcy's. It was only a fleeting glance, however, as he quickly turned his attention to the floor. She sighed quietly. At that moment, the sound of approaching footsteps drew her attention. When she turned to discover the source, she saw a small group of their neighbours and friends also making their way to the front of the house, their murmurs of curiosity and excitement evident.

Sir William Lucas was the first to speak. "Mr Bingley, we have heard rumours of a most intriguing gift outside, and desired to see it for ourselves."

Jane looked at Mr Bingley with widened eyes, and Elizabeth could not help but smile. Despite Jane's efforts to be covert, the news of the mysterious gift had travelled fast. Mr Bingley gave Jane a wry smile before shrugging slightly. Looking back at Sir William, he said, "You are correct. It is on the front drive."

With that, a small crowd drifted towards the windows; Elizabeth joined the others following Mr Bingley through the front door and found herself standing next to Mr Darcy. She felt her heart flutter being close to him again but refused to look up at him.

Once she arrived outside, she immediately recognised the gift as the beautiful carriage that she and Mr Darcy had taken refuge in. She had almost forgotten it was to be given to Jane. Elizabeth's eyes widened and she felt a blush overtake her as she remembered what had occurred inside of it only days ago. Mr Darcy, however, looked upon the carriage with a closed expression. Had he already forgotten? She only wished her emotions could be as easily diverted. And now it would only be more difficult, she groaned inwardly, as she would have to be reminded of those wonderful hours every time she rode with Jane in her carriage.

As the crowd was admiring the vehicle, Elizabeth heard Sir William's jocular voice. "It is beautiful and solidly built, Mr Bingley," he exclaimed, "and well able to protect a lady from wind, rain, and unexpected snowstorms."

She risked a look towards Mr Darcy, but he remained impassive, staring at the carriage. A hot blush accompanied the keen sense of mortification that assailed her, and she immediately turned and walked into the house. Several others followed her; it was still too cold to be lingering out of doors.

Soon after, the new Mr and Mrs Bingley boarded the

carriage and left for Netherfield amidst the cheers of all their guests. Not long after, Miss Bingley and the Hursts departed for London and the crowd slowly began to disperse.

Elizabeth glanced over her shoulder, wondering where Royce had gone. *Did he leave without me noticing?* As she turned her gaze forwards again, she was taken aback to find Mr Darcy standing right before her.

"Miss Bennet, if you will permit me, there is something I would give you before I leave."

The formality of his tone and the rigidity of his stance made her ache. "Oh? What is it?"

"Er...well, here." He handed her a book. She looked at the cover. It was *Charlotte Temple*, the novel she had lectured him about during their first meeting in Hertfordshire when she had argued with him rather than admit to herself how thrilled she was to see him again.

"I did not realise you had taken it."

He briefly inclined his head. "Forgive me...I really have no excuse," he said quietly, and paused for a moment. "I wanted only to understand why you defended novels so passionately. I did not intend to keep it so long, nor did I want to leave Meryton with it."

"Yes, well, did you want to...I mean, I have read it a number of times, and do not need it if you wished to keep—"

"No."

She drew back, stung by his quick objection.

"I think it would be better if it stayed with you."

Elizabeth swallowed, uncertain as to why she had offered him the book or why she felt hurt by his refusal. "Very well."

After another brief incline of his head, Mr Darcy was gone.

She watched sorrowfully as he nudged himself through

the crowd, pulling something from his pocket and rubbing it with his thumb as he walked. A moment later, a small black object slipped from his hand. He stopped, as if realising that he had dropped it, and turned, looking at the ground searchingly.

Kitty, engaged in conversation with Maria Lucas only a few feet away from Mr Darcy, bent down to pick it up and turned towards him. He appeared mildly alarmed as she turned the small object around in her hand, unabashedly curious.

"Oh! I see now that it is Lizzy's. I do apologise," she said, looking up at Mr Darcy. "I must have imagined that I saw you drop this."

She turned and walked towards Elizabeth, handing her the object before returning to Maria. Elizabeth looked at her palm and immediately recognised the thin, black hairpin lying there. It bore the initials 'EB' on it. *Her* initials. *Her* pin. It was the same pin that she had given him outside the parsonage all those years ago. Looking up she saw that he had not moved, but was watching her closely. Her insides twisted, her breath quickened, and she was unsure what, if anything, to do. It was Mr Darcy who solved her dilemma by turning round and leaving the room. The front door opened and closed, and moments later she watched as his carriage went down the lane, away from Longbourn, away from her.

CHAPTER THIRTY-SEVEN

Elizabeth sprinted towards the oak tree. The cold wind whipped her face and stung her lungs, and the only sounds she heard were her panting breaths and her boots pounding the ground.

Upon reaching the tree, she tagged it and ran past it before slowing her pace. After stopping, she laughed at herself, thankful no one was around to witness her actions, for she was certain she had the appearance of a lunatic. Recovering her breath, she walked towards a stump, sat down upon it, and began observing the quiet country scenery around her. Wind rustled through the bare-branched trees around her as she gazed upon the snow-covered fields. Slowly, the peace she had gained from running faded, as did her smile, and her mind quickly filled with memories from the last few days, from her stay at Netherfield until Jane's wedding on Saturday. It was the last time she had seen Mr Darcy, as he had not attended church services. It was now

Monday, and she could not help but assume he had left Meryton.

If Royce was not already at Longbourn, she knew he would be there soon to offer her his hand in marriage. Though still heartbroken, she knew she had made the right decision to let go of Mr Darcy. No matter how much it hurt now, she would move on. She would always love him, but they could not have had a happy marriage if trust, and her family and his dislike of them, was a wedge between them.

She stood, took a deep breath, and began the walk back to Longbourn to see Royce. Her mind inexplicably jumped to a scene in one of her father's history books, of Anne Boleyn walking towards the executioner. She cast the thought aside and marched towards and into the house.

To her surprise there was a loud commotion from within the drawing room. After hanging her coat, she entered the room, expecting—nay, dreading—that she might find Royce; to her relief he was absent, and instead, her entire family, including the Gardiners and their three daughters, were there making a fuss about something. Mr Andrews stood beside Lydia, smiling happily. Kitty was on the periphery of the activity, and Elizabeth asked her as to why there was so much excitement.

"You have not heard? With as much as you and Mr Darcy are in each other's confidences I would have expected that you would have already known."

Her stomach lurched at the mention of him. "What is it?"

"At the wedding, Mr Darcy pulled Mr Andrews aside and offered him the living as a clergyman in Kympton—at the church he attends regularly, in fact. Mr Andrews's income will now be enough to support him and Lydia. He proposed this morning, Papa consented, and they just announced their happy news."

Elizabeth covered her mouth in disbelief. She was delighted for Lydia, even if she worried about her age and her readiness to be a wife, but it was a good match for her sister and she would be happy. She quickly went to congratulate the happy couple, and after so doing, retreated to her room.

She sat on her bed and could only stare at the wall in contemplation. Why would Mr Darcy do such a thing? Though much reformed, Lydia remained the most officious, the wildest of all her sisters. She often skirted the rules of propriety, was loud, untamed, and unrepentant in most of her mischief. After everything she had told Mr Darcy, he must have known Mr Andrews would propose to Lydia after receiving the offer.

And now Mr Darcy will find himself in Lydia's presence constantly. Elizabeth did not know whether to laugh or cry about that. It must try his patience to be with her, and he would surely feel concern of exposing his sister to such an acquaintance. Why would he do this?

She thought it over without devising any suitable explanation when she heard a knock on the door which interrupted her thoughts.

"Yes?"

It was her aunt Gardiner. A shadow of concern lay beneath her eyes as she asked, "May I come in?" At Elizabeth's encouragement, she came and sat on the edge of the bed. Her eyes met her niece's as she remarked, "I was quite shocked to hear the news of Lydia and Mr Andrews."

"Yes, it has been obvious to everyone for quite some time that they preferred each other. But this happy outcome is so sudden..." Elizabeth furrowed her brows as she contemplated Mr Darcy's role in bringing about Mr Andrews's ability to marry Lydia.

Her aunt cast her a searching look. "Does it upset you?"

Elizabeth let out a soft, half-hearted laugh. "No, although I do believe Lydia is quite young to be marrying, she and Mr Andrews truly love each other. And it is a far better match than I could have ever expected for her."

Mrs Gardiner's gaze lingered on her, but neither spoke further. They sat in silence; the only sounds that could be heard were muffled voices drifting up from the drawing room. Elizabeth's sadness overcame her again and she looked down at her hands. She desired to release the secret that she had kept for better than three years but hardly knew how, or if, she should. She said a quick prayer for guidance on whether she should remain quiet or confide in her aunt.

Her aunt's next words decided her course.

"Lizzy, dear, I only came up here because..." she said gently. "Well, is there something you would like to speak to me about? I have felt you have not been your usual happy self these past weeks—even Lillian has noticed it—you have seemed to me rather melancholy since returning from Netherfield."

As often happens when finally releasing a secret, Elizabeth wept before she could speak audibly. Her aunt held her hands while she cried and waited patiently for her niece to regain equanimity.

Once able to speak, Elizabeth told her everything. Her history with Mr Darcy, her reawakened feelings, the events that occurred at Netherfield, and her decision to let him go and accept Mr Royce when he came to ask for her hand. Only the deeply personal and intimate details of her moments with Mr Darcy in the rainstorm at Rosings and in Jane's new carriage did she keep to herself. Some things were too precious to bandy about, even to a beloved aunt.

When she finished, Elizabeth took a deep breath. Already she felt soothed from the mere act of sharing her burdens with another. Aunt Gardiner was quiet for a moment. "You have been holding on to a great deal, darling Lizzy."

"You must think I am the biggest fool."

"I could never think you were a fool. You have had some very hard decisions to make."

"Do you think I have made the right choice?"

"In choosing Mr Royce? Or letting go of Mr Darcy?"

Elizabeth considered that for a moment before answering, "Both."

Mrs Gardiner grew thoughtful for a moment, her hand smoothing down a bit of the counterpane next to her. "I suppose that I think it is a surprise."

"A surprise? What is?"

Her aunt studied her before answering, "I have never known you to make decisions from a place of fear or resentment."

"I am not afraid or resentful," Elizabeth replied. "I simply do not trust Mr Darcy. I think it would be foolish if I did not learn from the way he treated me before."

"If he had not changed at all, I would see what you mean, perhaps even agree with you. But you did see a change in him, yes?" On Elizabeth's nod, she continued, "I have thought him a rather agreeable, if slightly taciturn, man. He is very high, as you know, and yet condescended to play with my daughters. He has been unfailingly polite to your family, and has taken your verbal barrages quite in stride it seems."

Elizabeth felt herself nearly sinking under the weight of

the truth Mrs Gardiner spoke and still her aunt had not finished.

"He encouraged Mr Bingley to propose to Jane, cared for Mary when she was ill, and offered Lydia's beau employment so that they could marry. As an unbiased observer, he does not appear prideful. Indeed, he seems quite gentle and kind."

Elizabeth sighed. "I agree he has acted generously, but you do not know what it was like for me. We were on the verge of an engagement. I was so devastated by his spurning me, it took months of pretending to be in good spirits, and trying to forget him…it was a terrible, dark time of my life."

"Are you so determined to punish him for hurting you that you will not see that he has altered? And in being wilfully blind, you will let your own happiness pass you by?"

Is that what I am doing? Is happiness passing me by?

Her aunt patted her hand. "I think you are acting quite rationally, which would make sense, as it is how most people approach decisions after a big heartbreak. You are trying to balance heart versus head, and that is not easy."

"Anyone can be kind for a few weeks. How can I know with certainty that he could suffer my family on a regular basis? And that he would not grow to hate me because of them eventually?" Her voice shook. "What if he were to hurt me again? I do not know whether I could endure it."

"There will always be some risk associated with true love. To make oneself vulnerable is part of what makes the outcome so rewarding."

After both were quiet and reflective for a few moments, her aunt shifted on the bed. "I will support you in whatever you decide. But I ask you to reflect on this. If you choose Mr Royce, you still cannot completely shield your heart. If the two of you were to have children, you would still be vulnerable to pain. Your children will always have your whole heart, even if your husband does not. Loving your children can open you up to more pain than you ever thought possible, but more joy as well." Elizabeth noticed tears brimming in her aunt's eyes as she spoke. She cleared her throat and with a wry tilt of her head, she said, "Perhaps you will decide that is too much for you as well and you will marry but not have children? But what of your family whom you already love? You will always be vulnerable to pain there. Lizzy, unless you completely isolate yourself from others, you cannot control who has the ability to hurt you. Grief and heartache come hand in hand with love."

Mrs Gardiner rose, kissed her on the head, and walked to the door. Pausing, she turned back. "You are angry with him and still heartbroken for how he treated you. But it was more than three years ago. You do not have to stay that way forever."

She then quietly exited the room.

Elizabeth stared into the silence. She leant her head against the bedpost and closed her eyes in contemplation. A moment later—or perhaps an hour, she had no sense of how much time had passed—she opened her eyes and looked over to the table where she saw the book Mr Darcy had returned to her after the wedding breakfast. She reached over and picked it up, gently running her fingers over it. It was not far from her mind that he had been the last person to touch it.

Mindlessly she opened the cover, and as she did, a letter slipped out. *'Miss Elizabeth'* was written neatly across the front of the paper in a familiar, undeniably masculine hand that made her gasp. She looked at it for long minutes until at length, she picked it up and unfolded it.

She had scarcely read the salutation before a knock on the

door made her jump and quickly shove the pages behind her pillow. "Come in!"

It was Mary. "Mr Royce is here and he wishes to see you."

Elizabeth closed her eyes a moment, feeling dread, fear, confusion, dismay…everything in a tumult in her mind. For a brief moment, she considered sending him away, telling Mary that she was unwell and asking her to pass along the message. But no, she could not. It was time to face the consequences of her fear. She opened her eyes and cleared her throat. "Thank you, Mary. I will be down in a moment."

CHAPTER THIRTY-EIGHT

Elizabeth stood up and smoothed her gown. She went to the mirror to ensure that her hair was tidy and her eyes neither red-rimmed nor swollen. *A little pale but you will do,* she told herself. Taking a deep breath, she prepared herself to go downstairs but found herself frozen to the floor. She needed first to read the letter. She quickly went back to her bed, pulled it out from behind her pillow, and began to read.

Miss Elizabeth,

You have asked me to leave you alone. I respect you and your wishes too much to ignore them, so I will cease my attentions. I would never wish to wear you down to accept me, but would only desire you to come to me willingly and happily.

By now you will have heard that I have offered the living to Mr Andrews in hopes that Miss Lydia could obtain the future she desired. I assure you, this was not done to entice you to accept me. I wish merely to see to the welfare of your loved ones, and to reward those who have shaped and been close to the only woman I will ever love.

While I shall not beg you to return to me, please know that my wishes and affections will always remain unchanged. I will wait forever for another chance with you. If you marry another, I will maintain a small glimmer of hope that if circumstances ever change, you will find me as an old man with my love enduring and unwavering. Even if you cannot give me your heart, you will always have mine for the keeping.

I was not strong enough to stand up for our love as a young man, and I am prepared to pay the price for that for the rest of my life. While I will always regret hurting you, I am not sorry for what has passed since then. I would have been a terrible person and husband to you if not for your set-downs. I owe everything good in my character to you.

I begin each day with a prayer of gratitude for having known you. Even if a second chance with you does not come to pass, I will feel gratified and fulfilled for having loved another with my whole heart and for having at one point been loved by the person I respect above all others.

I have taken rooms at Meryton's inn and shall depart for town on Tuesday morning. If you wish to see me, I will be there, awaiting you. If not, please know that I am forever yours,

Fitzwilliam Darcy

She put her hand to her mouth and gasped. She read the letter again, more slowly this time.

He had given the position to Mr Andrews simply to help Lydia, knowing full well he would probably have to interact with her for the rest of his life? *And only because of her connexion to me?* Elizabeth could not be insensible to the compliment of being responsible for the change in a man of such great standing.

He would simply wait for her...forever? Even if she were to marry another? She shook her head in disbelief. He would risk never producing an heir for Pemberley in the hope that he might one day have another chance with her? *How can this be? How could someone love another so much?*

She did not know what she felt but knew that she needed to go to him. He had given her this book on Saturday, and it was now Monday afternoon. He probably thought she had read the letter at least a day ago and did not wish to see him. Was he still at the inn, as he promised, or had he given up and left? Had she missed him already?

She pulled on her boots and mittens, chose her warmest bonnet and scarf, wrapped a shawl around herself, and left her bedchamber, where she almost collided with her aunt and young cousins.

"Amelia, Annabelle, and I have been sent to retrieve you," Mrs Gardiner said. "Mr Royce is here."

"He gave me a biscuit," said Amelia.

"And me!" cried Annabelle.

Elizabeth flashed a smile at the girls before saying, "Aunt, I need your help. I must go. He is likely already gone but still...I have to go see."

"Who is likely gone?"

Amelia's question was echoed by her mother, who shooed

the girls off to join Lillian in the nursery. Then Mrs Gardiner turned back to Elizabeth, a puzzled frown on her countenance.

"Mr Darcy. He…well, I will tell you later. For now, I must hurry and hope that he has not yet gone. Pray, distract my mother so I can slip out the door?"

"Are you choosing Mr Darcy now?"

In an instant all of Elizabeth's doubts vanished. "Yes!"

Her aunt moved to embrace her, but Elizabeth neatly sidestepped her. "There will be time enough to hug once I have stopped him from leaving, and he has accepted me."

"Accepted you? You will propose?" Mrs Gardiner laughed before asking, carefully, "What will we do with poor Mr Royce?"

"I cannot even think of him now. I feel awful for abandoning him so, but I must go to the inn at once."

Mrs Gardiner gave a quick nod and disappeared down the corridor. Knowing she could depend upon her, Elizabeth followed and waited at the top of the stairs, her heart beating wildly. After a minute, she heard mumbling and footsteps walking to the east side of the house. She knew this was her chance, and stealthily crept down the stairs, flinching with every creak of the wooden steps until she made it to the bottom. She eyed her cloak near the front hall, but dared not risk retrieving it. Instead, she turned abruptly into the kitchen, determined not to be seen by the others in the drawing room. She quietly tiptoed in, passing the scullery maid and Cook, their backs to her, as she walked quickly towards the door.

Darting outside, she felt all of her senses tingle as she began running as fast as possible towards Meryton.

Although Elizabeth had always prided herself on her

strength and speed, she found running so quickly in the cold and snow was more difficult than the day's earlier frolic. Her muscles burned and her side began to cramp; her bonnet loosened and with it, her curls tumbled out.

With every step she took, Elizabeth was more certain of him—and that her aunt was right about love. She would have to take a leap of faith and trust that he would not hurt her again. No one could know the future with certainty, but surely moving her youngest sister up to Derbyshire gave her the confirmation she needed that his feelings could withstand whatever her family might throw at him in the future. It gave her the confidence she needed to feel safe with him.

She knew now that she had allowed her wounded pride to dictate how she felt about him instead of her heart. She had been determined to see that he had not changed since their time in Kent, when in fact he had. She had been fighting a battle within herself, navigating between her hurt from his earlier rejection and what was authentically there between them. Now she understood his own struggles, and the grief and responsibilities he had faced.

How foolish she had been! To risk the happiness of the rest of her life to nurse her dignity and overlook what he too had lost. She prayed, fervently, that somehow, some way, he would not have given up on her and left for town.

A carriage came towards her as she neared Meryton's outskirts. It was a fine equipage, pulled by a team of gleaming black horses. Even before she saw the crest on its side, she knew it was the Darcy carriage. She wanted to wave her arms at the driver but instead found herself frozen in place, doing no more but staring, silently willing Mr Darcy to look out the side-glass and order the vehicle to stop.

And then, shockingly, the carriage came to an abrupt and

swift halt. The door opened before the coachmen could climb down to perform their office, and Mr Darcy stepped down, confusion on his handsome face. Without missing a beat, he tightened his coat and ran over to her, closing the distance between them quickly with his long strides. He stopped a few feet away from her, staring at her, clearly concerned.

Out of breath, and uncertain what to say, Elizabeth struggled to regain her composure. She was sure she looked the part of a madcap: running down the lane without a coat, her cheeks red, and hair undone.

"Elizabeth? What are you doing?" he asked gently.

"I need to speak to you."

He nodded, looking at her expectantly.

"Are you leaving?"

"Not until tomorrow," he said earnestly.

She looked down at the snow by his feet, then slowly moved her eyes up to meet his. She saw his love and admiration and smiled at him as tears filled her eyes.

"And what of you?" he enquired. "Are you coming into Meryton to see your aunt?"

"No." She had been so worried about finding him that she had neglected to prepare what to say when she saw him. "Yes, I am coming to Meryton, not to see my aunt, but because I read your letter, and I-I just wanted to tell you that do not…I do not want you to wait for me."

The look of pain that flashed across his face made her realise, immediately, her error. "No! Oh no! That is not what I meant." Trying to think of her next words, she put her hand to her forehead. "What I meant was, I do not want you to wait for me. I want us to start our life now."

She hardly knew how it happened but in the blink of an eye she found herself in his arms, being tenderly kissed. "Do you mean that?" he demanded breathlessly. "Will you trust me again? No—will you allow me the chance to prove myself worthy of your trust?"

"I trust you," she managed to gasp out. "I entrust my heart and my soul into your care."

He pulled back, gazing at her as he tucked her hair behind her ears. His eyes were shiny but there was only joy in his countenance. Then he opened his greatcoat and pulled her close, enveloping her within its warm woollen folds. Leaning down, he kissed her deeply, only pausing to declare his love and his devotion to her for the rest of their days.

CHAPTER THIRTY-NINE

February 1814, Hertfordshire

Elizabeth took a long sip of tea as the lively chatter of her family filled Longbourn's parlour. Mrs Bennet, in her usual fashion, was fretting over Mr Darcy's extended stay in London for business. He was expected to return tomorrow, and remain at Netherfield until their wedding, which was now just a se'nnight away.

"I cannot understand it. Three weeks away and so close to the wedding seems quite excessive!" Mrs Bennet complained as she placed her cup back on its saucer. "I hope he has not changed his mind about the wedding. Mr Bennet, what will we do if he does not return? It is unlikely that we could ever find another suitor for Lizzy…"

Elizabeth held back a sigh. She knew this was far from the truth, but even so, it did little to soothe the ache she felt for her loved one's absence.

"Mama." Jane, who was visiting from Netherfield for the

day, sighed gently from her seat beside Elizabeth on the sofa. "Mr Darcy is attending to important business matters. He would not delay his return without good reason."

Mr Bennet, lounging in an armchair by the fire, did not look up from his paper as he said drily, "If he does not return, fret not, my dear. After Bingley first came with five thousand a year, and then Darcy with ten thousand, I daresay another eligible gentleman with fifteen thousand a year will ride into the neighbourhood. We seem to be on an upwards course, after all." He shook out his paper and gave Elizabeth a wink.

Mary responded stoically, "Papa, it would not be wise to count on such an event. It seems highly unlikely."

Giggling at her father's joke, Kitty stole a look at the seat Lydia used to frequently occupy. "At least if one did, Lydia would not be in the competition for his heart now that she is married and gone off with Mr Andrews."

Elizabeth nodded absently, her gaze drifting back towards the window as the conversation carried on without her. Then, she saw something that made her heart skip a beat. There, in front of the house, sitting atop a horse and dressed far too fine for a day of travel, was the most handsome man she had ever seen. Darcy must have just returned to Netherfield, and ridden directly to Longbourn, arriving a day earlier than expected too!

Eyes wide with excitement, she glanced at Jane and tilted her head towards the window. Jane followed her sister's gaze before she understood the unspoken message, and without hesitation, she rose from her chair.

"Mama, I believe you had said you desired to have another look at Kitty's and Mary's new gowns for the wedding. Let us have them laid out in their chambers, so we can be assured the lace and beading are as you hoped."

"Oh, yes, of course," Mrs Bennet said. "We must make sure everything is acceptable. Mr Darcy's relations will expect nothing short of perfection! Kitty, Mary, come!"

As her sisters followed Mrs Bennet out of the parlour, Elizabeth sat still, her hands quietly folded in her lap, as her father read his paper.

Mr Bennet shifted a little, glancing out the window beside him, where he surely caught sight of Darcy's figure, before settling back into his chair with a sigh. After a moment, he folded his paper and stood up slowly. As if reading Elizabeth's mind that she desired some time alone with her husband-to-be after their separation, he cleared his throat. "And now, I believe I shall retreat to my library," he said as he gave Elizabeth a knowing look. "Please let it be known that I do not wish to be disturbed until dinner, unless of course that gentleman of fifteen thousand a year arrives."

Once he was out of the room, Elizabeth wasted no time. She rose from her seat, hurried through the front hall, grabbed her cloak and bonnet, and opened the front door. The cool February air brushed against her face as her boots trod the gravel, but her eyes never left Darcy, who had his back turned towards her. With each step, she found herself almost gliding towards him in eager anticipation.

He had handed his horse to the stableboy, who led the creature away, and Elizabeth soon realised Darcy had disappeared behind a hedge where he could no longer be seen from the house. Hastening her steps towards it, she called his name. He turned just in time to catch her in his arms as she embraced him with all the joy she felt at his return. He chuckled, wrapping his arms around her, though his voice took on a teasing reprimand. "Elizabeth…What if somebody sees?" Yet, even as he glanced over his shoulder, a smile played on his lips, and he held her tightly, seemingly determined to not let her go after their time apart.

"I suppose you would be forced to marry me," she said in a playful tone as she looked up at him. "But as fortune would have it, this spot behind the shrubbery is quite concealed, and I assure you, no one is watching. My family is on the other side of the house."

"Well, if that is the case." He quickly bent down and gave her a gentle kiss. He took a deep breath as he pulled away. "How I have missed you, my dear," he said as he drew her back into his arms.

"And I as well. Now that you have returned, I forbid us to ever be apart again."

"I believe we can arrange that," Darcy responded with a charming smile, still holding her close.

She shifted out of his embrace, and pulled his hand in the direction away from Longbourn. "Come, sir, before someone sees you," she said, glancing back over her shoulder with a mischievous grin. "Let us go to the stream behind Longbourn. I have been with my family all morning, and I wish to be alone with you before returning to the chaos of the wedding preparations that shall consume us for the next week."

They walked hand in hand through the fields until they reached a stream situated on Longbourn's property, a spot that they had often visited since their engagement. Though it was cold outside, the water was not frozen over and offered a soothing babble as a backdrop to their conversation. They stood at the bank watching the water flow by, their fingers intertwined as they spoke of the wedding trip that would follow the ceremony and a brief stay in town. At Elizabeth's request, their plans included a stop in Brighton so she could have her first glimpse of the sea.

"Are you certain you do not mind returning to a place you have already been?"

"It will be my first time seeing the sea with *you*, and that is all that matters to me." He added softly, "I could have done something a hundred times before, but with you by my side, it would still feel as if I am experiencing it for the first time."

As they spoke, Elizabeth's heart swelled at the thought of their future together. Eventually, she leant against Darcy's shoulder and closed her eyes, listening to the gentle flow of the water and feeling the crisp wind caress her face. When she opened them, she was surprised to find Darcy watching her with that familiar intensity she had come to recognise as a reflection of his deep feelings for her. It always made her feel shy to be admired so.

"I must ask you something," she said softly.

"Go on," he encouraged her. "You know I can deny you nothing."

Elizabeth hesitated before finally asking, "Do you ever wonder how things might have been different if we had married three years earlier?"

His gaze grew distant as he appeared to ponder her question. He paused longer than she had anticipated before finally answering in a low voice, "Do you still have the letter I gave to you at Jane and Bingley's wedding?"

Elizabeth, still nestled in his embrace, giggled softly. "Yes of course, I still read that letter almost every day because it has come to mean so much to me." She continued as she added softly, "It changed the course of our history."

Darcy nodded. "I meant every word, especially that I became a better person because of our parting. I would not have been the husband I should have been—that I hope to be—if we had not gone through our trials. Our separation, having to live without you for three years, and your sharp rebukes, permitted me to grow in ways I did not know were possible."

Elizabeth shifted to gain a better view of him as he continued, his voice becoming very serious. "I shudder when I think of my pride then, and that I believed you were beneath me or the Darcy name."

He shook his head and after a deep breath, wrapped his arm around her and pulled her closer; he continued as his voice became softer again. "Except that you had to endure heartache, I am endlessly grateful for every moment that led us here. Instead of having a marriage that would have been fraught with tension, we will begin our marriage more in love than I could have ever imagined. I never thought I would experience such happiness and warmth in my life."

Elizabeth laid her head on his chest as he drew her in even closer, his chin resting gently on the top of her head as he spoke again. "You are without a doubt the biggest blessing I have in this world. I will get to spend my days with a woman whom I respect, adore, and laugh with. If I had not had to spend three years apart from you, I might not have appreciated everything you are as deeply." She felt her cheeks flush with such a compliment.

"Yes..." she said slowly, a pang of guilt still gnawing at her, "but I wish I had forgiven you more easily when you first arrived, or had been willing to hear what you were trying to tell me. I fear I made you suffer unduly."

"I do not," he said firmly. "I had treated you abysmally,

and you needed time to regain trust in me to see that my character was truly amended."

"But..." she continued, still unconvinced.

Interrupting her thought, he lifted her chin so that she was facing him as he continued, "Even though there was much pain in our journey, I could never wish it would be altered because of what it has led to. Because of everything we have endured, there will not be misunderstandings, or lack of trust, or pain in our future. And that is what matters most."

She smiled gently and he looked on her warmly before placing a tender kiss on her lips. When he pulled away, he tucked her hair behind her ear as he had done so many times before.

"Well, my soon-to-be Mrs Darcy," he said with a sigh, as his voicing of her new title sent a thrill through Elizabeth. "I suppose we should return. Your family must be wondering where you are."

"You are correct, sir. Let us be on our way," she replied with a smile.

Before they left, she looked around at the idyllic stream and the surrounding natural beauty. "You know, this place reminds me a little of Lady Catherine."

"Excuse me," he said with a mock sharpness. "I do not wish to associate her with this peaceful place."

Elizabeth laughed softly. "I only mean that the stream here reminds me a little of the river at Rosings, where you and the colonel used to swing on the rope as boys."

He conceded with a nod as he gazed out and observed the landscape. "Yes, I agree."

"And it reminds me of a certain rainstorm we got caught in..."

"Oh?"

She held her hands out in the air, with her palm up as if she were detecting something in the air.

"What is it, dearest?"

"I daresay, I worry some rain might detain us, causing us to be delayed by at least a few more minutes."

He glanced up at the clear blue sky, which showed no signs of an impending storm. When he looked back at her, she grinned at him impishly and arched an eyebrow.

"I fear we must take shelter over there," she said, pointing to a large tree.

Now clearly understanding what she was about, Darcy's face broke into a knowing smile. "I believe you are correct. It seems we have a few minutes to spare for an unexpected rainstorm," he said with a chuckle.

Hand in hand, they walked towards the tree and settled into its wide roots. As Darcy sat beside her, Elizabeth gazed into his eyes and saw reflected there the depth of his love for her. Her heart was so full it felt as though it might burst.

She leant towards him and kissed him deeply. They carried on in that manner for quite some time.

CHAPTER FORTY

A week later, Elizabeth stood quietly in the middle of her bedchamber as the gentle morning light seeped through the room, casting a delicate glow. Sarah, Longbourn's lady's maid, worked diligently behind her, fastening the final buttons on her gown. Once she had finished, Elizabeth turned slightly to face her, and smiled. "Thank you, that is all." Sarah's eyes quickly flickered to Elizabeth's undone hair. "My sister shall assist with my hair," she explained. The maid nodded and with a graceful curtsey quietly exited the room.

Left alone, Elizabeth moved with slow, deliberate steps to stand in front of the mirror and view her reflection. Her dress, made of pristine white satin with sleeves and bodice trimmed with Mechlin lace, looked elegant as it hung delicately over her form. As she continued to study her appearance in the mirror, she took a deep breath; her lips curved into a gentle smile. On this, her wedding day, she felt more beautiful than she ever had before.

She moved to sit at her dressing table, where her mother's suggested hair adornments lay neatly arranged. With a slow exhale, Elizabeth thought of the whirlwind of activities that had occurred over the last week, from welcoming out-of-town guests, attending parties in honour of Darcy and herself, and making—or overruling—Mrs Bennet's innumerable last-minute decisions. She felt the weariness of it all; it had seemed as though the day she had been long anticipating would never arrive.

A gentle knock at the door drew Elizabeth's attention. She turned to see Jane entering the room, her eyes softening as she gazed at Elizabeth.

"Jane," she said calmly with a smile.

Her sister stepped closer, her eyes brimming with tears. "Lizzy," she said as her voice wavered. "You look radiant. I have never seen you more beautiful."

Elizabeth felt her own eyes begin to sting with restrained tears as she reached to take Jane's hands. "Thank you."

Jane cleared her throat. "Would you still like me to arrange your hair?"

Elizabeth nodded gratefully, and watched her sister's reflection quietly as she brushed her hair into an elegant style. When she finished, Jane gazed on the assortment of hair pins and combs. She picked up a jewelled comb, and brought it close to Elizabeth's hair, as if to assess how it might look.

"No, I would prefer this one," Elizabeth said, leaning forwards and pointing to the delicate black pin with her initials on it.

Jane examined the pin thoughtfully with pursed lips. Her eyes met Elizabeth's in the mirror. "Are you certain? It may not be visible in your hair."

"I know," Elizabeth replied softly, "but it is significant to us."

"Mama seemed to think—" Jane stopped herself before continuing and shook her head. "It is of no consequence."

Elizabeth settled back into her chair with a wry smile. "I know she would not approve." She shook her head as she continued. "Lydia's wedding to Mr Andrews was a modest event, but every decision about mine has been a battle with her. She wishes to impress Darcy and his relations and I have tried to let her have her way as much as possible, but on the things that matter most to me, I must stand my ground."

"I understand."

Elizabeth looked up at her sister's reflection, her expression softening. "Although, I must confess," she said, her voice catching slightly, "as tiresome as it has been to prepare for this wedding, I will miss her deeply, and all of you, when I leave."

After Jane placed the pin into Elizabeth's hair, she paused and glanced at her sister with brows furrowed in concern. "Is that why you were quieter than usual last night?"

Elizabeth nodded. "Yes. I daresay, I was thinking about leaving Longbourn and making my home at Pemberley. It will be wonderful, I am sure, but I have never been there and for a moment, it seemed difficult to imagine a new life. So much is changing so quickly."

Jane nodded, as she placed her hands on Elizabeth's shoulders and gave them a gentle squeeze as she offered a reassuring smile. "I believe that is a very common feeling. But today, you seem more collected. You are radiant."

Elizabeth's smile grew warmer. "I am."

"What helped you find peace?" Jane asked, tilting her head slightly.

Elizabeth's eyes grew distant as she spoke. "As I said, I was feeling uneasy," she began. "But when I lay in bed last night, I imagined walking down the aisle and seeing Darcy at the front of the church. What he might be doing, what he might look like. The way he might look at me..." Her voice trailed off, and a soft smile played on her lips as she continued. "I then thought of how much I love him and everything he has done for me, and for this family. And the realisation struck me, like an arrow through the heart, filling me with warmth. He is my home."

Jane smiled tenderly as a single tear escaped her eye. She quickly wiped it away with a handkerchief. Elizabeth continued, "As much as I love Hertfordshire, and Longbourn, and our family, my home is wherever he is."

"And that is exactly the way it should be, Lizzy."

Elizabeth's smile faltered slightly. "And now I only want to be married." She let out a small sigh. "I do believe I am feeling a bit overwhelmed with all the preparations, the people, the parties..." Her voice trailed off as she looked around the room and furrowed her brow. "Perhaps we should have eloped."

Jane's eyes widened. "You would not want that!"

Elizabeth giggled. "No, but sometimes it feels as if all of these preparations are too much."

Jane's face brightened, and the corners of her lips lifted. "Perhaps you need a distraction. I have news that might do the job well."

"Oh? What is it?" Elizabeth asked, her curiosity piqued.

Jane barely concealed her smile. "Mary says that Mr Royce came over again yesterday."

"Again?" Elizabeth's eyebrows lifted in astonishment as a

surprised laugh escaped her lips. "While I was with you at Netherfield? That is the third time this week!"

"I would not be surprised if we are back here in a few months preparing Kitty for her big day," Jane said.

Elizabeth smiled. The day that she and Darcy had reunited had been the most beautiful of her life. Yet, there had been one difficult task that followed—returning to Longbourn to tell Mr Royce that she could not marry him. He was a kind, respectable man who had wanted to take care of her, and delivering such unwelcome news, which would undoubtedly hurt him, was an arduous duty. It was difficult to tell someone who had shown her such kindness that, despite all his virtues, she could not offer him her heart.

He, however, had made it easy, accepting the news graciously, even offering his congratulations to Elizabeth and Darcy. Before he left, Elizabeth asked him not to stay away from Longbourn on her behalf. She assured him that if it was not too difficult for him to be around her, her family would be exceedingly pleased to have him visit, as they were very fond of him.

To her surprise, he accepted her invitation and began visiting Longbourn the following week. He came as often as he ever had, and soon began paying special attention to Kitty, who appeared thrilled and received his attentions with equal excitement. Although it was a little strange that the man she almost married was now likely to marry her sister, Elizabeth was genuinely happy for them.

Her laughter softened, and she gave her sister a warm hug. "Thank you. That is indeed distracting and helped me forget about the whirlwind of wedding preparations for a moment."

Jane returned the hug. "You are welcome. Now, let us go to the church. It is almost time for the ceremony to begin."

As Elizabeth and Mr Bennet ascended each stone step of the church, her heart pounded. When they at last reached the top, she took a deep breath to steady herself. "Let us wait just a moment, Papa," she said softly.

She gazed around at the countryside before reaching out to lightly touch the cool, weathered stone of the church walls. Despite her mother's desire for a wedding in town, Elizabeth had firmly decided on marrying in Longbourn's church. It was where Jane and Lydia had wed their husbands and would likely be where Mary and Kitty would marry as well. It contained countless childhood memories, a place that had witnessed her grow into who she was today. It was the perfect place for her passage from girlhood to womanhood, from daughter and sister to wife.

Her breath caught as she looked at the ancient oak doors, knowing that her soon-to-be husband awaited her behind them. Just then, a chorus of birds sang out, their melodies seeming to ring in the significance of the day. Elizabeth closed her eyes briefly, allowing the gentle beauty of the scene to fill her senses as she attempted to memorise every detail. The notion was not lost on her that this would be the last time she would see this place as Elizabeth Bennet.

"Lizzy, are you ready?" Her father's voice broke the silence.

As she opened her eyes and looked at her father, she saw the slightest trace of a glimmer in his eyes. Her fingers trembled slightly as she adjusted her dress, and she took another steadying breath.

"I am," she replied with quiet resolve.

Mr Bennet cleared his throat and glanced away for a moment. When he looked back at her, Elizabeth linked her arm with his, and he gently squeezed her hand. With a final nod, he opened the door, and together they walked into the church. Sunlight streamed through the windows, casting rays of light in the air and shadows across the old wooden pews and the people who gathered to witness the ceremony. Her eyes quickly sought out Darcy, who stood at the front of the church next to the minister. He had not yet heard her enter, and his focus was absorbed in meticulously adjusting his cuffs as his brows furrowed in concentration. Elizabeth's lips curved into a smile at the sight of his simple, yet endearing habit.

The sight of him standing and waiting for her brought on a wave of calm, and she stood straighter. Any lingering tension dissipated as she began walking towards him.

When Darcy's eyes finally lifted to meet hers, his face fell for a moment, as if the sight of her overwhelmed him. He took a deep breath and looked up again, and his gaze locked with hers. Elizabeth's smile widened, but his eyes remained fixed on her with the intensity she had only ever seen from him. To an outsider, Darcy's expression might have appeared stern, but Elizabeth knew it was a testament to the depth of the feelings he was struggling to contain.

Her steps quickened towards the altar, towards Darcy, towards her home. Darcy's gaze on her remained unwavering and once beside him, she could detect a mistiness in his eyes. A profound warmth spread through her, causing her to lose her breath momentarily.

The voice of Mr Trammell, the clergyman whom she had known since childhood, broke through their mutual daze. "Dearly beloved, we are gathered here in the sight of God, and in the face of this congregation to join together this man and this woman in holy matrimony."

Her gaze softened as she looked at Darcy, her eyes never leaving his. Mr Trammell guided Elizabeth to place her hands in Darcy's; he continued staring at her as he gripped her hands tightly in his. He then repeated after the clergyman with a thick voice, "I, Fitzwilliam Darcy, take thee, Elizabeth Bennet, to my wedded wife, to have and to hold from this day forward, for better for worse, for richer for poorer, in sickness and in health, to love and to cherish, till death us do part, according to God's holy ordinance; and thereto I plight thee my troth."

Darcy's words, almost palpable, lingered invisibly between them as he gazed at her with profound emotion. As he finished reciting the vows that had been spoken by countless couples through the ages, Elizabeth felt a surge of pride and adoration. She was completely assured of the truth in his promises, for his actions had already demonstrated his unwavering commitment. His love, steadfast and enduring, was as timeless as the tradition of these vows themselves, promising to sustain them through every trial and triumph.

She blinked back tears as she made her own pledge, and soon, Darcy was placing a delicate gold ring on the fourth finger of her left hand. His voice then spoke the final words which would bind them in holy matrimony.

"With this ring I thee wed, with my body I thee worship, and with all my worldly goods I thee endow: In the Name of the Father, and of the Son, and of the Holy Ghost. Amen."

As the service concluded, Elizabeth turned to face their

loved ones. She saw the faces of her family and close friends sitting among the pews, all beaming with joy. Looking up at Darcy one more time, she saw the man she loved above all others, the man who had become her closest friend. Her heart swelled with pride that this was now her husband, and she thought, *I am home.*

ACKNOWLEDGMENTS

I would like to acknowledge Quills & Quartos, for caring about this book and for taking what I had to offer and shaping it into something far better. Their support has played a pivotal role in turning my dream of becoming an author into a reality.

In addition, I would also like to acknowledge Jane Austen, for writing such captivating characters that people still want to read more about them over 200 years later.

1

ABOUT THE AUTHOR

Abigail Sheffield is a longtime lover of historical fiction novels. After discovering an annotated *Pride & Prejudice* in a bookstore, she became enthralled by learning about the customs and nuances of the Regency Era. Her enthusiasm only grew as she continued reading other Jane Austen titles as well as watching film adaptations of her work. After finding the world of Jane Austen variation literature, she became captivated by plotlines writers created that were shaped by altered circumstances, and eventually became inspired to imagine her own.

When she is not writing, she enjoys spending time with her family and traveling. Abigail resides in the United States where she shares her life with her very own Mr Tilney.

Printed in Dunstable, United Kingdom